Climbing the Date Palm

by Shira Glassman

This is a work of fiction. Names, characters, places, and incidents are either the product of the author's imagination or are used fictitiously, and any resemblance to any persons, dragons, lizards, snakes, swans, or cats living or dead, business establishments, events, or locales is entirely coincidental.

Climbing the Date Palm by Shira Glassman, edited by Jessica St. Ama

Prince Kaveh, the youngest son of the king of the City of Red Clay, is bisexual and completely besotted with Farzin, the engineer his father hired to oversee the improvements to the city's roads and bridges. However, the king doesn't share his positive feelings. After Farzin ends up at the head of the protest that ensues when the workers are only paid a third of their promised wages, he's thrown in prison and is scheduled to be executed.

Queen Shulamit, who rules over the neighboring nation of Perach, is eager to assist the desperate prince. She, too, loves justice and has a same-sex partner. She's also hoping Kaveh, with his royal blood, is willing to give her and her sweetheart a legitimate heir in exchange. But can she find a peaceful solution that will pacify the king next door, get his workers fairly paid, and free Farzin? Or will she and her dragon-riding bodyguard Rivka have to go to war?

Cover art by Rebecca Schauer and Jane Dominguez

Songs 7:8, as translated by Dr. Alana M. Vincent, Lecturer in Jewish Studies, Department of Theology & Religious Studies, University of Chester, UK

Don Karlos, Infante von Spanien, Friedrich Schiller. Act 5, scene IV, as translated by Shira Glassman

All quoted literature sourced from the public domain.

Dedicated to the labor rights activists of north central Florida.

Those who are rooted in justice shall flourish like a date palm.
--Psalms 92:13

Chapter 1: The Horse's Baggage

Aviva was not surprised, only annoyed, when a strange horse interrupted her walk home from Market and tried to nose its greedy way into her purchased bag of malabar spinach; the surprise came a moment later when she realized that sprawled across its back was a very attractive, well-dressed young man who seemed near death.

"Oh!" she exclaimed. "My goodness, Horse, what stall were *you* shopping at?"

But beneath the askew pile of hair, the talk of nonsense, and the constant turmeric stains beat the heart of a woman who had tended to a sick mother and then a sick sweetheart for nearly all her young life. Slipping into the caregiving role to which she was accustomed -- or as she thought of it, God's purpose for her -- she put a finger to the man's temple and saw that he yet lived. She also saw that dried blood had collected around several places that looked as though they might have brought him to the edge of survival.

Hefting the lightweight but unwieldy sack of leaves over one shoulder, she took the horse by the bridle and led it back toward the palace. Aviva was the second cook there, but her primary duty was as Queen Shulamit's personal chef. She had a habit of going to market herself instead of sending kitchen servants like the head cook of the palace did, because it gave her ideas to wander among the colorful bounty of the stalls, and it gave her pride to manage the quality. This way, she could buy what had grown well that week, or what struck her fancy. She could also keep track of the cleanliness of her products that way -- the queen's body had odd reactions to both wheat and fowl, and although Shulamit wasn't so sensitive that she couldn't bear to be in the room with it, Aviva felt safer buying the malabar if she knew it hadn't had a chicken's carcass resting up against it in a basket.

1

Aviva protected the queen's health with a devoted fierceness, for she was also the queen's sweetheart. Or "favorite," as the fashionable word went. What a word -- it did make her feel a little bit like a halvah or something. Ooh! Halvah! When she could coax a true, full smile from Shulamit's usually intense and studious face -- for Shulamit wasn't one to smile unless genuinely happy -- a sweetness just like halvah flowed through Aviva's body, and she resolved to tell her so the next time they had a comfortably private moment.

Even during this frivolous mental wandering, however, she never took one eye off the man on the back of the horse. His hair, like hers, was dark; it was curly and a bit of a mess. His skin was a little lighter than hers. Most likely this meant he had come from the west. A bit of stubble had grown across his face, but only just enough to hint he had stopped shaving because of his wounds. He was thin but healthy, except for all the blood. There was so much gold decoration on his clothing that her first thought was that he must be some sort of actor. Surely, nobody would wear anything like that *on purpose.*

Then she noticed the royal ring.

Queen Shulamit, sovereign of Perach, was sitting in the shade just inside the palace gates with her ladies in waiting. Her face broke into a broad smile when she saw her love returning, but of course she noticed the horse and its rider right away and raised her eyebrows inquisitively.

She opened her mouth to ask who it was, but Aviva beat her to the punch. "Your Majesty, we need a peaceful room and the doctor. A horse showed up with a dying prince on its back."

❀ • ❀ • ❀

The doctor and his nurses spent two hours with the prince in that quiet room, tending to his wounds and treating him with herbs and salves. Meanwhile, Shulamit paced outside, her thoughts dancing nervously around memories of her father's deathbed. The resemblance of circumstance was only superficial, of course, but waiting outside a room, worrying while doctors worked, reminded her of those awful days in the past when she'd been inches away from a throne she was about to purchase with every last tear in her body. Then she was only a child-woman, and now she was grown and had settled into her crown. But she would never forget.

An open door and movement shifted her reverie back into attendance. "Is he awake?"

"Yes, Your Majesty," said the doctor.

"Will he live?"

"It's too early to tell."

"May I come in?"

"I suppose so," said the doctor, "but don't overtax him."

"I'll try to be gentle." Shulamit stepped inside the room and took her first good look at the foreign prince. Yes, he was definitely from the west. There were several small city-states beyond the borders of Perach, but she wasn't sure which one was his. Most of them had multiple princes. She began to narrow it down by age and style of dress. Poor man! She hoped he wasn't going to die so far away from home. Did his family know where he was?

She had moved closer to him with each thought, and now she stood directly over him. "Who are you?"

With great effort, he opened his eyes. His lips moved, but no sound came out.

"Would water help?"

"He's had water," said one of the nurses.

3

"I'm going to give him more. He's trying to speak." Shulamit picked up a jug and poured some water into her hand. She cupped it against his lips and tipped it up.

He did his best to drink. His breathing sounded strange and dangerous. "Do you know who I am?" Shulamit asked. "Blink once for yes and twice for no."

He blinked, deliberately enough that she knew he had heard her, and understood.

"Can you tell me who you are? You're among friends. Whoever did this to you, it wasn't us. We'll protect you."

His lips moved again, and finally, with what seemed like all the effort from his entire body, he spoke for the first time. "Captain... Malabar. Only."

Shulamit's jaw dropped. What?

"Aviva found you, and she was carrying malabar. Her name is Aviva. She's my cook. Do you want her to come back?"

His head twitched to the side. Was that no, or an involuntary gesture?

She reminded him about the blinking, and he blinked twice.

Then he said one more syllable, "Riv," and passed out.

Shulamit clapped her hands to her face. Riv. Riv of Bitter Greens, Riv Maror. A strong warrior with a peppery personality, the captain of Shulamit's palace Guard had easily earned the nickname, which was a variant on the original "Beet-greens" that had referenced an illegitimate conception and a farmhand father. Shulamit realized it must have gotten twisted into Riv Malabar as the legend of the northern mercenary had gossiped its way across into the west, into the prince's land. For a moment, she was struck by how ill it fit Riv, given malabar's mildness.

4

Captain Riv Malabar indeed.

But what did the prince want Riv for, anyway? "Where is the captain?" Shulamit asked the guard who was attending her at the moment. "I know it's his and Isaac's day off, but are they still hanging around here someplace?"

"No, Majesty," said the guard. "They went off this morning out into the countryside."

"We'll just have to take care of him until they get back." Shulamit felt strangely reluctant to leave the room, but she also wanted to see her darling, bizarre Aviva. Trust her to go to the marketplace for greens and come home with a dying prince!

Chapter 2: The Warrior and the Dragon

A coach drawn by two horses wound across a wide swath of high grasslands that cut between stands of banana plants. Two light-skinned men sat in the front of the coach, driving the team and talking in the northern tongue about horses and women.

"I swear, one more night in that place and I would've had *both* those women's names." The man on the left slapped his thigh and then drank from his canteen. "I don't know why she made us keep going, anyway. The letter said to wait in Ir Ilan and send word."

"Maybe to keep you away from the fruit sellers," quipped the other.

"Aw, she doesn't care what I do. She didn't care back in Riachinho Estela."

"Estrela."

"Whatever. I can't speak Imbrian." He scratched his beard. "How much longer 'til we get to Home City?"

"The map says that we need to go through that valley--" He pointed down across the sloping landscape, but as he followed the line of his own finger, he saw unexpected movement in the foliage. "Hey! Tiny! Look over there!"

"What?"

Down in the valley that lay directly before them, a battle was unfolding between a ferocious dragon and a sword-wielding warrior. The dragon was several times larger than the man, with wings almost as long as its body, a powerfully muscled tail, and enormous back haunches. Two golden horns were the only parts of its body that weren't a green so dark it was nearly black. Here and there, silvery whips of light emerged from its claws, and it was these that the warrior met with sword strokes as he crashed

6

through the ground cover of lush green philodendrons. Big, broad leaves shook and waved violently in the combatants' wake.

What glimpses they could catch of the man as he darted in and out of sight around the dragon revealed him to be well-built and an expert fighter, clad in a sleeveless leather tunic and loose-fitting trousers. He was wearing a helmet and a mask obscured the lower half of his face, but they could still see the light skin of his bare arms and the space around his eyes, and the explosion of dark-blond hair pouring from beneath his helmet.

"He looks like he's from up by us!"

"What do you think he's doing in Perach?"

"Fighting a dragon."

"I can see he's fighting a dragon, you schmendrick. But why down here? Unless you think he *followed* the dragon all the way from--"

"Oh! *Ouch!*"

"No, he's okay. Oh, wow, look at that!"

"Nice."

"Good one."

They were watching the battle now almost as if it were a tournament. "Hey, do you think we should go help him?"

"He doesn't look like he needs us."

Just then, the dragon pounced on the warrior with all four limbs, knocking him to the ground. The sword wasn't in his hand anymore, and they appeared to be grappling in a tangle of arms and legs, blocked from view by leaves as big as shields. "Are you sure about that?"

"But what about *her?*" Tiny jerked his head back at the coach.

7

"Milady, we're going to go rescue someone," his companion called back loudly, spurring on the horses. "Hyaa!"

"What?" called a female voice from behind them as the coach picked up speed, moving bumpily across the landscape.

"There's a man fighting a dragon, and we think the dragon's winning."

"A dragon? I don't want to get close to a dragon. What are you doing?"

"What's that, Milady? I can't hear you over the hoofbeats," lied her escort, his blood fizzing inside his veins at the prospect of adventure. This whole journey had been far too tedious, schlepping a wealthy passenger miles and miles from home with only the female-obsessed Tiny for company.

As they got deeper into the valley, it became harder to see what was going on; from above, they'd been able to follow the fight, but down here there was too much tropical foliage and underbrush. They followed the sounds of thrashing wings, and when they could see bits of the dragon up close through the leaves, the two men sprang from the coach with swords unsheathed. "Back, you!" yelled Tiny, thrusting his sword at a patch of dark-green scales.

The next thing they knew, a whirlwind of humanity had kicked Tiny to the ground with one bootprint to the groin and now held his friend against a tree, a sword at his neck. "*Al tigu bo!*" the warrior hissed in a guttural voice from beneath his cloth mask.

"What?" squeaked the imprisoned man, dropping his sword. "We were just helping! We were saving your life! He was gonna eat you!" He was still talking in his own language, even though he understood some Perachi. He thought maybe the man had said *Leave him alone.*

The warrior glared as he kicked away the sword on the ground. "You're going to be very embarrassed in about ten seconds." Then his eyes narrowed and he squinted, leaning his face in closer. "Wait. *Hersch?*"

"How do you know my--"

The warrior peeled away the cloth mask. "Hersch, it's me. What are you doing down here? Who's that? Is that *Tiny?*"

There was a woman under the mask. And he knew that face. "R-- Rivka?"

"You haven't changed at all," moaned Tiny from the ground, where he was clutching his gonads.

"Well, I'm *sorry,* but you were stabbing at my husband with a -- *that,* you call a sword?" She snorted. "I just acted on instinct."

"Husband?" And then Hersch looked over and noticed that the dragon had nearly finished transforming into a husky middle-aged man in clothing similar to Rivka's -- the powerful tail quickly disappearing into his backside and the horns melting back beneath neatly cropped dark-blond hair. His mouth was ringed by an afterthought of a beard and mustache that seemed sketched on with a paintbrush. "Is that Isaac the wizard? I thought he died in one of the Apple Valley attacks."

"It's a long story," said Isaac, holding his hand to his thigh oddly.

"Did he get you? What's wrong?" Rivka released her grip on Hersch and rushed to him.

"Just a scratch. Don't worry about it."

Rivka turned back to face her bewildered countrymen. "Why are you down here?"

Just then, a well-dressed woman stepped out of the coach. "I hear a lot of chatter. What's going on?"

The warrior's face lit up. "Mammeh!"

Rivka pressed her sword into Isaac's hands and ran through the foliage to her mother's side. She hadn't seen her in three years, and she was glad her journey had been a safe one.

The two women hugged, and then Mitzi held her daughter out at arm's length. "My goodness, you look so big and healthy. I would have taken you for a man." She stared wide-eyed at Rivka's huge biceps.

"That's the idea," said Rivka. "Everyone at the palace except for the queen and her sweetheart call me Riv and think I'm male, so nobody gives me any trouble about being captain of the Guard. And Isaac turned Beet-greens into Bitter-greens. *Riv Maror* -- doesn't it suit me?"

"But what about him? What's he doing here?" She cast her eyes over to Isaac, who was standing placidly at a distance, watching them.

"Remember in my letter how I said I was married...?" Rivka grinned awkwardly.

"*Him,* you married? But the wizards are all celibate! What about the curses that would make him explode if he even touched a woman?"

"They thought he broke his oath and cast him out of his order under a curse -- it's a long story. Why didn't you wait for me in Ir Ilan like I said in my letter? We'd rather have come to get you.

It's easier to keep my secret without those two running around the palace, now that they know."

"We can go back to Ir Ilan now, if you can take Lady Miriam's luggage back with you," Tiny promptly offered.

"He wants to go back and chase women at the market," Mitzi whispered to Rivka, far too noisily to have genuinely meant it as a secret.

Rivka looked at Isaac. "What do you think? Can we fit all this on your back, somehow?" She waved her hand at her mother's things.

"Can he carry some of it in his paws... hands... legs... whatever dragons call them?"

"Hand injury," Rivka reminded her, making a little grasping motion with her hand.

"Oh. Right." Isaac's right hand had healed improperly from being sliced open in battle, leaving him unable to close his grasp. He made no attempt to hide the scar across his hand and forearm, and it had led to their compatriots' belief that their Captain Riv's mask hid a similar and even more horrifying scar.

"I think I can get all this if we use some ropes to tie it around my waist," said Isaac, approaching them.

Luckily, Hersch and Tiny had ropes.

"If I transform back, you'll leave me be this time?" Isaac asked them wryly.

They quickly nodded. "We're sorry, sir, we didn't know," Hersch pointed out.

"It looked like you were going to eat him -- her--"

11

Isaac raised one eyebrow, folded his arms across his chest, and leaned back slightly, giving them an impish half-smile.

"...*Oh.*"

"Hey, man, I'm sorry!" Tiny grinned and slapped his own face. "Oy vey, do I feel--"

"I *said* you were going to be embarrassed, didn't I?" Rivka pointed out. But she was embarrassed now too, because her mother was four feet away and nobody wants their mother around when they're talking about sex.

The dragon Isaac accepted his burdens graciously, and Mitzi bade farewell to the men who had transported her down to her daughter's adopted homeland and protected her along the way. "Make sure you let the baron know we're all well down here," she reminded them. "And remember to eat healthy."

"She's mother enough for seven," Tiny muttered to Hersch. "How long do you give her before she starts pestering Beet-greens for grandkids?"

Rivka could tell they hadn't intended her to hear, but since she wasn't sure she disagreed, she let it go.

The two men climbed into the front seat of the coach and drove away the way they'd come. Meanwhile, Rivka helped her mother climb aboard a dragon's back for the first time. "I didn't know he had serpent powers," said Mitzi as she steadied herself, leaning back against her daughter's broad body.

"Neither did I. The first three years after I left home, I rode him into battle without having any idea who he really was. Turns out, he was under a curse, but once I got rid of that, he could turn human again and I married him."

"Were you already fooling around before you left home?"

"*Mammeh.*" The answer was an emphatic no -- in fact, the years of being called *Rivka bat Beet-greens* in ridicule as a child, as if she'd been fathered by the vegetables themselves rather than the farmhand who grew them, had left such an impression on the warrior that she had waited to exchange makeshift wedding vows before claiming her dragon. But she wasn't about to discuss that with her mother.

Isaac flapped his wings and carried them skyward. "Ooh! Whoo!" Mitzi made lots of strange, excited noises as they soared through the air. "Wheee! What if we fall off? I feel like I'm going to fall off."

"We're not going to fall off. Besides, he'd double back around and catch you."

"Then the luggage would fall off."

"It's only luggage."

"But it's all my things."

"Then don't fall off."

Mitzi's head was swiveling from side to side constantly as she gazed around at the unfamiliar southern landscape. Her wide-eyed curiosity made Rivka overly conscious of the scenery herself. Everything glowed under the direct sunlight pouring from a clear blue sky. The plants were so much showier than their northern cousins, with enormous leaves that weren't content to be bigger, glossier, and more brightly green, but sported flashes of yellow and orange as well. One type had even produced misshapen fruit as big as two-year-old children in clusters sprouting directly from its trunk. Its rind was knobbly and yellow-green. "Does something hatch out of that?" Mitzi almost sounded frightened of it.

"Breakfast," said Isaac.

13

"Jackfruit," Rivka explained. "It's yellow and fruity inside. You'll probably get your first taste soon."

"What's wrong with those trees?" Mitzi pointed at a thickly planted grove of silver palms, their leaves spread out in a fan of shining swords.

"Nothing. They look pretty healthy to me."

"They're all gray."

"That's how they grow. They're silver palms."

"They look sickly."

"That's just how they grow."

"I still think they look sickly."

On the way, Mitzi updated Rivka about the family she hadn't seen in years. Rivka was stunned to learn that the war between her people and the folks in the next valley was over. "Your uncle married Gitel and that was the end -- the valleys are united now."

"*Gitel?* What is she, seventeen at this point?"

"Nineteen."

"I can't count. Still -- he has daughters older than that."

"Oh, speaking of them! Liba is engaged. And Bina has three children. Frayda was pregnant again when I left."

"He has grandchildren and a nineteen-year-old wife."

Mitzi shrugged. "He's the baron. He's worked hard to keep the valley safe and the people fed. He deserves a little fun."

Rivka thought he also deserved a good kick in the jaw, for constantly belittling her youthful attempts at fighting to defend his keep. From where he stood, letting a woman fight for him

14

made him look weak and desperate, and he had done everything in his power to prevent her from becoming the warrior she was today. But there was no point in getting into that now. "I can't believe the fighting has stopped. I'm still stunned."

They continued along this vein the rest of the way home. Rivka was amused at the way her mother's gossip gave way to more awed gawking and staring, distracted by one marvelous view after another as they flew past the splendor of Shulamit's tropical capital, Home City. Tall, slender palms stood guard over the gleaming white buildings with their rooftops of curved, red tile. People teemed everywhere amidst the arches and columns -- selling and buying, moving things from place to place, stopping to chat with friends, or sitting down to eat. Rivka sat up even straighter on the dragon's back, proud of her new home and the effect she knew it made.

"We're the only people here with light skin," Mitzi observed suddenly.

"So?" Rivka dearly hoped for that to be the end of that.

Mitzi was a little overwhelmed from her very first dragon flight and the other surprises of the morning, so she was glad when Isaac began his descent. The palace was shining, white, and built in a square around an open-air courtyard. Isaac touched down in the center of that courtyard, beside the lily pond. She saw a tiny young woman with dark skin and black hair in two tight braids coiled at the base of her neck rush toward them in a flurry of elegant clothing. "Riv, Riv, Riv, Riv, Riv!" called out the woman in frenetic greeting, her fists tapping each other along with her speech. "Good, you're back. There's a--"

Then she noticed Mitzi and cocked her head. "Is that your mother?"

Mitzi scrambled to keep up with the foreign tongue, familiar from prayers but so different to hear in ordinary conversation.

"Yeah," said Rivka. "Uh, *Mammeh*, this is Her Royal Majesty Queen Shulamit."

"Is she always this...?" Mitzi asked, under her breath, in her own language.

"Something like that. She's as tightly wound as those braids," Rivka murmured in response.

"Lady Miriam, right?" Shulamit approached Isaac's back, squinting as she looked upward because looking at Mitzi also brought her eyesight directly in line with the sun.

"Yes, Your Majesty. Thank you for your hospitality," said Mitzi, speaking carefully in the language of Perach.

"Mammeh, we have to get down off Isaac's back and unpack or he can't transform," Rivka reminded her.

"Oh, sorry!" Shulamit's guard reached out for Mitzi, and she climbed into his arms. "Sorry, thank you." He was a nice-looking older man, dark-skinned like the queen, of course, and suddenly Mitzi found herself smiling nervously. Well, what was the harm in that? Even if he was only a guard. But then, she reminded herself, here, she was only a guard's mother. Even if Rivka -- Riv -- was their captain.

"Tivon, please get Lady Miriam settled in." Shulamit drew close to Rivka.

"Yes, Your Majesty," said the guard.

"What's going on?" Rivka asked the queen.

"Aviva came back from market with a dying man on horseback, and he won't talk to anyone but you."

"*Me?*"

"I have no idea." Shulamit shook her head. "Come on." She dragged the surprised warrior off into a distant room, with a transformed Isaac following them.

Mitzi was left by herself in the courtyard watching them disappear, standing by the lily pond surrounded by her luggage. She *thought* she'd been able to follow the conversation, but then, it had nothing to do with her. She blinked a few times, a little disoriented.

"Please come with me." The guard beckoned, lifting her heaviest bundle by the handle with his other hand.

Oh well, if Rivka was going to run off like that, at least Mr. Attractive was still there. She picked up the rest of her things and followed him across the courtyard.

Chapter 3: The Priorities of Riv Bitter-Greens

The mysterious prince slept, but he was so fixated on finding "Riv" that in fevered dream he relived the moment he had first heard of the Captain of the Royal Guard of Perach.

"Bitter-greens or Malabar or something. His first name is Riv. Tall, and broad, and hair of bronze that sticks out in every direction, past his shoulders," the traveling merchant was saying. "He keeps his face inside a mask -- they say it hides a horrible scar."

"From fighting a dragon? Didn't I hear something about a dragon?" asked my older brother, the Crown Prince. He seemed glad that they'd stopped talking about the cancellation of his arranged marriage. He hadn't been in love with her, but it embarrassed him to hear so many graphic details of his former future father-in-law's exposure in the brothel. My father already disapproved of whores, and it would have been unacceptable for the city's future queen to have a father who visited them so voraciously.

"No, the dragon..." Here, the merchant snickered lewdly. "The dragon is his lover."

"I've heard that too," said my father, the King. "Some wizard or sorcerer or what have you. I think it's nonsense. Everything I've heard about this Riv person has been one triumph after another -- he caught the ring of blackmailers, he rescued a temple full of celibates, he wins competitions. Men who see each other as lovers aren't capable of that. It's a sign of weakness and lack of focus. Lack of priorities."

My heart sank. The lamb on my fork became dry and unchewable; the rest remained on my plate untouched for the rest of the meal. It had been delicious.

18

"Maybe in this kingdom," remarked the merchant, "but over there I tell you that's the way it is. No question. They don't even make much of a secret of it."

"He disgraces his queen, then," was my father's response. "Has he no respect for her reputation?"

"He's probably more concerned with protecting her life and her people," pointed out my fiancée, Azar. "If I were queen, I wouldn't care if my bodyguards were sleeping with sheep. What matters is how good he is with a sword, and how loyal he is. That's what I have to say about priorities." Her dark eyes flashed as she dared to defy the king, even though her tone was demure and quiet. She grew more beautiful to me in this moment, as she defended Riv -- and as she defended me too, without realizing it.

"I wouldn't have Riv as my captain, at any rate," said my father. "And you, Azar, are not going to be queen anyway, only wife to my youngest. So maybe you'd better keep your mouth shut."

She said nothing more, but gave him a look full of defiance.

Later, in the moonlight on the balcony, I thanked her. I took her by the hand and gazed into those big glistening eyes of hers and told her how much I loved her, and how brave she was to challenge my father, and she told me that she was glad she was marrying me and that she liked me best of the three princes, even if it meant she wouldn't be queen.

And then I was foolish enough to be honest.

"I loved you even more in that moment," I said. "I despaired when he said that men who looked at other men that way were weak. I know that I'm not weak, and I--" Azar's face alarmed me, and I stopped talking. "What?"

"Why do you speak of yourself that way?" She drew back slightly.

19

I kept holding her hand. "I've looked upon both men and women with love. But you're the queen of my heart, and I hope that you'll be the only--"

"What?" She pulled away entirely now, and looked at me as if my face had sprouted pustules. "You're lying."

"Why would I lie about something like that?"

"You can't be serious. I love you!"

"And I love you too," I protested. "I don't understand -- you said--"

There was more, but "You're broken," were the last words I heard from her before she ran from the balcony, back into the palace.

Into my brother's arms, apparently. Now, she will be queen, someday, after all. And she won't have to marry a man she thinks is broken.

But I knew I couldn't be broken, because Riv -- Captain Riv -- wasn't broken.

Somehow, the prince could tell that Riv was sitting at his bedside before he opened his eyes.

For several silent moments, they beheld each other, Rivka's gray-blue eyes tenderly gazing down on his dark ones.

"I'm here," the captain said at last, and took his hands in hers.

"Captain Riv," said the prince, with great effort. "Please... please help us."

20

"I hope I can," said Rivka.

"I love him."

"All right," said Rivka, nodding. Someone handed her a fresh wet cloth, and she replaced the one on his forehead with this newer, cooler one.

"My father... the prison... he's... he wants to kill..." The prince disappeared into himself a little bit.

"Who does he want to kill?" Rivka prompted him.

"We're like you," said the prince slowly and deliberately. "Like you. You're our only chance."

"Like me," Rivka repeated, and then the light turned on. "Like us. Like Isaac and me."

"Isaac...?"

Rivka cocked her head backward slightly, and from the other side of the room the wizard approached. "This one. The one who puts up with me."

The prince smiled slightly. "Save him..." Then he started to faint again.

Rivka grabbed him by both shoulders. "Wake up," she demanded. His eyes rolled open, but she wasn't sure if he was *there*. "Do you love him?"

"Yes. More... more than life."

Rivka tightened her grip on him and stared into his eyes. "You have to love life *as much as you love him,* do you hear me? Because if you don't live to tell me *where he is,* or *how I can rescue him,* he'll die. So *try harder."*

Slowly, the prince nodded.

✿ • ✿ • ✿

Shulamit was in her library reading correspondence when she heard Rivka come in. "Did he tell you anything?"

Rivka nodded. "His name is Prince Kaveh."

"Oh! That's the youngest son of Jahandar from the City of the Red Clay."

"So he tells me. He also said he's in love with another man--"

"He's like me!" Shulamit's eyes widened.

"--and his father, he just threw his lover in prison. He's supposed to be killed at the end of some sacred month they celebrate where they can't execute prisoners. Kaveh rode all the way here, and why? To beg help from *me,* of all people."

"Why you? Oh my God, those poor men," she added at half-volume.

"Think about the way everyone else sees Captain Riv and Isaac," Rivka pointed out.

Shulamit smirked and nodded. "Two big, strong, heroic men who love each other." As a genuine lover of her own sex, but one who often felt frail and vulnerable thanks to her small stature and overactive mind, it comforted her to think of the image of strength they projected to those from whom she wanted respect. "Why was he falling apart when he showed up -- bleeding and barely alive?"

"I'm getting there. King Jahandar hired an engineer named Farzin to design a series of public works projects for the city: a new bridge, repairs to the roads, *fershtay?* During the project, Farzin and this Kaveh got pretty close -- they'd been friends since boyhood. Then at the end of the whole thing, the king decides he's only going to pay everyone half wages. In his mind, that should be enough -- everyone should work to improve the city 'out of patriotism' or else they aren't true Citizens of the Red Clay.'"

"That's ridiculous. I'd never do that."

"We know. Anyway, between Farzin -- and Kaveh -- working hard to oppose him and support the people, and him finding out that Farzin had, uh, debauched his son... I'm sorry... Please don't make that face... Oh, *Shula.*"

Rivka had to tell the rest of the story from one side of a tight hug, for the young queen took all such insults to heart very deeply. "Farzin's in prison, and Jahandar wants him dead. Kaveh, he went to the prison to tell him he would ask me for help, but some of the guards didn't recognize him and on the way out -- zoom! With the arrows. He didn't want to stop to get treatment because he knew he had to get to me and convince me in time. He figured it was more important just to ride all the way here. Only, now he might not live. Isaac said he's full of infection. He might have to use magic to cure him. He says he'll try his best, but..."

"Poor man," said Shulamit, hugging the stuffing out of Rivka. Her late father hadn't been a big fan of the direction of her attentions, but the idea of anyone trying to have Aviva *killed...* Things like this made her glad she had a sword-slinging loudmouth and a dragon-man on her side.

Whereas it sounded like Kaveh had only the persistence of his own determination.

Well, maybe *now* he had Rivka. And Isaac. And herself.

"So Isaac is going to work on him now?"

"No, he has to wait for some of the prince's strength to come back. He hasn't had enough fluids or eaten enough yet. But he will -- tonight."

Shulamit nodded. "Keep me posted. Sorry about your day off."

"My what?" Rivka quipped wryly.

On her way out into the central courtyard, Rivka crossed paths with her mother, who was exploring the cultivated flowers. "Oh, hi, Mammeh." It was novel to be speaking her own language within Shulamit's walls with someone other than her husband after three years. Her Perachi was fluent but heavily accented, as was Isaac's.

"Nice of you to notice me," said Mitzi crossly. "Why did you invite me all the way here if you didn't even have time to get me settled in and show me around?"

"I--" Rivka was caught sideways. "Now that I've got a job, I wanted to give you a place to live where you'd be treated with respect."*Because nobody here knows that you got knocked up by a vegetable gardener when you were a teenager,* she added silently. *Except the queen, and she doesn't care about things like that.*

"I didn't mind," said Mitzi. "I had learned to live with it. It was no more than I deserved. I was happy up there!"

"Then why did you *come?* You didn't have to." But by looking at her face, Rivka knew she'd made a mistake.

"Yes, I did." Mitzi looked away. "Your uncle got ahold of the letter and decided it was a good idea for me to come down and

24

live with you. And now he doesn't have to be responsible for me anymore."

"I'm sorry."

"I--"

Then both women looked over sharply, because they realized they weren't alone anymore. A gentle-faced woman about Mitzi's age, with long hair held back with a scarf that had been folded into a headband, had limped over to them with a pretty little cane. "Are you Riv's mother? So nice to meet you, finally. I'm Leah -- Aviva's mother. You must be so proud of Riv. And you have such beautiful hair! I've never seen a woman with golden hair before."

Mitzi blinked a few times. Rivka knew her mother wasn't used to random castle-inhabitants treating her so kindly. "Please call me Mitzi."

"May I show you around the palace? I only just moved in a few years ago, just after Riv came."

"I'd like that."

"We love Riv here," said Leah. "You really did raise him right."

As far as Rivka knew, it was the first time Mitzi had heard anything like that in her entire life. Her mother's face made it clear she was soaking it up like dry soil in a rainstorm. "See you at dinner, Mammeh," Rivka called out to them as they walked away.

Isaac was at her side. "Leah to the rescue?"

"She could charm the stone out of a peach," said Rivka.

"Now you sound like Aviva."

"'Vivaleh would have said something even weirder. Something about peaches with wings, and a flute in there someplace. Or maybe snails."

"Come on, Captain. We still have a few minutes of 'day off' before sundown." He could say so much with just his eyes, and with that subtly smirking mouth.

Rivka followed him inside their room, their little 'dragon cave.'

The door panel was barely shut before his powerful arms snaked around her, pulling her into the cushion of his belly. She caramelized into his heat like a ripe plantain, sizzling at the feeling of his hungry lips all over her face and neck as he pushed her down onto their bed. "I wanted you so badly out there in the brush when we were sparring," she told him huskily, "and then when Hersch and what's-his-name showed up swinging swords I just couldn't believe..." She began to remove the leather armor that both protected her and kept her breasts -- and therefore her womanhood -- secret. "Need to feel your skin on mine."

He seized her wrist. "Not in the palace. Put it back."

"Don't *wanna*! Your tongue... everywhere..."

"Not here. Someone might see. And you know I can't do that here, either."

Her growl sounded like a charging bear.

Propping himself up on his right elbow, he untied the laces between her legs with well-practiced fingers and purred into her ear. "I promise, Mighty One, I promise I'll make it so good you won't mind so much."

"Aaaahh," Rivka moaned.

"And then, on another day off, I'll take you back into the woods and you can have as much dragon's tongue as you want."

26

Her legs were wrapped around him now as she rubbed herself eagerly against his bulging trousers, trapping his left hand between them. "Waited... all... day..."

"For this?"

Rivka threw her head back and let out a deep groan of abandon as she was filled. He began to thrust, and she overflowed with pleasure at the feeling of his bulky torso bearing down on her, his fingers working at her, himself inside of her stretching her and colliding with the parts of herself she couldn't see that buzzed and shuddered. True, they were separated by layers of heavy clothing that preserved her status and reputation and sometimes her ribs ached, but it was still so *very good.*

She seized up and came, her fingers grabbing his back hard enough to leave marks.

"Would it be so terrible if they found out? If the world finally learned to cheer a lady warrior?" Isaac's head rested on her shoulder as he idly stroked her thighs.

"If they don't learn, I'll lose everything." Rivka feared practically nothing; for years she had gone into battle with a strong heart and a ready temperament. But a childhood near her bullying, misogynist uncle had given her one thing of which to be scared: that even after they'd seen her succeed, if the rest of the world found out she was female, her great reputation would shatter into unbelievable lies, and she'd have to start anew.

"You wouldn't lose me," Isaac reminded her. "But I'll help you protect your secret."

"I know you will. Keeping secrets is kind of your specialty."

He grinned. "Not from you, Mighty One. Never again from you."

And she knew he meant it.

Chapter 4: What They Built

"Wake up, Your Highness." The voice was a deep, quiet bass he didn't recognize.

"Can't."

"Yes, you can. The herbs are wearing off. Open your eyes. I need to know you're listening to me."

"Who is this?"

"Isaac."

Prince Kaveh's eyes snapped open. The room had grown dark in the nighttime, with moonlight sneaking in at a window. Its pale light merged with the light from an oil lamp at his bedside to illuminate a round face with a trim beard and mustache. "You're Captain Riv's--"

"Wizard."

"How did you meet?"

"I taught him to sword fight," said the wizard.

"So you're a warrior too?"

"Was a warrior," Isaac corrected. Drawing back his sleeve with his other hand, he showed the prince the raised, gnarled scar across his right palm and forearm, then strained his right fingers to show how they no longer closed properly. "I prefer other ways of fighting now, and if I have to use a sword, I still have my left hand."

"I feel normal around you," Kaveh blurted suddenly and irrelevantly.

"I think we all feel that a little bit, sometimes," said Isaac. "Sometimes, I only feel normal around the Captain. Whatever 'normal' is."

"Is Riv going to save Farzin?"

Isaac met Kaveh's pleading eyes with his own sky-blue stare. "We're all going to do everything we can. For my part, I'm supposed to save your life tonight. You're so full of infection I could almost draw it all out and make a whole second Kaveh."

"What are you going to do?"

"My magic will kill the infection. Your part is to think of something that makes you happy. I need you to keep your mind on pleasant thoughts."

"Farzin." Kaveh's word was almost a sob. He immediately thought of the last they'd seen of each other, with Kaveh outside the prison window, straining against the bars to touch his beloved's face and hands as best he could.

"*That is not what I meant!*" Isaac growled, and Kaveh believed the dragon rumors.

"I'm sorry," he said, quickly.

"Happy moments, Highness."

"I'll try harder."

Kaveh slipped into a reverie, and Isaac used his magic to convert the happy thoughts into that which would fight the infection.

My despondent meditation ended as my father jerked me up from the floor by my shoulder. "I can't believe I have to pick my own, grown son up off the ground," he complained to whatever aide stood beside him. "At least he has two brothers that know how to be men, so that I know I did something right."

"What do you want, Baba?"

"Show a little respect. And clean yourself up. I'm sending you on a mission."

I tried to tidy the dark, messy disaster of my hair, insulted that he'd treat me like this in front of his aides -- but not altogether surprised. "What is it?"

"Everything is ready to go for the improvements to the City," said the king. *"I've selected the site for the new bridge across the river, and all the places where the road needs to be repaired are marked on the map. The bridge is going to connect all the new houses with the new market, so that the people won't have to walk to the old bridge on both sides of the river to get back and forth. You'll go and oversee the entire project."*

"Public improvements?" My brow furrowed. I knew nothing about roadwork and bridge building. "Me?"

"Just the thing to take your mind off Azar," my father added cruelly. "Surely you realize how ridiculous you are to mope after her to this degree. Why, all it took was one joke from me about how she'd never be queen, and the next thing she does is go off and change her allegiance. A woman like that isn't worth all the fuss you're making over her."

My chest heaved as I simply breathed in and out, unable to defend the maligned, innocent Azar without incriminating myself. And that had been no joke. Baba always tossed off his insults as jokes later. "I don't know how to build a bridge."

"You dizzy boy." My father rolled his eyes. "I'm not asking you to build it, just babysit the project and make sure my money's being spent properly -- and the glory of the City made great. I've got a real engineer working on the practical details -- that fat fellow you were friends with in school. Farzin, I think he calls himself."

30

"It'll be good to see a friend," I said softly, almost to myself.

"Go -- I told him to expect you at the bridge site."

That was how it started, with me trudging toward the new marketplace, a pack on my back, looking for Farzin.

I found him standing at a table under a makeshift canopy, at the edge of the high, steep riverbank. The table was covered with parchment, and he was alternating between marking things off and staring at them when I approached.

He looked different and the same. He was still pudgy, the way I remembered, with a softness to his belly and arms, and a face that was a little bit flabby. But he seemed taller, somehow, and simply by standing there he created a presence. He radiated confidence, and he hadn't always been like that.

I watched a commoner approach him with a brick in each hand and ask a question. Farzin studied both bricks, then pointed to the one on the left. The commoner nodded and scurried off. The decision had been made with complete self-assuredness. What would it be like to have that kind of confidence?

Then Farzin must have sensed my eyes on him and looked up. "Prince Kaveh?"

I grinned and joined him under the little tent. "You remember me!"

He greeted me with open arms, and we hugged briefly. Then I laid my pack on the ground beside his table, and he began to show me the plans he had designed for the new bridge.

I put in my best effort, but I couldn't keep my mind focused on what lay before me. "Farzin... it's so good to have a friend."

"What's eating you?"

"Everything."

31

"Intense as always. You haven't changed."

"You have. You're so full of... power." It wasn't the word I wanted to say, but it must have been what I felt.

"I'm so full of math," said Farzin. *"Maybe math can fix your problems. It's going to fix the problem of how to get those people home with their groceries without dying of exhaustion."* He pointed at the houses across the river, then at the market in front of them.

"I'll give you a math problem," I said. *"One prince minus one fiancée equals an absolute wreck."*

"Oh. Azar. Well, I heard about that."

"What did you hear?" I gasped, a little more frantic than I would have preferred.

Farzin put a hand on my shoulder to steady me. *"I heard that she was marrying you, and then all of a sudden she was marrying your brother, that's all. Why, is there more?"*

I blinked, not having enough room in my brain to figure out whether my distress was at his question -- or his touch. As I looked away into the river, I heard him softly calling me. *"Hey."* It didn't help.

"She found out something about me." He had coaxed that admission from me with that one soft word, and the warm, firm hand on my shoulder.

"Must have been quite the secret," said Farzin. *"What--"*

"I can't tell you." I pulled away from him and took a couple of steps toward the river. *"Maybe you'll hate me too."*

"I'm not like that," said Farzin. *"I could never hate you. I'll always be your friend -- nothing could ever make me feel*

otherwise. I knew that the minute you stood up to those boys on my account, the first day of school."

"I'm glad I did it, even if it got me beaten to shreds. They were being horrid to you."

"They wouldn't have beat you up if they'd known you were the prince," Farzin pointed out.

"Once they found out they kept trying to make it up to me, but I never had any respect for them."

"Instead, you chummed around with me -- the fat nerd."

"You were the nicest."

"See? I'm the nicest. You should trust me. Tell me what's so bad that it drove away Princess Ficklepants."

"She's not technically a princess yet." I chuckled in spite of myself at the ridiculous name. "I--" The scene with Azar replayed itself in my mind, the suddenness with which my admission shattered her love looming before me. So I said nothing. "Explain to me again what a keystone is?"

Farzin laughed outright. "That wouldn't fool a kitten."

"Fine. I don't see any kittens."

"Since you're not telling, I'm just going to guess. Tell me if I get it, all right? She left you because you... roast small animals alive and eat them."

"What?"

"Well, it can't possibly be worse than that -- I know you well enough to be sure. I'm just starting big and working my way down."

"Roasting small animals alive? Where do you even come up with--?"

"So that's a no, I take it?"

"A big no. I don't even like rare meat."

"I think I remember that. Okay, another guess... You... you're in love with your own stepmother!"

"I don't even have *a stepmother anymore," I pointed out. "She and Baba quarreled, and he had the marriage annulled."*

"See? Your way is clear! Now you can marry her right away."

"Very funny. I'm not into older women, and I'm especially not into older women who have slept with my father."

"You're right. That's a bit disturbing. Well, how about... You eat shoes!"

"What do you *eat, that you're able to come up with these off the cuff like that?"*

"You beat the maid."

"I never beat anyone."

"You cast spells on rabbits."

"I've never done magic."

"That's it! She left because you can't do magic."

I shook my head, grinning at his silliness.

"You tried to juggle oranges and dropped one on her foot... You caught a fish and named it after her because of the smell... You stole enchanted gold from mermaids... You got into a knife fight with a hashish girl... You threw the wrong baby into a fire."

"Since when is there a right *baby to throw into a fire?" But he made me grin and laugh at my own misery, and I realized I was*

really enjoying his company, even more than I thought I would when I first heard my father say his name.

"Mmm, babies."

"You're ridiculous." It was my father's word, and it wasn't quite what I wanted. Somehow, he understood anyway. Maybe it was because of the giant silly grin plastered across my face. My cheeks hurt from smiling so hard.

"But I'm helping," he pointed out.

"Yes, you are. Okay, I'll-- I'll tell you. I-- "

Then a pair of workers walked up, each holding rolls of parchment. Farzin threw me a look of resignation, murmuring, "Your secret is safe with me -- or without me, I suppose!"

I grinned again and returned to looking at the designs for the bridge. This time I was able to concentrate, and I lived my first productive hours since Azar's defection.

I didn't get a chance to tell him later, either, because when the work for the day was done and it was time to head off to Mother Cat's for bread and meat and wine, I found that we were accompanied by three of the workers. Farzin had invited them, which surprised me, but I went with it because I trusted him. The five of us sat at one of the bigger tables, all sharing a conversation as if we were equals.

Farzin often did things like that. He himself was of noble birth, but he had a passion for ranking men based on ability, not class. I learned as I worked with him those happy months that some of his brightest assistants had begun as brickmakers or errand boys. It was a wise way to structure an operation. Sometimes I was grateful and confused that I had made the cut. I had no special aptitude for math, although he was patient with my efforts and seemed pleased by the double effort I poured into understanding things that didn't come naturally.

35

He hadn't forgotten the secret, although he wasn't too mean about it. He would just say things in quiet moments, like "I still haven't answered your question about keystones, but maybe you should go first." And I'd start to say something, but I liked him too much to open my mouth.

Brick by brick, the bridge was built.

And moment by moment, I fell in love.

This was a love deeper than what I had experienced with Azar. She was intoxicatingly beautiful, and her strong will was exciting. Farzin wasn't beautiful, although I found his appearance pleasing in a baffling way that defied everything I had always been told about beauty. He was also admirable and principled and gentle and just and brilliant.

There came a night when the bridge finally stretched in completed glory across the City's river. The following morning, my father would host a ceremony to open it to the public. But for tonight, it was still ours -- mine and Farzin's.

I stood beside him on the riverbank, marveling at what human mental and physical strength had created.

"Isn't it amazing? I'm so proud of our team. We must have had some of the best workers in the world."

I gazed out at the bridge, my eyes sweeping over the enormity of the silver-white stones, standing out against the night sky as if made from moon-stuff. I relished the places where they were solid and strong and loudly proclaimed their right angles, but also the more graceful bits of flair and decoration where flowers and fruits and images of the sun and moon had been carved by more artistic hands. "It's magnificent," I agreed. "But it'll never again be as magnificent as it is right now, in this moment. When I see it in the future, that magnificence will be tempered by sadness. I'll think of these months we've spent together, and the bridge will remind me that we're apart."

"Oh, no! I don't want anything to ruin the bridge. We've worked so hard on it. For the sake of the bridge, then, we should never be separated."

I turned to face him, inspecting his mild face in the moonlight for an answer to this mystery before me. Would he be my brother, or was this something else? "Then do you promise to stay with me? And I'll be by your side as well?"

He took both of my hands in his. "Enthusiastically!" Heaven knows what expression he read on my face, because he soon added, "What's wrong?"

The words were out of my mouth before I could even think them. "I'm afraid that I'll kiss you, and then you'll throw me in the river."

I didn't even have time to get nauseated or loud of heartbeat before he drew nearer and replied in a tone far too jaunty for the moment, "Then why don't I kiss you, and then you can throw me in the river instead?" And he did. It was quick and unbearably light, like a leaf brushing against my lip as he pounced and retreated.

He hadn't gone far. I pulled him closer, our lips nearly touching again. "Why are you always such a wiseass?" I felt his breath on my face, and my body was alive with heat like a torch -- no, like a night full of torches.

"I'm ugly and nerdy." He was so close that I could feel movement from his mouth as he spoke. "I figured if I were extra entertaining, it would make up for it and you'd like me."

"If you're ugly, why does my heart beat faster when I look at you?"

"I don't know. Maybe you should visit the docto--"

Enough of this; I couldn't bear it. Against his mouth, open in speech, I pressed my own. He yielded into my kiss and dropped my hands so that he could enfold me in his arms.

He was the first man I ever kissed, and deep within my pleasure I had one thought of clarity: this act, this kiss, it was the same as kissing a woman. In that moment it mystified me why this kiss should be so forbidden where Azar's had been ordinary and expected.

Then I stopped thinking and just wallowed in the feeling of my tongue against his.

When the kiss broke, he leaned against me. "How I have loved you."

"Why?" I didn't mean to say it, but it was the first thought in my head.

"Who couldn't?" He was all smiles as he beheld me. "You're adorable, smart, good-looking, kindhearted, hardworking..."

I had expected to be called handsome, of course, and I knew I worked harder than my father would have thought possible -- but all that at once was too much for me. I'd never heard so many nice things said about me at once, and it scared me.

He seemed to sense my discomfort and persisted in a reassuring tone. "Kaveh -- my Kaveh. I know what I'm talking about. I'm smart -- you should listen to me. I'm an engineer!"

"A great one," I agreed. It would be easier to turn the compliments back on him than to explain.

"You know it." His face took on the look of a child unwrapping a roomful of presents, and he added, "And I'm such a good engineer that they let me design that bridge. I know there's a space beneath it, just beside the river..."

"Where we won't be seen?"

Where he sat against the bridge foundations in the black of the night, and I leaned my back against his chest and let his arms encircle me and caress me as I had caressed myself. Where I leaned my head back onto his shoulder and kissed his neck and his ear and sometimes his lips, if I could reach.

Speaking of bridges, this was one Azar and I had never crossed. But it was even more glorious than the edifice above me.

Above him, the wizard Isaac worked deep into the night. The sky was a fuzzy gray when he finally crept into bed beside Rivka, who stirred and wrapped her arms and legs around him in sleepy greeting. "How's the prince?"

"He'll live."

"I knew you could do it."

"I did it, but I've lost my magical abilities for a few days. Too draining."

"Wow. That's some serious stuff."

"But he'll live."

She hugged him hard and then fell completely back asleep.

Chapter 5: The Alliance

It was late morning, and Shulamit was pacing by herself in the Hall of Ancestors. White sunlight poured in through the windows and lit up the mosaics as she passed them over and over, studying the faces she knew so well.

She paused to examine her great-grandfather, who was famous for his great love of music. He had commissioned a wealth of dances and ballads from his court composers, and they were still very popular across her kingdom. He had very bushy eyebrows.

Beside him was her grandfather, who looked stern and intimidating in the mosaic, but whom she remembered being gentle and patient with her when she was a little girl. The way he glared out from the portrait made him look as though he could snap you in two by looking at you, but she remembered running across the courtyard and falling down, and him picking her up again as carefully as if she were a paper sculpture.

Next, her father... She wondered if the tears would come, as they sometimes did -- but not today. She looked into the tiled eyes of the mosaic and heard him singing as he lit the royal menorah in Chanukahs past. Would there have been anything else he would have wanted to tell her, if he'd known she would be queen so soon?

At the end of the row of portraits glittered the brand-new tiles of her own likeness. She studied the image, dryly amused by how different it was from all the stern middle-aged men to the right. A young woman with thick black hair parted in the center and braided in two plaits, twisted back up at the nape of her neck and pinned like two coils of rope, looked back at her with as much of a regal expression as she had been able to muster for the portrait sketch.

And then... to the left...

Looking at the blank wall beyond her reign, Shulamit pawed her abdomen slowly and imagined what it would be like to have a *little person* growing inside her.

From outside the door, Tivon, who was on guard duty, called out, "Your Majesty, Aviva."

"Thank you." They still announced Aviva even though the two women slept in the same bed every night.

"The experiment with the tapioca flour didn't work, so I brought you figs and cheese instead," said Aviva, placing a platter on a small table near Shulamit.

"Thanks! I'd almost rather have this anyway."

"Are you feeling all right?"

"What? Oh!" Shulamit realized she was still touching her womb. "I'm fine. I was just thinking about Prince Kaveh."

"So you're definitely going to ask him... to help you make the next mosaic?" This wasn't a new topic, but now that the prince's survival was no longer in question, it had become more practical.

"I'd be silly not to. All this time I'd been wishing for a prince who liked men to come along so I wouldn't have to worry about anyone wanting to take me away from you."

Aviva squeezed her shoulder affectionately. "Even with a husband you'd need a cook."

"I know you wouldn't feel like I was being unfaithful to you, but *I* would. Although, I realized a long time ago that being queen means I have to make choices that are good for the kingdom, and sometimes that means things that make me uncomfortable. There's also my complete lack of interest in lying down with men," Shulamit added. "Every time some neighboring prince or king comes sniffing around wondering if he suits my fancy, my skin crawls. I don't even know what I'll do if Kaveh says yes.

41

He'll still have to touch me -- I know where little monarchs come from!"

"But he's so *pretty!*" said Aviva, grinning.

"I'm not *like you.* I don't like men at all, not that way. I--" Shulamit covered her cheeks with her hands and rubbed her face nervously. "I need to stop thinking about this. I need to get him to agree to marry me before I worry about how to cope with the next step."

"Whatever you face, I'll help you." Aviva took both of her hands and lifted them to her mouth. She kissed each set of knuckles sweetly, then led Shulamit over to the food. "Some fuel before your hunt."

Isaac and Rivka had carried Prince Kaveh out into the courtyard to breathe the outdoor air. He rested in the shade of a coconut palm, propped up against its fat trunk with the aid of many pillows. To his right sat Rivka, who was mending a piece of her armor, and Isaac stood to his left against the tree.

Rivka hopped up when she saw Shulamit and Aviva come out into the courtyard. "And now, Your Highness, I can properly introduce you to our queen. May I present her Majesty Shulamit bat Noach, and this is Aviva, with whom she shares her life."

The prince gazed up at the two approaching women with questions in his big brown eyes. Then he looked at Rivka. "Excuse me, are-- is--?"

"Yes, I meant share a bed. You wanted help -- you certainly came to the right kingdom!"

A cloud lifted on Kaveh's face, and he looked happy for the first time since they'd met him. "Then I'm truly safe!"

"Nobody will hurt anyone for loving someone of their own sex in my kingdom," Shulamit informed him in her best queen voice. "Pleased to meet you, Kaveh of the City of the Red Clay."

"Thank you for everything, Your Majesty. I'm sorry to have been so much trouble."

"I'm just relieved that you're doing so much better." She sat down beside him on the grass.

"I never imagined there would be a queen -- or king -- like me," Kaveh breathed, wonder still in his voice and face. "Your kingdom now seems like a paradise. Farzin and I -- we'd talked about sharing a home after the construction project was over. We would have been happy here. He's an engineer. He was always good at math in school, and putting things together... You could use someone like that, right?"

"Sure. There's plenty of work for anyone with either a strong back or a strong mind," said Shulamit.

"A little house together..." He turned to Rivka sharply. "You'll rescue him, won't you? I rode all the way here without stopping because I couldn't think of anyone else who would help... men like us."

"I want to help you both," said Shulamit. "I'm sick inside thinking about what you're going through, you and him. Traveling this road -- our road -- hasn't always been easy, but never has anyone tried to kill me or kill Aviva just for loving each other." She paused strategically.

Kaveh took the bait. "What kinds of problems have you had? I would have thought a monarch could do as she pleases."

"Mostly, yes," said the relieved queen. "But queens need heirs, and my line of the family is a straight branch with no twigs. My

43

kingdom goes to my closest blood relation when I die, and I can't in good conscience let that be someone I don't love or even know. Kings and princes know this, and they visit me and pay me court. I've refused all of them so far -- they all wanted me as a wife, not just an alliance. I've always known that it would be wrong for me to lie down with them. I can't explain it. But to you, I don't have to."

"I don't know," said the prince. "I think Farzin is like you and only likes men. But I've always known I liked more than just one or the other. I don't see why it should matter what kind of body someone has. Don't we fall in love with our hearts and minds anyway?"

"I wish it were that simple," said Shulamit, trying not to be cross with him. "I don't know what it is about me that refuses men. I have a strange body. It refuses wheat and fowl as well, although I probably wouldn't be the same kind of ill if I lay down with a man as if I ate a chicken pita."

"I hope not. That would make this heir business even harder!"

"Mmm. It's hard enough figuring out what I'm going to do. I need to do something before people decide I'm not ever getting married and then I'll have to deal with scheming nobles fighting over which third cousin to support for succession."

"What about-- What's your name again? Aviva?"

Aviva nodded. "Yes, I'm Aviva. I'm not worried for myself. Climbing vines twist around each other and reach for the sunlight. Butterflies land on them but don't speak their language. They fly off and don't matter."

Kaveh blinked. "What?"

"She knows she has the queen's heart and all this is immaterial," Isaac explained.

"She does that," Shulamit added sheepishly.

44

"That was beautiful," said Kaveh.

"Thank you!" Aviva smiled broadly.

"So, whatever your plan is, your real love will always be Aviva, right?" Kaveh confirmed, looking back at Shulamit.

She nodded. "For life. That's the plan, anyway." *Until my elephant comes along,* came the thought with no warning, and she found herself momentarily stony-faced as she forced away the moment of grief. In the years since her father's death, moments like this had grown fewer and farther between, wild hares instead of a cageful of mice, but sometimes one still ran across her path. At least, that was the way Aviva had put it once.

"And that means, if it were me, you'd let me stay with Farzin, right?"

Shulamit's plan had worked. "Of course! I'm glad you saw where I was going with this."

"Are you kidding? I grew up hearing nothing but hate for people like me from my father -- not that he knew -- and hardly meeting another, and then I find this... *enchanted* place where even the queen has a lady friend. You sit there talking about needing a prince who won't trouble you too much. Am I enough of a prince for you? I'm only a third son, and the City of the Red Clay isn't all that powerful, no matter what my father likes to think."

"You're definitely enough. Do you mean it? Will you?"

"I will if you rescue Farzin."

"I'm pretty sure that was our plan, although we hadn't really worked out the specifics." She looked at Rivka.

"Isaac won't be able to turn dragon for a few days," Rivka reminded her. "Last night wore out his magical strength."

"Which means we have time to discuss plans," said Isaac.

45

"Don't forget, my father wants to execute him as soon as the Sacred Month is over."

"That gives us... three weeks?" Shulamit calculated. "Isaac, how long is your dragon-flight to the Red Clay?"

"I can get there in a day, especially if there's only one person on my back."

"Why don't we start with you and another emissary going over there on a reconnaissance mission," suggested Shulamit, "on the surface, to ask King Jahandar for his cooperation in my marrying his son, but also to figure out where we stand and what we're up against."

"You've got the superior military power," Kaveh observed. "Can you also threaten him a bit? Get him to pay all those workers? Farzin might feel like he was deserting his people if he left without getting that sorted out."

Rivka struck a pose. "That father of yours sounds like he needs a good kick in the *tuchus,* and I've got two kicking feet right here."

"You're not going with Isaac, not this time," said Shulamit. "I'm sending Tivon."

"What? Why?" Rivka made a face, though the only parts of which could be seen over the cloth mask were her furrowed brows and piercing gray-blue eyes.

"Because you're too eager to start a fight," said Shulamit. "This time I just want information. If you go over there and tip tables over, Jahandar's likely to see it as an act of war. Besides, I need you here. I need your help with something. I know I have the stronger military and more resources. But I feel like if I think about it hard enough and put enough smart minds to the task, we can come up with a peaceful way -- of both getting Farzin out and getting the king to pay his people."

"And for *that* you need your star warrior?"

"I know you're really well-read about strategy. Well, both you and Isaac are, but I need him over there because he can use one of his forms to sneak around and snoop. Plus, he's the transportation."

"Hm." Rivka folded her arms.

"Don't worry, Riv; if there's butt-kicking to be done, I'll make sure you're at the front of the charge."

"If only my father could see him," said Kaveh happily. "He doesn't think men with male lovers are any good at fighting. Riv's so brave!"

Beneath Rivka's cloth mask, a very female brain remembered her uncle, the baron, saying similar things about women and fighting. "You're brave too, Highness," she said softly. "People who aren't brave don't ride all the way to a foreign capital bleeding from multiple arrow wounds to beg for help from a stranger."

"Thank you. Nobody's ever called me brave before."

"Bravery isn't all swordfighting and riding dragons," said Rivka. "Sometimes it takes bravery just to be who you really are inside."

Chapter 6: The Army of Brains

Shulamit clapped her hands. "Hey!"

The roomful of chattering, well-dressed women instantly fell silent. Each lady-in-waiting's eyes snapped to her queen, curiously waiting to find out why they'd all been gathered here in the Hall of Records. Shulamit greeted their curiosity with her characteristic awkward smile, her head held high but the fingers of one hand clutching the end of her filmy scarf.

Riv was there too, with her recently arrived mother beside her. Mitzi had made a pleasant, if shallow, impression on the ladies of Shulamit's court; her conversation, halting as she navigated their language, had been mostly about clothing and jewelry and whether or not men were good-looking. Of course, Aviva was hovering near the queen as usual.

"All of you know by this point about Prince Kaveh from the City of the Red Clay," Shulamit began, "who joins us as a fugitive from his own father, King Jahandar. He's healing up well and should be back on his feet soon, thanks to the doctor and to Isaac."

"What did Isaac do?" whispered one woman to another.

"Who knows? Isaac scares me. He can turn into a snake, and he has so many secrets," replied the second.

Shulamit ignored the chatter. "When he's well, I hope to make Kaveh my prince consort. *Quiet!*" she had to add as the room erupted.

Several of the women looked at Aviva. The cook responded with grace to everyone's stares, throwing up her hands and smiling wistfully. "What can I say -- too many hens, not enough roosters."

The room fell into an uneasy silence.

"Now that everyone's good and embarrassed," Shulamit continued, rubbing her eyebrows with both hands, "I'll explain why I need you to help me right now. Kaveh and I will have a political marriage only -- I need an heir, and he needs someone to help him rescue his companion from his father's prison. Yes, his male companion. See why this is so perfect?"

"Where do you keep finding these people?" piped up a voice from the middle of the crowd. Lots of the women were looking at Riv.

"God must want everything to make sense, is all I can figure," said the queen. "Let me explain the situation. Kaveh will only marry me if I can rescue this Farzin of his, and also get his father to pay some workers who built a bridge for him. I know I can send Riv and the rest of the guards in there to do this by force, but I don't want to make an enemy of the king. Besides, people could get hurt. It's my theory that if we look into Jahandar's life, and become scholars of him, we can find a peaceful way to accomplish this goal."

She gestured to a pile of parchments and books that rested on a table beside her at the front of the room. "Each of you will take one aspect of Jahandar's life: his childhood, his views on love, his views on war -- Riv, I guess that'll be you -- his offspring, his rise to power, whatever. You'll read these books and become an expert on that one topic. Then you'll report back to me."

"I want to be the expert on Prince Kaveh," said one of the women. Those around her tittered slightly.

"I'll look into anything to do with King Jahandar and food," offered Aviva.

"Good."

"Why aren't each of us reading an entire book?" asked one of the ladies-in-waiting.

"If you did that, you'd only know one biased author's opinion of lots of topics on a surface level," Shulamit explained. "This way, you'll get a broader, more objective picture and be able to see one specific topic more clearly."

"Why can't we just ask Prince Kaveh about his father?" asked another.

"Each of you will interview the prince after you've already read about your topic in the literature. That's the best way to ensure the information he gives you is in addition to what you've read -- you go to him and tell him what you've already discovered, and then ask if there's anything he can add. Otherwise you're likely to get only the same obvious information that would be in the books anyway." Shulamit paused to sip at a goblet of guava juice. "We can't afford to miss any information -- even the tiniest detail may prevent a war."

"Excuse me, Your Majesty," said Mitzi, putting her hand up slightly. "If we're supposed to learn all this about a man, shouldn't we have a man in here to help us do our research, for some perspective? I mean, a real man. I mean--"

Rivka was staring at her, and everybody else was staring at Rivka.

"I'm sorry," Mitzi added hastily. "I just-- you know-- eh..."

Shulamit cringed, ruefully glad that Mitzi's slip could be passed off as prejudice.

"I can get my father," offered Aviva. "I'm sure both he and Ima would be happy to help."

"That's a good idea," said Shulamit. "The more people we have helping us, the better our chances are of not missing something." She paused for emphasis. "We have three weeks. At the end of three weeks, Farzin's scheduled to be executed, and even if we don't have a peaceful solution, we'll have to rescue him however we can."

The women filed up to the front of the room, to collect their parchments and books and pick out the aspects of Jahandar's life on which they were to focus. When Leah and Benjamin, Aviva's parents, joined them later, they received topics as well.

"What are you going to research, Majesty?" asked one of the ladies.

"Everything," was the queen's answer. "I'm going to read all the books. Like I said, I don't want to miss anything."

More than one pair of eyes grew as large as oranges in awe.

"Aviva, while you're reading about food, don't forget to keep the snacks flowing," Shulamit reminded her. "One feeds an advancing army, and what are we if not an advancing army of brains?"

Then she sat down and opened the first book in her stack to page one.

Over the next few days, the research team read and digested the material in the library pertaining to King Jahandar, his family, his reign, and his city. Shulamit stayed up late into the night, sometimes reading by candlelight while Aviva dozed in her lap. She turned pages as quietly as she could with one hand while idly stroking her sweetheart's hair with the other. So much did she absorb that she began to have dreams about the king. None of them made any sense, and she awoke in disappointment, realizing that the brilliant solution her sleeping mind had concocted sounded very silly now that she was awake.

Meanwhile, the other women of the court, plus Benjamin -- and Rivka, who behind her mask didn't count herself as one of the court women -- began to come to her with their reports. Most of them had enjoyed their interview with Prince Kaveh, and everybody agreed that Shulamit must indeed not like men at all "that way" if his dark, curly hair, sympathetic eyes, and tall, regal nose had been unable to turn her head. How lucky, then, was this unknown man they were working so hard to rescue! Sometimes they wondered about Riv and Isaac -- Isaac definitely had his own way of being attractive but he was *weird,* and while they admired Riv as a great hero, they had never seen his face -- but with Kaveh they could definitely understand anyone wanting him, male or female.

"Ow!"

Aviva shook herself awake. She'd fallen asleep again on the divan beside her partner. "What's the matter?"

"Paper cut." Shulamit had balled her hand into a fist.

"You're up too late." The bosomy woman unfolded herself from the position in which she'd been napping, reaching out a hand to languidly close the book Shulamit held. Then she wrapped her fingers around the queen's offended thumb and pulled it over to her mouth.

A low, pleased sound came from the back of Shulamit's throat, and she leaned back into the generous softness of Aviva's arms. "Don't forget, I'm doing all this work so that we can keep on living like this forever." But she didn't stop Aviva's creeping hands from traveling across her nipples, her waist, her thighs.

"I thought you said that any man you marry would be prince consort, not a real king who could boss you around and take over Perach?" Aviva's lips moved against Shulamit's tender neck while she talked, and the response of Shulamit's body reminded Aviva of sunlight emerging from behind thick clouds . "Why would that only apply to Kaveh?"

"No, you're right. Aba set it up like that because he raised me to be queen... But I feel safer with someone like Kaveh -- someone like us. I mean, I trust him."

"But can you bear to wade in his pond?" Aviva felt Shulamit's body tense up at the idea, and tried to soothe her with calming caresses.

The queen swallowed before answering. "I don't know. I guess all I can do is try. But..." She paused. "I've been spending a lot of time around him to make sure. At least he seems like he'll be gentle, and careful, and listen to me if I say something hurts."

"We can always practice that part," Aviva reminded her.

"I wish you could do the whole thing!" Shulamit whimpered. "I never wanted to *love* men... but... this is so inconvenient."

"What do you think Kaveh would say if he knew about Rivka?" Aviva wondered, out of nowhere.

Shulamit drew in her breath sharply. "That doesn't sound like a fun conversation. Right now I think the whole 'Captain Riv' mythos is the only source of pride he has. His father managed to convince him he's a waste of space. Riv is his proof that men who love other men can be... strong. Brave. Heroes."

"He needs to learn how to become his own proof."

"I think Farzin was helping him with that. Kaveh sounds really proud of his work on the construction projects." Shulamit shifted positions because parts of her body were beginning to get tingly from being scrunched up. "Rivka's keeping her secret, though.

That uncle," she shook her head disdainfully, "he hurt her badly. And her mother believes a lot of it too."

"Rivka doesn't chew her cud for days the way you do," Aviva pointed out. "She swallows her prey whole."

"Yeah," Shulamit agreed. "She's got ideas in her head she's just always going to have because she never thinks about them long enough to question them."

"Would she be wrong, though?" Aviva undid the cord on the edge of one of Shulamit's braids and began to run her fingers through her thick, wiry hair. "Sometimes I think about the path we walk, you and I -- the things we fight for. Rivka never has people thinking her thunder is only from monthly bleeding. They don't think Isaac is her master. They don't care whether or not she's pretty. She's there already."

"I guess we're taking the long way around," Shulamit agreed. "But I don't have to breathe into a mask in boiling hot weather."

After a few days, Isaac regained his ability to perform magic, and it was time for him and Tivon to leave for the City of the Red Clay. He stood with Rivka in the courtyard in the gray hour just before dawn, holding both of her hands in his -- as well he could, of course, in the case of his right hand.

"Kiss me so I'll be able to feel it when we're apart."

Pushing aside her cloth mask, he obliged.

"I can't wait to hear what it's like over there -- the king, the prison, Farzin," she commented when the kiss had finally exhausted itself. "We'll need to know everything we can if Shulamit's plan doesn't work and we have to attack."

"Of course."

"I hope this isn't all a waste of time and the horse that carried him here isn't really Farzin under a curse," she jested, thinking of Isaac's own history.

Isaac chuckled and gazed at her with impish eyes. "I've spent enough time around that horse to be pretty confident there's no human soul hiding inside."

"I'm glad we have an expert, then." She rubbed his beefy chest through his tunic. "You make a much better man than mare."

"How fortunate for us both that I prefer it that way myself," he said dryly. "However, for the next day or so, the man must give way to the dragon."

"*My* dragon."

He held her and kissed her again, then transformed. She remained by his side until Tivon appeared, carrying their provisions for the journey.

"Travel safely, and report everything you see," Rivka reminded them. She trusted Tivon, who was a reliable and honorable man, if more traditional than progressive, but it had been jarring to find him sent in her place.

Tivon nodded. "Good luck with your research."

"Thank you."

A noise over at one of the doorways made them all look. Prince Kaveh, who had been able to stand and limp about as of the day before, was hobbling toward them. His face was full of wonder as he beheld Isaac in his dragon form. The light of the sun wasn't yet there to show the black-green scales and golden horns to their best shimmer, but he was still a sight to see simply by being so large and powerful. Tivon fit comfortably on his back with room for two more passengers, perched between the enormous wings.

Shulamit had decided, however, that Kaveh would be staying in her palace for now to recuperate. As much as he longed to go and rescue Farzin himself, he was staying safely behind.

"You don't have to be scared of him," Rivka reminded him. "He's still Isaac." To illustrate, she wrapped her arms around his neck and kissed the scales of his cheek.

Kaveh was clearly impressed by how Riv approached that mouth of enormous teeth with no fear. "I've never seen a dragon up close."

"You can get closer. I promise he won't bite you."

"I save that for Riv, and you can't watch," growled the dragon flippantly.

Kaveh reddened a little, but he drew nearer cautiously, taking it all in -- the huge tail, the haunches, the claws... "You said you were going to use your lizard form to spy around and talk to Farzin?"

"That's the plan." Isaac's serpent powers didn't end at the dragon form. He could also transform himself into an unobtrusive lizard, and an enormous python of dappled cream and yellow.

"Please... please tell him I love him... that my love for him is like food to me, or like air, and make sure he knows that my agreement with Shulamit doesn't displace him in my heart."

"I will, Highness."

"I wish I could come with you."

"You aren't well enough. It's too dangerous for you, and Shulamit has forbid it," Riv reminded him promptly in a no-nonsense tone.

He nodded sadly. "In that case, good luck."

After affirming that Tivon was ready, Isaac flapped his great wings and lifted them up into the sky. Riv and Kaveh watched them disappear into the gray side of the sky as the sun rose behind them to follow them west to the City of the Red Clay.

Chapter 7: Our Bridge

In a prison built of bricks of red-gold clay, a young man languished in a dusty cell. Outside, he had been Farzin, the engineer; here, he was just Prisoner #15, a mouth to feed until the end of the Month of the Sun. At that time, by the orders of His Most Royal Majesty King Jahandar, he would be taken from the cell and hanged, in punishment for the treason of believing that workers deserved to be paid fairly, and for the decadence of daring to love the king's son.

When he had enough energy, Farzin kept himself occupied by deriving equations in the dust on the ground with a pebble he had found in the corner. When he didn't, he simply rested against the corner of the room and prayed.

People like me aren't supposed to wind up sentenced to death, except maybe for making really bad puns, he spoke into his head. *I'm an academic, not some violent firebrand trying to overthrow the throne. I should be sitting in Mother Cat's, talking politics with my mouth full of falafel and thinking up new ways to make Kaveh smile.* He was bewildered about how wrong things had gone, and the enormity of an actual death sentence was so hard to grasp that there were moments when he didn't believe it. It was easier to be upset about hunger pangs than about being put to death by the state. He fantasized about food, even though it was torture. Falafel, dripping with tangy tahini... chewy cheeses... chickpeas... At first, he kept his dreams meatless in honor of the Month of the Sun, to make the illusion more real. It was an attempt to hold on to his dignity even though he was beginning to smell awful.

There were different moments when he was too terrified for such distractions, but even then, he still thought about others. If he had done everything right and still wound up in here, was it possible there was no safe way to fix injustice? Maybe so, but he couldn't allow himself happiness if others were being exploited right there under his nose. The men on the bridge had families, and there was absolutely no pride in being a Citizen of Red Clay if all the beauty and grandeur and modern conveniences had been built by lies and coercion and cruelty.

He was convinced his actions on the bridge had been necessary. If he hadn't prevented the men from tearing down what they'd built, they'd have all gotten arrested or even killed, "defense" not counting in the Month of the Sun's prohibitions on executions. If he hadn't bought them food with every coin of his salary, they wouldn't have had the resolve to continue until word had gotten out to more supporters.

And if he hadn't come running after Kaveh and given himself up, his handsome sweetheart would have been murdered by a father who would never miss him. To comfort himself, he pictured Kaveh's face -- his sculpted nose and cheekbones, his smooth skin, his carelessly disarranged curly hair. Farzin felt bittersweet pride that in these last months he had been able to make Kaveh happy, and to give a direction and purpose to his restless energy. He often slipped deep inside his mind to relive their most recent memories together, their sweetness his most powerful balm.

Had Kaveh survived? He didn't know. Rather than face the uncertain and most likely bleak future, he wrapped the past around him like a cloak, a past where he held Kaveh in his arms.

They had been so blissful, that night underneath the newly completed bridge. After bringing each other pleasure, they'd clung together and kissed -- thorough, minute-long kisses that lived in a time between times. It wasn't today, and it wasn't yet tomorrow; they existed in a little world inhabited only by themselves.

"I don't think I've ever felt so good in my whole life," Kaveh murmured, resting his curly head on the cushion of Farzin's shoulder.

"That was the idea," Farzin replied. "I've always wanted to make you feel good. Even before I knew it made me even more of a weirdo."

"How so?" Kaveh asked as he snuggled closer.

"When we were friends in school," Farzin explained, "especially after you were so nice to me and treated me like you actually valued me as a person, thinking about you made me happy. I wanted to make you feel the same way. You always looked so glum and unloved."

"My family is..."

"I know."

"*You* never treated me like I was worthless. I used to wish you were my brother."

"I think I did too. I didn't understand."

"What made you understand?"

"As I was saying, I noticed you were always sad and needed affection. I knew a way to bring myself warmth and peace, and I figured that if I did it for you, it would feel good for you. It didn't even occur to me that what I wanted to do was related to what everyone was talking about doing with girls. I just... I think I was silly enough to think it was something different that I'd come up with all on my own -- something that only applied to me."

"When did you figure out what it really was?"

"I was reading the second page of a love poem one day when I was bored and waiting for my mother to finish with something so I could show her a clockwork eagle I'd built. I was really surprised and fascinated because the speaker in the poem felt about the subject the way I felt about you. I was excited and turned the page back in her book so I could see what was going on, so I could remember to tell you about it the next time I saw you." Farzin paused to steal another kiss. "Sorry, I just like kissing you so much that I had to do it again!"

"You can have all the kisses you want for the rest of my life," said Kaveh enthusiastically. "Let me guess -- the poem was about a man and a woman, right?"

"Exactly," said Farzin. "You can imagine my surprise. I immediately asked my mother if a man can love another man the way men love women, and she said she didn't see why not."

"But you never told me..."

"No, and you were engaged to Azar anyway."

"That's true."

"Did you ever like a man besides me?"

"There were some of my father's guards that I... Well, I've always known I was different, but since I liked women too, and knew I'd enjoy being with Azar, I wasn't worried about it..." He shuddered with pleasure as Farzin wrapped his arms around him and pressed him close. "Is this real?"

"I sure hope so. Otherwise you're lying on the ground under a bridge that doesn't exist humping the grass on the riverbank."

Kaveh chuckled. "Madness. Like eating small animals roasted alive, right?"

"That's the idea."

"I suppose we'd better get back to the barracks or they'll come looking for us."

"It wouldn't look good for the king if they found you with your tongue down my throat," Farzin agreed.

Kaveh was slightly aroused by these final words, but since Farzin was right, he stood up. Helping his companion to his feet, he said, mostly as reassurance to himself, "Someday we won't have to say goodbye to each other at night."

"Soon," Farzin reassured him. "We'll live together always. It's fairly easy for me to find work. I can build or design anything that needs creating, and if nobody hires me, I can sell clockwork toys to the children." They began the climb up the stairs back to the top of the bridge where the roads lay, several stories above the river.

"I can do anything as long as someone teaches me how to do it," said Kaveh. "My father thinks I'm useless, but I learned to work with you on the construction project pretty quickly, didn't I?"

"I was impressed," agreed Farzin. "Honestly, if I hadn't already loved you... I might have started just from seeing how hard you worked to learn all the things you didn't know."

"I didn't know math would have such practical uses."

"One prince plus one engineer equals..." Kaveh seized him again, there on the bridge steps, and glued their mouths together one more time.

They were careful not to kiss each other again once they reached road level, but they walked close together back to the workers' barracks, their hearts full of dreams. And when they lay down to sleep in their bunks, sharing the room with four other men as they'd been doing throughout the project, their last sight before falling asleep was each other, from across the room.

If hands were moving around under blankets, well, let the other inhabitants be none the wiser.

Back in Home City, Kaveh was himself clinging to the same memories, reliving those few intense days at the start of the holiday. He woke with them, dressed with them, and in waking moments when he was alone, ate with them and prayed with them as well. He told Shulamit the less intimate parts, whenever she wasn't asking him questions about his father. It made him feel closer to Farzin.

Kaveh remembered every detail of that dangerous day when Farzin had first defied his father.

Everyone rose with the dawn to begin the glorious Month of the Sun, during which no meat was eaten, no prisoners were executed, and no morning was wasted. Joy was in the hearts of every resident of the City of the Red Clay, and none so more than the two men who had found each other's embrace the night before. They dressed in the finest clothing they had brought with them and went along with the rest of the workers to the site of the bridge and the road repairs, all of whom were ready to meet King Jahandar to hear his blessing and proclamation -- and to receive full payment for the work they'd performed.

Kaveh hadn't seen his father in a long time, but neither had he missed him. Nevertheless, he looked forward to the dedication of the bridge, because it was recognition of the grand work accomplished by his beloved Farzin.

The king gave a grand speech about the Month of the Sun and about the glory of the City of the Red Clay and how all its Citizens deserved this new bridge, which connected the new neighborhoods with the new marketplace and made it easier for them to get their things back home from market. He spoke about how the Sun would light up the red clay of the city all month long with brilliance and splendor, and how the new roads helped the city live up to its potential as a modern paradise. The workers and all those who had come to see the bridge dedicated clapped and cheered.

When the speech was over, the king instructed the workers to line up to collect their wages. Farzin, as the project leader, was first in line, and he put the purse inside his jacket without opening it. Then he hurried back to Kaveh, who was still standing in the crowd. "I wonder if there's enough in here to buy that little house we talked about. I'm afraid to count it in the crowd -- I know it's going to be a lot more than they got, and I feel self-conscious."

"Of course you deserve more than they do. You built that bridge up out of your head!"

"But they did most of the heavy lifting," Farzin reminded him.

"They wouldn't have known what to lift without you."

"I couldn't tell that to the man who's torn his muscles and sweat himself sick in the sun to move stone and brick."

"If you weren't so precise and perfect at your job, the bridge would collapse."

"If they don't lay the stones right, the bridge-- What's going on over there?"

A commotion was growing among the workers. The two men hurried over and quickly learned what was wrong. Apparently, the purses received by the workers contained only a third of the payment they'd been promised. "It must be some mistake," Kaveh reassured them. "I'll go figure it out." He fought his way through the throng of agitated men to the dais where his father stood.

"Oh, Kaveh. Good. Good job with the bridge," said his father in greeting. "Looks like everything went pretty smoothly. Do you need a servant to help you bring your things home?"

"The men who built the bridge say they got lighter purses than they were expecting," said Kaveh. "Where's the rest of it?"

Jahandar shook his head, a puzzled and innocent expression on his bearded face. "That's all. A true Citizen of the Red Clay works not only for bread but for the pride in his native land. Now that our roads are smooth and our new bridge shining, their hearts should overflow with patriotism, as does mine." He smiled warmly and looked out over the structures that his promises, if not his money, had built. "This truly is the dawn of the Month of the Sun."

Kaveh stared at him stupidly. "Do you mean you did it on purpose?"

"Are you arguing with me?" In a flash, a terrifying look came onto the king's face.

Kaveh wanted to turn and run, but courage flowed into him as he realized Farzin had joined him at the edge of the dais. "Your Majesty," said the pudgy engineer. "These men have worked hard, under heat and under rain, lifting backbreaking weights for you. Why can't you pay them what you promised?"

"They don't need more than what's in those purses," said the king, obviously shocked that someone, even the son of nobility, was talking to him like that. "All they want for is food. Anything extra, and they're liable to spend it on this vice or that. Why, just the other day I saw a working-class woman wearing a silk scarf on her hair."

"Most likely a cast-off or gift from a rich employer," Farzin countered. "Should she have declined it simply because it made you think she had wasted money on it that she doesn't have? Besides, the money in the purses might buy some food -- but what if the man has a large family, or a sick wife who can't work? And what if someone needs a doctor? There's nothing in the purse for that, and many of the men have injuries from their toil."

"That's the lot of the working class, I suppose," said the king. "Those who deserve it, rise above. I can't do anything to help those who are where they are."

"But how can they rise above if you--"

"I am grown weary of this conversation. Kaveh, come."

The king reached out his hand, but Kaveh, who had grown increasingly horrified with his father's callousness, having seen the lives of the workers up close in these past months, would have none of it. Instead of accepting his father's invitation, he glared at him with anger and sadness, then whirled around and ran back into the crowd. "Please," he begged a man who had just taken off his own outer robe because of the heat, and when the man acquiesced, Kaveh quickly covered himself so he looked like all the other workers.

Soon, he was beside his beloved in the middle of a throng of chanting men. "Give us back our promised pay!" they chanted, over and over again. He heard a sound like coins being thrown, and soft thuds, and when he peered through the milling crowd, he realized that the workers were hurling their deficient purses back at the king.

"What is this insurrection!?" Jahandar bellowed. "And on the first day of the Month of the Sun?"

"We should have given you a third of a bridge!" yelled one man.

"Who said that?" The king's eyes blazed.

"Tear up the roads!"

"Knock down the bridge!"

"No, no!" cried Farzin under his breath. "Spread the word. Fill the bridge. Stay on it and refuse to leave. He'll have to listen to us eventually, and the people will see us there and support us. Until they buy it back from us, it's *our* bridge."

The king didn't hear him, but some of the men did, and they spread the word. Kaveh, inspired, darted around the group, telling all workers within earshot.

66

Finally, all the men had gathered on the bridge, chanting. Their fists pumped in the air, but they had run out of purses to throw.

Jahandar rolled his eyes and shrugged. "I've had enough of this," he muttered to his guards. "If they'd rather do this than work, I can't stop them. You -- collect that." He pointed at the pile of purses at his feet. "It's not my fault if they won't accept what I tried to give them."

"Sire, what about the prince?" asked one of his guards.

"I can't figure out what he's up to," said the king, "but I suppose he'll come home eventually. If everyone on the bridge threw back their purses, then none of them have any money for food -- even the prince. And he's probably the least used to sitting in the sun with nothing to eat or drink. I expect he'll be home in a day or two, in time for his brother's wedding."

He and his men filed away, leaving the chanting, angry men on the bridge shouting at the sun. But he was wrong about the food, because Farzin had taken the bigger purse containing his own salary to Mother Cat's and spent it all on bread and juice for the men.

Chapter 8: The Non-Reign of King Farzin

"Is our labor worth nothing?"

"Are we slaves?"

"Our time is worthless!"

For two days, the men on the bridge shouted and chanted. Strengthened by the food Farzin had provided, they were able to keep up the vigil until the clamor attracted the attention of sympathetic supporters. Some joined them on the bridge; others brought food or water. There wasn't much to go around, but they tried to keep up hope.

The king ignored them at first, hoping they'd get tired and give up. On the third day, when he realized the group was growing larger, not smaller, he sent a guard patrol to keep an eye on them. They prowled the streets menacingly, focusing their stares on the workers. Blinding sunlight glinted from their weapons.

Farzin did his best to keep morale up. He spoke quietly, but he spoke about justice and fairness and how all should be respected equally who had done equal amounts of work. Having impressed them with his compassion on the first day, he now impressed them with his zealotry and wisdom.

Kaveh began to overhear things.

"You'd never know one who looks so funny would be so wise."

"I can understand why they were so angry, but aren't you relieved that he stopped those guys from ripping up everything we'd done? I know I am."

"A decent man. Decent, honest man. Not like our king."

"Farzin should be king."

"I'd gladly go to war for a man like that."

"Aren't we already at war?"

What he heard both thrilled him and scared him. In his deepest heart, where the thoughts without words lived, he relished the strange and dangerous idea of his beloved as king. He imagined Farzin covered in richly dyed clothing embroidered with gold thread, and a crown on his head, and himself at the engineer's side as royal favorite. He had no doubt Farzin could run the City of the Red Clay as well as he'd run the construction project.

On the other hand, the murmurs of the crowd were treasonous, and the penalty for treason was death. He was nervous that the campaign to restore the workers' rightful wages would get mixed up in a more radical dream of revolution. Such a dream might be a lethal, if seductive, poison -- given the glares of his father's guards.

A melon seller who had been blessed with a bumper crop brought some of her fruit to the men on the bridge, and they were cutting up the fruit to share for supper. Kaveh brought a slice over to Farzin, keeping another for himself. "I needed this," said Farzin between bites as he wolfed it down. "It's getting hot."

"Do the people have enough food?" Kaveh gazed out over the throng pensively. "I still have this. I can sell it and get us more than melons and pitas." He reached inside the proletariat brown robe he still wore, the one he'd begged off one of the workers when he had first darted into the crowd to avoid his father, and drew out a gold medallion.

"But that's from your mother..."

"I know, but... if you can give up all your money for these people, I feel like I should too."

Farzin took his hand and squeezed his fingers. "I think we have enough for now, but it's good to know we have that in reserve."

Kaveh gazed up at him adoringly. "I thought I cared for you already, but when you spent all your money making sure everyone was fed, I fell in love all over again. My heart is completely consumed, and recreated to exist within you."

"I'll tend it well and keep it safe, here -- with my own," said Farzin, pulling Kaveh's fingers to his own chest.

"What will you do without payment?"

"I'll have to take you as payment," said Farzin playfully, pulling him closer with his other hand, "to be mine forever. And even if they build up a mountain of gold as tall as you, and try to hide you behind it, if I can still see you through the cracks looking at me with those stars in your eyes just like you are now, I'll kick the money aside and hold you close."

"Oh, sweetest delight... Oh, blessed king of my heart."

Farzin chuckled. "If your talk was any more flowery, you'd be attracting bees instead of just engineers. And I wish you didn't call me a king. It makes me feel like I've got an honor I don't deserve." He kissed the corner of Kaveh's mouth. "I'm just your engineer."

"Some of the people in the crowd think you should be king."

"That's not going to help convince the king to pay them."

"Do you really think this is going to work?"

Farzin looked at him with sad eyes. "I don't know. I'm making this up as I go along, and I'm doing my best. I want to believe... And with each day, the crowd with us grows bigger. That's got to count for something."

"I'll trust in hope," Kaveh decided firmly. "And if hope fails, let the sword that will save us come bursting from my breast, born from the righteous anger in my heart."

"I thought your heart was here with mine," Farzin joked. "Kiss me. I'll taste of melon." He was right.

The next morning, some of the king's guards dressed themselves as workers and infiltrated the crowd. They asked innocent questions and listened to gossip and kept their eyes sharp, and it didn't take them long to find Prince Kaveh. The group of men pounced on him before he knew what was going on; one minute he was waking up snuggled into Farzin's side with his back against the bridge's safety wall, and the next he was being dragged to his feet and marched at swordpoint out of the crowd, surrounded by enemies.

Disoriented and frightened, he looked for a way out -- but there was none. Six or seven men dressed exactly like the workers flanked him on all sides, and maneuvered him deftly off the bridge and into the street.

There stood the king, in full royal ceremonial regalia. Guards and advisors surrounded him, but they scattered when they saw the prince approach.

"Kaveh."

"Baba, what--"

"What is this I hear of the people seeking a new king?"

"What? I-- Nothing! They just want their money."

"That is a *lie.* I know there's been unrest, and that someone in there's deliberately keeping rebellion in those men's minds."

"If you paid them, they'd go home."

"I think it's you. I think you're jealous that your brother is my rightful heir, and that you're nothing."

"I don't want to be king."

"You made them adore you by speaking to their interests and implanting in them this unpatriotic greed that makes them sit down and act like useless children."

"If they like me, it's because I recognize their worth."

"Spoken like he who would steal my crown if he would."

"Baba, I'm not *like* that!"

"I don't know *what* you are. You were always quiet and different. I thought you were weak. Now I'm not so sure. Perhaps you were always just crafty -- waiting... watching... looking for weakness."

"Baba-- I'm your *son.*"

"If a goat attacked the rest of its herd, it had better become a stew or the rest of the herd is in danger. If I was an imperfect enough father to bring disruptive treason into the world, it's my responsibility to remove it."

"Remove-- What are you *talking* about?"

"I still don't know the truth," said King Jahandar, "but if you started this mess on the bridge, I have a responsibility to the City of the Red Clay to sentence you to death at the end of the Month of the Sun."

"All because I wanted you to pay people what you *promised them?*" Kaveh leapt at him, but was caught by four guards and wrestled to the ground.

Jahandar looked down at him with an expression of driftwood. "Well, I guess that settles that." He closed his eyes. "May the Sun cleanse me for having raised a betrayer for a child."

"You betrayed the people who worked themselves weak for you," Kaveh muttered into the dust, since a guard's foot was on his head.

72

"At the end of the sacred Month, you will be hanged--"

"No," cried a breathless, familiar voice.

Kaveh felt the guard's shoe scrape painfully into his ear as he turned his head to see.

"Majesty, it was never the prince. It was me. I encouraged the people to resist you. He never betrayed you. He only agreed with me, but he never--"

Several pairs of eyes focused on Farzin the engineer, and he took a step back and gulped.

"That makes more sense," grumbled the king. "Kaveh, get up." He yanked his son off the ground roughly. "Get him back to the palace to get cleaned up for his brother's wedding."

"What? That's today?"

"I should have known better than to think you had enough direction to be the villain I sought," said Jahandar. "You!" He jabbed a finger in Farzin's direction. "You sowed this hatred against me?"

"You sowed it yourself," said Farzin quietly. "I just told the men what to do with the harvest."

"The penalty for treason, since I am destined to repeat myself today, is death," said the king. "Take him away to the prison, and at the end of the Month of the Sun, hang him."

Kaveh broke free of the men who were trying to escort him away and threw himself at his father's feet. "No! Please, by the Sun's light, if you have a heart in your body, don't kill him."

The king furrowed his brow and studied Kaveh suspiciously. "Why?"

"Because..." Kaveh's chest heaved as he breathed heavily, not knowing what to say next. "Baba, *please.* I'll do anything."

"So Azar *wasn't* lying," the king mused in a voice of deadly calm.

"What?" Kaveh could barely get the word out.

The king turned to look at Farzin again, then down at his prostrate, pleading son. Suddenly, with a whirl of spangled robes, he charged at the engineer and flung both his hands on his neck. *"What have you been doing to my son?"*

Farzin's protesting voice disappeared into choking noises, and Kaveh, who was already underfed and too hot, succumbed into a dead faint of despair.

Chapter 9: The Elegant Harp Shattered In His Iron Grasp

People were slapping Kaveh's face with cold, wet hands, and something pungent and bracing attacked his nose. "Farzin!" he called out in a cracking voice.

"Majesty, stop! The Month of the Sun!" pleaded a clamor of male voices. "Executions are forbidden! You must wait!"

Jahandar released Farzin by violently hurling him to the ground. "Fine, then. It is as you say. Put him away. Let his presence insult the Sun no longer, in this, its sacred month. When its light shines on him again, a twisted braid shall take him to his fate."

"Baba, *no*... If he dies I'll go with him..." Kaveh was still too nauseated to move his body, but he reached for Farzin across the dust of the road.

"Please live." Farzin's lips were moving but they barely made a sound. "I'd be so sad if you didn't."

"But I want to be with you," Kaveh pleaded.

"I know."

"Guards, take my son back to the palace and get him ready for the wedding."

"I can't stand up," Kaveh reminded him.

"Carry him and bring him juice, then. Who asked you to go wasting your time and ruining your health with the likes of this traitor on the bridge?" The king kicked at Farzin with his toe. "I always said men like him didn't have their priorities right."

"One breath of air exhaled by him... carries more moral weight than all your might and power."

"And I suppose he told you that as he used your body, and you believed him."

Kaveh wished he would faint again if all his body could do was lie there and torture him instead of letting him get up and attack his father with both fists -- even if it would have resulted in his own execution. But he was a member of the upper class who hadn't eaten properly in three days of sitting outside on a paved bridge, and that was something no amount of anger would change.

"You haven't used me," he whispered to Farzin. "You made me whole."

"You mean I made you get in a *whole* lot of trouble."

"How can you still joke?"

"Because I'm still me. And even when they kill me I'll still be me, and that means I'll still love you. I'll always love you."

"This is patently disgusting. Guards, *please* carry my son back to the palace and get him in a fit state to attend the royal wedding." Jahandar scratched his temple. "Take *that* to the prison. I don't want to waste any more time on this, and I hope those layabouts on the bridge won't, either -- now that I've got their false king locked up. Go and spread the word that Farzin the Pretender has fallen, and will be eliminated at the close of the Month."

Some of the guards hefted Kaveh up between them and began to carry him off. As the other guards forced Farzin to his feet, he mouthed one more word at Kaveh as they parted.

"Pray."

Back at the palace, a weakened and dazed Kaveh was force-fed fruit juice and falafels and then stuffed into ornate celebration attire, covered with gold embroidery depicting suns, moons, and bunches of grapes. He spoke to no one, and followed along with the rest of the wedding party as they mounted a team of horses.

76

The men and women rode in separate clusters, which kept him from laying eyes on Azar. He would have broken away from the team and ridden straight to Farzin, to hold hands through the bars if nothing else, but the pack was too tight and he was surrounded.

The wedding party arrived at the Temple of the Twenty Date Palms, and everyone quickly dismounted and left their horses in the care of the groom they had brought to watch them during the ceremony. Crowds of cheering Citizens on foot awaited them outside the temple; some threw flower petals.

Among the flowers came a rotting, moldy apricot. "Who threw that?" demanded the king, who had been near the front of the procession.

"Pay the men who fixed the roads!" shouted a female voice from the crowd.

"Silence her!" Jahandar turned his back to the crowd and continued his procession, and two of his guards searched in vain for the woman who had melted away into the population.

From the midst of the men's group, Kaveh's older brother, the Crown Prince, emerged in his wedding finery. He was dressed in a suit of white, embroidered all over with gold images, and around his shoulders he wore a shimmering golden cloak. It was the Month of the Sun, and he was now made in its image.

If he was the sun, then pale Kaveh was the moon. He gave no light of his own, and with empty eyes he watched the women's group for the first sign of Azar. Soon, there she was, in a dress made entirely of golden cloth. A white veil covered her hair. The bride matched her bridegroom in solar splendor.

She had told the king his secret. Kaveh looked upon her and expected to hate her -- but he didn't. He had loved her once, and she hurt him to the very core with her first betrayal -- but her second just made him sad with its consequences. Somehow, he didn't think she'd outed him out of malice; most likely, the king

77

had insulted her one too many times with the accusation that she'd changed her mind in order to gain the throne, and she just wanted him to leave her alone. With Kaveh working on the construction project, out of the palace and out of her sight, he could easily imagine her starting to forget their friendship that had once been love.

Mechanically, he filed inside the temple with everyone else. A group of young women danced in rings and then made way for his father, who gave a speech at the altar at the far end of the temple. Kaveh wasn't listening. He was staring down the pathway to the altar, succumbing to a disturbing fantasy. He imagined himself walking that path, the festival girls throwing their flowers at him, and then Farzin following him, wrapped in a cape of gold. But when they got to the end of room, instead of the wedding altar they found a noose. It bound them together in a single loop, fixed around both their necks, locking them in intimacy as it prepared to strangle them.

He could almost feel Farzin's cheek against his, as if it were really happening. Pain tore at him, and he wondered if he had gone crazy. Then Azar appeared, maidens to either side of her throwing flowers beneath her feet as she walked, and Kaveh suddenly felt several pairs of eyes turn to *him*. What was that about? Oh -- he had loved her once. They knew he had been... "unwell"...and they were expecting him to make a scene.

Well, let him make it. Like a butterfly upon a flower, the thought landed in his head that he had already fainted once today, and it would surprise nobody if he were to faint again -- especially when his former fiancée was walking down the aisle to marry his brother. Surely such a thing was not only plausible, but expected. And if he fainted, they'd probably take him outside for air. Whatever happened next would be up to the divine, but he still had hope.

Deliberately, his eyes rolled back in his head, and he let his body go limp. There was a quiet shuffling in the crowd as people of less importance struggled to keep him upright, propping him up under each armpit, and he was quickly scuttled out of the temple. Their priority was to keep the disruption of the wedding to a minimum, and they succeeded by laying him down on a stone bench outside the temple. "Watch over the prince," Kaveh heard someone command the stable-groom who was looking after the horses. "He's had a spell. Poor man, it can't be easy watching your older brother marry the woman you were promised since youth."

He kept his eyes shut and waited.

The sound of wondrous music came from within the temple, and the voices of a chorus rose up to join it. Kaveh heard the stable-groom walking away from him, and he opened one eye slightly. The stable-groom was standing close enough to the temple entrance to watch the celebration. Distracted by all the fuss and finery, he wasn't paying as much attention to the horses he had been assigned -- or to the prince.

Perfect.

With the grace of something blown about on the wind, Kaveh slipped off the bench and made light footfalls toward one of the horses at the far edge of the herd. He mounted the animal and forced himself to let it walk away from its compatriots slowly, so that the sound of rapid hoofbeats wouldn't alert the stable-groom.

Not that he would have been able to hear, anyway. Song and cheering filled the air, and he could still hear it when he had gone far enough away that he felt safe moving to a faster pace.

He made straight for the prison.

Like everything else in the city, it was built of bricks of red clay. An imposing fortress of many sides, intended to convey both power and hopelessness, it was perched beside the river far beyond the Old Bridge. Kaveh slowed his horse and cast his eyes over the building, looking for a good angle of approach, but there was a guard on each side.

Finally, he just dismounted, took a deep breath, and led his horse toward one of the guards.

"Stop! The fortress is forbidden."

"I know," said Kaveh, reaching inside his shirt. "I was hoping you could help me with that."

The gold medallion sparkled in his hand as it reflected sunlight into the guard's greedy eyes.

The man led him to a far corner of the fortress, where a small window near to the ground and set with thick iron bars let indirect light into the sunken cell inside. Kaveh left his horse beside the building and waited for the guard to go away as promised, then knelt to peer into the window.

Inside, far below on the ground -- which was several feet below the earth outside -- Farzin sat with his fingers to his lip in thought. Kaveh reached through the bars for him, overcome with emotion and unable to speak.

Farzin sensed the movement and looked up. "Kaveh! Kaveh, my prince, my own passionate prince." With a slow, deliberate motion that revealed the pain in his limbs from how the guards had treated him, he picked himself up from the floor and walked toward the window.

If he stood on his toes, he could stretch himself high enough that Kaveh's fingers could caress his face. This he did, with all the strength he could muster. For several moments, this was everything.

Then Kaveh bent down and tried to kiss him through the bars. They managed as best they could. "Oh, my love, you're the best thing that's ever happened to me, and I'm the worst that's happened to you." Kaveh swept his fingers over Farzin's cheek again and again.

"You aren't -- you aren't... but your father might be."

"If he kills you, I can't call him my father anymore."

"Do you think you can persuade him not to?"

Kaveh was silent for a moment. "Not really. What are we going to do?"

"And what about our men? Will they ever get paid? Are they keeping up the fight?"

"I don't know – they dragged me away to the royal wedding" said Kaveh. "You're so selfless – you're going to make my heart burst. Here you are in here--"

"Well, you're not exactly Mr. Selfish, escaping from right under your father's nose just to come find me. How did you get away?"

"I pretended to faint again and escaped when they put me outside."

"I'm glad you're here with me. I'll tell you what a keystone is now, if you want. It's only fair, since I know your secret now. A keystone sits at the top of an arch, holding the two curved halves together... It strengthens the bridge." He paused. "That *was* the secret, wasn't it? That you can love a man? That's why Azar..."

Kaveh nodded. "She told my father... but I'm not angry. Just hurt. And she's already hurt me so much that I think there's no room to top it off."

"Would had it been me in her place," said Farzin. "What she gave up--"

"I should have brought you food," Kaveh suddenly realized, interrupting. "The wedding feast--"

"I've got food," said Farzin, trying to sound cheerful. "Here we have..." He held up a stale piece of bread. "The finest cake made by the pastry chef at Mother Cat's! See how moist it is? Think of all the butter he must have used."

The piece of bread looked as though it could have been used as a building brick. Kaveh smiled sadly.

"They've also given me this wonderful wine," Farzin continued, gesturing at a clay bowl full of river water. "Crisp flavor, smooth finish." He could tell he was cheering up Kaveh a little bit, and searched around the cell for more things to turn into 'food' for his imaginary feast. "Over here," he added, pointing to some slick green algae growing on the stone floor where river water had seeped into the cell, "is a platter of malabar just off the vine, and fried in fresh butter. The leaves are tender, yet firm to the--"

"What did you say?" Suddenly, Kaveh's eyes were flashing, and he looked twice as alive.

"Malabar...in...butter? What? You look like ants crawled up your legs."

"Malabar. Captain *Malabar.* What's that man's name? Riv?"

"What are you talking about?"

"The queen of Perach. Remember? I told you about how the captain of her Guard has a male companion?"

"Yes, I remember. Wha--"

"I'm going to go to him. He can save us -- I know he can! Think about it: a man like us, but a fierce warrior, fluent in multiple fighting styles and expert with a sword. He's got a whole team of guards behind him, and his lover is a--"

"--a dragon, yes, I know. Which makes the whole thing sound a bit like a bedtime story."

"It's *true!* It's not a *wild* dragon. He's a wizard with a dragon form."

"You know," Farzin began, but Kaveh never got to hear the rest, because there was a great noise behind him. He turned around to see several guards approaching him with arrows already lifted to their bows.

"But I bribed the guard! I--"

"It's probably a new shift," Farzin pointed out, his heart sinking.

"Get that man!" shouted an angry voice. "He's working with the traitor!"

"I'm going for Riv! I love you! Don't you dare die!" Kaveh shouted, jumping onto his horse and kicking its sides.

Arrows flew through the air toward him, and several found their mark. "You *dogs!*" Farzin cried in agony. "You've hit the king's son!"

The guards scurried about in panic, realizing he spoke the truth. Kaveh's horse galloped away with Kaveh astride it, but he was swaying unevenly and there was blood forming at some of the places the arrows had hit. Farzin watched the horse until it was out of sight, unable to tell how Kaveh had fared. He clasped his hands to his heart, imagining Kaveh's beat there as well beside his. "I'll tend it well, and keep it safe, here with my own," he repeated softly to the empty cell.

Then he sat down in the dust and, picking up a pebble from the corner, comforted himself with math.

Chapter 10: The Masked Warrior

King Jahandar sat on his throne in his great hall, listening to three musicians play and enjoying being full from a satisfying lunch. Strong sunlight streamed in through the windows, making the red clay of the walls bright and alive like fire. To his right sat his oldest son, the Crown Prince, and beyond that the Crown Princess, Azar. To his left sat a courtier, who was falling asleep.

"A livelier tune next, I think," Jahandar said when the song had ended, one eye on the man to his left. "We're all overly soothed by good food and good music." But a slight cough from the guard at the far end of the hall drew his eye, and he held up his hand to stay the musicians before they could start. "What is it?

"Sire, there are two Perachis at the door asking for audience with you," said the guard. "They've come from Queen Shulamit's court, and they bear gifts and news."

Jahandar lifted his eyebrows. "Very well -- thank you. Musicians, you may rest. I'll see you during the next meal. Guard, permit the emissaries to enter."

The guard disappeared and came back leading two men. One of them had the darker skin of their neighbors to the east; the other was much taller and broader than anyone in their region and had lighter skin. His dark-blond hair was cropped short, and the lower half of his face was hidden behind a piece of cloth.

Azar stared at him, blinking and without saying a word.

"Come closer," the king invited.

The two men approached the throne and knelt on one knee.

Jahandar studied them carefully. The darker-skinned man was of advanced-enough age that his shoulder-length hair was streaked with gray. He was slender but looked powerful. All he could see of the blond man's face was blue eyes that were both piercing and beady under thick eyebrows of dark gold. Both men wore what looked like ceremonial armor: tunics of black leather over simple black clothing. The center of each tunic was decorated with Shulamit's court seal, crafted in metal. "Welcome to my court, men of Perach," said the king, holding out his hands in greeting. "You may rise."

"Thank you, Your Majesty," said the older one as he rose. The other simply nodded solemnly.

"What brings you to my court?"

"We have news, Your Majesty," said the masked man, speaking for the first time with a heavily accented voice so deep and booming that Jahandar noticed everyone around him start a little from its unexpected power.

"We also carry gifts from our most esteemed queen, Shulamit bat Noach," said the older man, holding up a wooden box covered with intricately carved designs. The king beckoned for him to approach, so he stepped closer and placed it into the king's hands.

"Ahh, I love the scent of jasmine," Jahandar murmured as he opened the box. Briefly, he inspected the scented oils, teas, spices, and tiny carved figurines the foreign queen had given him. "Tell your queen I give her my thanks. For what purpose does she send me these gifts?"

"She seeks unity with your house," said the older man.

"Your son, Prince Kaveh, took refuge within our walls," said the masked man.

Jahandar's eyebrows went up again. "Has he?"

"Queen Shulamit wishes that you would grant your blessing to her marriage with your youngest son," said the older man.

Off to his right came a sharp gasp that told the king that power-hungry little vixen Azar was indeed paying attention.

"My son's mind is unbalanced," Jahandar pointed out dismissively. He wanted no angry retaliation if she discovered her mistake when it was too late.

"Her Majesty finds him agreeable," said the masked man. "Perhaps she thinks his face will look good on the other side of the coin of the realm."

Jahandar considered this development for some time without speaking. Kaveh was less than a man and more than an embarrassment, and he couldn't figure out what value this foreign queen saw in him. But accepting the marriage would not only rid him of any obligation to count Kaveh as part of his immediate house, it would also strengthen him as a nation linked with the powerful -- and much larger -- lands to the east.

"Very well. I consent. Give she who is to be my daughter my blessing for me, and I wish on them a happy reign and healthy children."

"Thank you, Majesty," said the masked man.

"How is my son? He collapsed during his brother's wedding and hasn't been seen since. He must have wandered into your country in his delirium." Jahandar was lying; he knew the guards at the prison had shot him as he escaped from where he'd been visiting that traitorous wolf, Farzin. Farzin the Fat. Farzin the Fool.

"He recovers well," said the masked man, drawing himself up to his full height. "A brave and a strong man, to ride so far while in so much pain. He nearly died, but he never lost his focus. You are wise to be proud of him."

Jahandar studied him, uneasy at this last sentence because it sounded like a challenge. He'd been thinking about the man's size, and his blond hair, but most of all the cloth mask over his face. "You'd know all about bravery, or so I hear, Captain Riv." Of course. Who else could he be, with his northern coloring, and the cloth mask, coming from the court of Shulamit? He said this to show these foreigners that he could guess who they were, that he was king and had the ultimate upper hand.

"I fought in wars in many lands, and now I guard the queen," said the masked man, "so, yes, I know bravery."

"Stories of your exploits have traveled beyond Perach's borders," said the king. "They say you ride a dragon into battle. The scar you hide behind that mask -- tell me, is it from an enemy, or from the dragon?"

An inscrutable glare came from the foreigner's blue eyes. "The dragon would never hurt the one he loves," he growled.

Jahandar eyed the other man, the older one, suspiciously, but he held up his hands. "I'm not the dragon, Your Majesty."

"My apologies," said the king.

"No offense taken, Your Majesty."

"Captain, we'd love to hear one of your adventure stories," said the king. "Will you take wine?"

"If you'll give it," said the masked man.

The king clapped his hands loudly, and two servants appeared from a side door. He ordered wine and fruit from one and bade the other bring chairs for the travelers. They sat down, and the masked man told them all about how Captain Riv -- before he was Captain Riv -- and the dragon, of course, had fought and captured the twin brothers who were highwaymen on the roads of Imbrio, to Perach's immediate north. There was also the tale of the rescue of the lady in blue, far away across the sea at Port Saltspray. Everyone was enthralled by his cavernous voice.

None had been as captivated as Crown Princess Azar. As soon as the masked warrior had opened his mouth, Azar momentarily forgot to breathe. As he continued his stories, she looked away in embarrassment, but she could feel his presence affecting her heart like the earth pulls on falling feathers. Though they float, they can't help but travel mercilessly downward.

Azar straightened her shoulders and sat upright in her seat, irritated with herself. Not only was she a married woman, but she was wed to the future king of the city! What right had this strange man to speak with such muscle in her presence?

Ah, but even when he was silent, those smirking blue eyes, those pointed eyebrows...

Haughtily, she looked away again. It didn't help as much as she hoped it would.

When the men had finally left, Azar turned to Jahandar, waiting for him to say what was on her mind. He didn't disappoint. "Hard to believe a man like that is one who favors men," he muttered thoughtfully.

Meanwhile, Azar was thinking to herself how hopeless she was, first with her ill-fated love of Prince Kaveh, then this sudden and infuriating attraction to a foreign warrior who also loved men! She loved her husband, but his voice didn't make her blood bubble the way the captain's had. "He said such nice things about Kaveh," she commented, because she was thinking about that too.

"Hm. Yes, I noticed that. I hope it doesn't *mean* anything." He emphasized the penultimate word in a grim tone.

"Surely nobody would cuckold a dragon," Azar pointed out.

"A comforting thought."

Outside the palace, when they'd turned a corner and it was safe, Isaac peeled away his mask. "That went well. Much easier to breathe now."

"You're a strange one! I don't think you told a single lie, yet you managed to convince him you were Riv." Tivon shook his head. "And I know for certain, because I know *you,* and I listened and kept track. If I were Riv, I'd be a little bit scared of you."

"Yes, well, Riv knows I'd die for him," growled Isaac with such intensity that Tivon mentally scurried back from the line he'd crossed.

"Our first mission is accomplished," Tivon pointed out. "We got the king to accept the marriage without him suspecting your lizard form is anywhere near his prison."

"I'm glad you found a way to mention that you weren't the dragon, either."

"I'm not as sneaky as you are, but I can still think on my feet. Meet you back at the inn?"

Isaac nodded. "Time to go find this engineer of Kaveh's." With that, he transformed into a small green lizard and scurried down the river toward the prison.

Chapter 11: Burnt Sugar

In the long light of the afternoon, the lizard Isaac scuttled over the rocks and clay of King Jahandar's prison fortress. He had poked his scaly nose in and out of several cells so far, and found a weeping and disheveled woman, two old men, and several men who were the right age but who were either too thin, too toned, or too short to match Kaveh's description of his beloved. When the next cell contained two attractive young women quarreling over which of them was at fault for their arrest for pickpocketing, he began to wonder if the king had hidden Farzin away in some secret underground chamber, reserved for only the most dangerous criminals. It didn't make sense for Farzin's personality or deeds, but Isaac knew Jahandar wasn't interested in any version of reality he hadn't made up himself.

However, he had better luck in Cell 15. A heavily built young man had fallen asleep in the middle of the floor, his head resting on his arm. Isaac remembered Kaveh thinking of his beloved's face as 'flabby' and he noticed with satisfaction that the man's cheeks puffed out slightly. A pebble had slipped out of his hand, and all across the dust in front of him were lines and figures.

Isaac crept through the window high in the cell and made his way down the wall, thinking carefully about his next move. He didn't want to startle Farzin awake in some way that might upset his nerves; he felt bad enough for him already.

A beautiful, bass voice cut through Farzin's slumber. The song was soft and soothing enough that it woke him gradually, before he could understand the words.

"Upon a tree beyond the lake
The golden apples grow,
Protected by a fearsome snake
Who sleeps coiled up below.

The knight approached to take the fruit
And fight the scaly beast
Who rests against the apple's root
And dreams to life a feast.

The snake became a dragon bold
To guard the magic tree,
But not all knights are after gold
And precious few are free.

'Please share with me,' cajoled the knight,
'Or I shall starve tomorrow.'
'Then share my life,' the serpent sighed,
'And end my lonely sorrow.'

So now the tree is watched by two
And flourishes--"

Farzin lifted his head from his arm, peering up at the window. He squinted as his eyes, used to the cell after so many days of darkness, met the tiny source of indirect light head-on. "Who's there?"

The song stopped, replaced by a spoken voice. "Kaveh's alive. I'm guessing who you are because of all those calculations on the ground."

Farzin sprang to a more upright position, and he pointed one trembling hand at the window. "Who are you? I can't see you!"

"Look down. I'm the lizard on the wall."

"What?"

91

"I'm Isaac, the dragon wizard from the court of Queen Shulamit."

Farzin's eyes bulged. "You're--you're the bedtime story! He found you!" He threw his head back in grateful prayer. "He found you -- and he's alive!"

"He wanted to make sure I told you he loves you."

"And I love him," Farzin replied intensely. "Can you help us?"

"We'll try," said Isaac. "Between my magic and Riv's mastery of multiple combat techniques, there are probably several ways we could rescue you -- especially if we wait until they take you out of the fortress for execution."

Farzin wiped sweat from his face and furrowed his brow. "Such a short time -- from here to the gallows."

"Then it may cheer you to hear that our queen has another plan," Isaac continued. "She's convinced she can find a peaceful solution, one that will save your life but won't anger the king. Even though her armies, wealth, and power surpasses his, she doesn't like to make enemies."

"She sounds like an interesting woman," said Farzin. "Maybe I'd like her."

"I hope you will," said Isaac.

"I did think of an escape plan," said Farzin, rushing over to the corner where several bits of rubbish sat in the sand. "Look -- one of the guards felt bad for me and slipped me some butter, and here's a piece of broken bottle that someone threw away near my window. If I rip off a bit of my shirt and ball it up and put the butter all over it, I might be able to use the bottle to catch the sunlight just right and make a torch."

"And then what?" asked Isaac politely.

"That's where it falls apart." Farzin hung his head. "The door's wooden, but there are guards everywhere outside of it. I'd get outside, and they'd beat me again."

"It's still an interesting idea."

"What about the workers? Did Kaveh tell you the whole story -- how his father denied them fair payment?"

"We've heard everything," said Isaac. "If Queen Shulamit's plans work, she's committed to find a way to persuade the king not only to free you, but to restore the proper wages to you and your workmen."

"I don't need any money for myself," said Farzin. "I just want to make sure the men get what they worked for. Just get me out of here. A quiet life with Prince Kaveh is the only wages I seek."

"On behalf of the queen, then, I ask you -- will you share those wages with us?"

"What do you mean?"

"Queen Shulamit doesn't care for the caresses of men."

Farzin blinked. "Oh! You mean -- you mean like me? I mean, the other way around?"

"Exactly. She's always hoped she'd come across a prince who felt the same way she did, so that she could produce an heir with someone who wouldn't trouble her for physical intimacy otherwise."

"I see where you're going with this." Farzin felt blood rushing into his face. "How does Kaveh feel about it?"

"He agreed, but made us all promise to rescue you and get the king to pay everyone their promised wages."

"He agreed," Farzin repeated. "Your queen -- is she beautiful?"

"Her looks are average," said Isaac. "It doesn't hurt my eyes to look at her."

"Is she smart?"

"She has a brilliant mind."

"Is she interesting?"

"Farzin, *please*. Kaveh rode straight to our courts without stopping to have his wounds tended, nearly dying from infection and thirst, because he was so desperate to reach us and beg for our help. *To save you.* We try to talk to him about other topics, like his father, or what the Month of the Sun is like, and all he wants to talk about is you. He loves only you. Besides," Isaac added in a deep grumble that made Farzin believe that he really could turn into a dragon sometimes, "Shulamit is more to me than my queen -- she's like the daughter I don't have. If she doesn't want a man to touch her, I won't let him."

"I believe you. I'm sorry. I just... It's easy to imagine that people have forgotten you, locked away down here."

"Kaveh loves you. I nursed him back to health myself, and his thoughts of happiness that fueled my magic were all of you. And your men -- they still demonstrate on the bridge, dwindling though their numbers might be."

"I still can't believe any of this happened. I'm just an engineer!"

"You're a very brave one, from what I hear."

"I was just standing up for what I thought was justice."

"Not everybody does that. It's very, very easy not to."

Isaac stayed until the sun went down, asking Farzin lots of questions about the prison, about the planned execution, and anything else he thought Riv might find useful in planning an attack strategy -- should Shulamit's quest fail.

"We'll save you -- not just because we care about you," Isaac reassured him, "but because without you, my queen has no heir."

"I still can't believe Kaveh's promised himself as a breeding stud to save my life." Farzin shook his head. "Please... tell him that thinking about him is keeping me smiling down here."

"I will." Isaac scrambled back up the wall to the window and slipped through its bars.

"Wait!" Farzin called after him. "On your way home -- find my mother and tell her what's happened--" But Isaac had already disappeared, and Farzin slumped with a sigh on his bench of stone.

Isaac ran over stones, clay, and dirt until he had cleared the prison, then hurried down the streets and alleyways, looking for a secluded place in which he could transform back into a human unnoticed. So focused was he on watching out for humans that he missed a nebulous gray form creeping around in the shadows behind him.

The cat had pounced only milliseconds after he realized it was there. With both front paws holding his neck to the ground, it purred in a human voice, "Gotcha! Now I'll find out what you're up to."

Isaac quickly transformed, leaving the cat's paws fastened around his neck as he grew into his full height beyond six feet. But it began to transform nearly as quickly as he had, and the next thing he knew, the arms around his neck belonged to a woman, around his age, with long hair and dressed in the clothes of the working class. She was so close he could smell her, cardamom and sesame oil and other cooking smells -- and the fragrance of a woman's sweat beneath.

He was disconcerted by how good she smelled. *Highly* disconcerted. Irritated, even.

"Hmmm!" she breathed, in that same purring voice as before. "Ain't *you* a tall, handsome drink of water. Hey, Serpent-Master, do you have time to show me your snake form?"

"Sorry, Pussycat -- I already have a snake charmer." *So this is a duel, woman?* ran his growling internal monologue. *I'm supposed to be impressed by clever speech? Too bad. I can match you blow for blow. You have absolutely no power over me.*

The woman's mouth broke into a wide grin, and she chuckled ribaldly. "That was great. Just for having such a way with words, I'll buy you a drink. Come to Mother Cat's with me. They're closed for the night, but that's okay -- I own the place." She relinquished her hold around his neck and stood back to look at him.

"Mother Cat's?" Isaac lifted an eyebrow and gave her a weak smile.

"I know. Isn't it an awful name? And inaccurate too -- I'm nobody's mother. But it was the name when I bought it, and I didn't want to make waves or attract attention by changing it."

"What else do they call you, Not-Mother Cat?"

"Eshvat. Who are you, and what are you doing here besides not coming home with me? I didn't think there were any others with animal form in this city -- the old Master who taught me's been dead many years, and the other woman he taught alongside me left town."

"I'm not from here."

"Ya *think?* You're from somewhere up north, aren't you? With that hair?"

"Yes, I'm from the north."

"What were you doing in the prison?"

"What prison?"

"Very funny. Nothing can creep in the dark places without being seen like a cat. I know you came from the prison."

"Since you know everything, why don't you tell me?" Isaac folded his arms and leaned back against the wall, focusing his blue-eyed stare on her as if it were a weapon.

"I think you came from the cell of that engineer," she replied promptly, "who built the bridge."

"What do you think of the king's decision?"

"I'm a business owner -- what *can* I think?" Eshvat threw up her hands in defeat, jangling the bracelets that hung from both her wrists, and looked at him innocently. "Of course I'm loyal to the king. It's not my fault if a stray cat that I feed sometimes steals my leftovers and drags them over to the men on the bridge." She shook her head as if in exasperation, her lips pursed.

"Do you also have a problem with your apricot supply going rotten before you have a chance to serve them?" Isaac inquired. An idea had crept into his mind about Kaveh's story of the woman who had thrown spoiled fruit and heckled the king, and then disappeared completely. It would be awfully easy to do that as a cat, slipping here and there between the legs of the crowd.

"You were at the royal wedding?"

"No, I arrived only this morning."

Eshvat's eyes widened. "What's your secret, Serpent-Master?"

"Who says I have one?"

"I do. I say you have nothing *but* secrets."

"The prince sends his regards."

She grinned and nodded slowly. "I think I understand. Tell him to be careful, this prince of yours. Love is delicious until it burns your tongue."

"Spoken like a true cook."

"I promise you'd like my food."

"I should get back to my colleague."

"Some other time, then. Look me up when you're lonely for your own kind."

With a last, deep look into his eyes, she slipped back into her cat form and disappeared into the night.

Isaac walked the rest of the way back to the inn with a cross expression on his face, missing Rivka fiercely. Somewhere along his walk, he plucked a cat hair off the shoulder of his cloak.

Chapter 12: If Only I Were Not Unworthy

"He compared you to a rabid *goat?*"

"It's really not that big of a deal. He's said stuff like that before." Kaveh looked away into the palace's inner courtyard and fingered the rim of his teacup. "He just..."

Shulamit hastened to return the conversation to a less sensitive topic. There was something specific she wanted to know, anyway. "The books say that you and your brothers all went to secondary school once you were old enough, instead of learning from tutors like I did. Wasn't your father worried something would happen to you?"

They were sitting on one of the shaded porches of the palace's inner courtyard with a pot of tea between them. The tea had gone cold, but the conversation was still piping along.

"He's far too confident in his reputation. I mean, I did get beaten up, but that was before they knew who I was. His power is absolute, accepted like... like the blue of the sky, and pretty much unquestioned -- that's probably why he reacted so badly to being challenged by Farzin. I'm still amazed he had the courage to do that. By holy Sunrise, he's the most incredible man--" Kaveh's hands clutched at his chest.

"The other students at the school," Shulamit interrupted deftly and not for the first time that day, "I read that they weren't just from the nobility, but also from wealthy commoner families. What's your father's attitude about that? Did he want you to choose your friends from among the noble-born?"

"Actually, no," answered the prince. "He always taught us that if a commoner amasses wealth honestly, it's an indication that he's fit for the upper classes. I'm a little bit ashamed to admit that I never really questioned it until Farzin came back to build the bridge. He'd take poor men from the working class out to dinner with us, and, honestly, they sounded just like us, sometimes... and it made me wonder, if Farzin hadn't been born into the nobility, even with that great brain of his, would his family have been able to afford to send him to a school fit for teaching him?"

"So your father's opinion of the poor among the common folk..." prodded the queen, holding out her hand.

"He thinks they have flaws that keep them poor. That day we finished the bridge, he said some pretty stupid things to Farzin--"

She nodded. "That pretty much reflects what I've read about him. It doesn't sound like he respects poor commoners, but rich ones pass muster."

"You'd be right about that. Whereas Farzin--"

"In other words, if he respected a woman greatly, so much so that if he put her opinion above his own, she'd probably--" Noises from the center of the courtyard attracted her attention, and she stopped midsentence to jump up and squeal, "They're back!"

Kaveh followed her over to the recently landed dragon. Tivon had already dismounted and was stretching his limbs, and Aviva was standing by, ready with cold drinks. "Isaac," Shulamit asked with a giggle, "why do you have a garland of flowers around your neck?"

"Because your sweetheart is a weirdo," growled the dragon affectionately. He poked at the queen's nose with one claw, then transformed back to human form. "Where's my--"

A blur of blonde hair and leather armor cartwheeled across the green and smashed into him with a hug. Rivka whispered into his ear before pulling away.

"I missed you too, Mighty One. That was impressive, just now. I love to watch you work." It had always been clear to Shulamit that some of Isaac's love was flavored with hero worship.

100

"I was going to say that he's off training, but I think that's a little bit obvious," said Shulamit.

"For the rescue?" asked Isaac. "What about the peaceful solution? Nothing yet?"

"I do have one idea... but I want to hear all about your trip too."

By this point, a group had gathered, so the men told them the two things they wanted to know the most. "In regards to the marriage of Queen Shulamit to Prince Kaveh -- King Jahandar has granted us his enthusiastic cooperation," said Tivon.

"Mazel tov!" said a number of voices.

One hurdle down, but am I ready for the next one? Shulamit wondered, relieved and slightly nauseated with panic at the same time. She smiled weakly at her courtiers.

"As for Farzin," said Isaac, looking pointedly at Kaveh, "he's fine, for now. They don't torture him in prison, and he wanted you to know that thoughts of you bring him comfort."

Kaveh's face shook with emotion. "I wish I'd been there with you."

"Now that we've satisfied everyone's immediate curiosity," Isaac continued, "Tivon and I would like to disappear into the kitchen and replenish ourselves."

"You may have been flying all day, but I was doing backflips. I need food too." Rivka trudged along behind them.

By the time Shulamit joined them in Aviva's kitchen-house, Tivon had finished eating and was off to go see to his own affairs. "Did Rivka already fill you in on what she's turned up on Jahandar's battle philosophy?" She kissed Aviva, who was puttering around her pantry mostly ignoring them, on the cheek and then sat down across from Rivka and Isaac at the table.

"No," said Isaac, flashing an impish look at his wife.

"We talked about something totally different," said Rivka. "Isaac met another wizard over there. Some woman who can turn herself into a cat."

"Yes, and she seemed to think I was her prey," Isaac grumbled. His brow was furrowed and he was frowning, but his unnerved expression melted away into relief when Rivka draped both of her muscular arms over his shoulders and rested her head against his.

Shulamit giggled. "Okay. Well, anyway, while you were gone, I ran out of books to read about the king, so I started looking at all the other books, leafing through them quickly to see if I could turn up any time he was mentioned briefly, even if the book or chapter wasn't really about him in particular."

"*All* the other books?"

Shulamit nodded. "I don't want a war."

"I guess you don't!" Isaac began peeling another litchi. "So, *nu*, what did you find?"

"Hardly anything, but...."

Then she picked up a piece of parchment that had been sitting on her lap, and slid it across the table to him. He read out loud in his sonorous bass voice,

"My love, my love, her eyes are figs,
Deeply dark, dripping with sugar, large and moist
Do they weep for me, that I am imperfect?
They weep for me, for I am unworthy,
Though I wear gold on my head, I am unworthy.

My love, my love, her breasts are melons--

He paused to lift an eyebrow at Shulamit, who was giggling quietly. She grinned sheepishly and fell silent.

Round and sweet and yet locked away behind the rind of cloth
That she calls a dress. I will never taste
Of their sweetness, for I am unworthy,
Though I wear robes of silk, I am unworthy.

She is a bird, and she has flown.
She knows compassion and truth and godly wisdom.
She knows justice and mercy alike,
And she has found me wanting,
Though I am earnest, I am unworthy.

She is a bird, covered in jewels,
And in some beautiful shell I have never touched,
She keeps a pearl I will never kiss,
For I am unworthy, and she is lost these many years.
She said I am heartless, and thus, unworthy.

If she had only stayed to teach me
All those years before we were grown.
If she were to return I should be her slave,
Though my house is a glorious house,
She knows Right as I only know Myself
I would give Myself solely to her.

If only I were not unworthy.

"I don't understand," he added when he had finished.

A little nervously, Shulamit explained. "This poem is
supposedly, possibly about King Jahandar, back when he was a
teenager. In fact, depending on whether or not you find one of the
sources credible, it might have been written by Jahandar himself."

"He wrote that when he was Crown Prince?"

"No, he wrote it years later -- after Kaveh was born, in fact," said
the young queen. "He went through a phase of poetic excess
between Kaveh's mother passing away, and his marriage to his
second wife."

103

"That must be who she was, then. She did come back."

"It can't be. He had only known Queen Maheen for a month before he married her."

"And we all saw how long *that* lasted," Rivka snarked.

"Then who's the woman in the poem?" asked Isaac.

"That's just it. Nobody knows." Shulamit leaned across the table at him, her eyes big and earnest. "But I feel like if we can find her, if we can piece together enough clues and figure out who she is, she seems like she'd be somebody who'd sympathize with Farzin and his men on the bridge. Justice and compassion and mercy..."

"And he'd listen to her." Isaac nodded.

"If she's even still alive," said Rivka. "And if the poem's not fictional."

"Right," Shulamit admitted.

"We really don't know anything," said Rivka.

"That's not entirely true," said Shulamit. "From my reading, and from talking to Kaveh, it doesn't sound like he'd give this kind of respect to a poor commoner. So she's either a rich commoner or a member of the nobility. Or foreign royalty, I guess. That's always a possibility."

"Surely, *Malkeleh,* Queenling, I don't have to remind you that the king might be a hypocrite," said Isaac. "Kings fall in love with scullery maids, despite their own professed beliefs."

"That's true, but someone as obsessed with his own power and prestige as King Jahandar -- I feel like if he'd gotten himself into a situation where he felt that someone who was supposed to be that far beneath him were his moral superior and held that much power over him, he'd lash out in anger instead of worshipping the ground she walked on."

Isaac lifted an eyebrow. "Good point. What are your ideas?"

"Rumors," said the queen. "I have to catalog all the women whose names have ever been linked with his."

"We know his two wives are out, Kaveh's mother and the Lady Maheen."

"The poem says he never lay down with her," Aviva added, "if that bit about the shell and the pearl means what it would mean if I said it."

Shulamit fought a sudden impulse to hide behind her own braids.

"Or at least that he didn't by the time he wrote the poem," Isaac reminded them. "She could have returned after he divorced Maheen. Maybe she even had something to do with that."

The queen shook her head. "Kaveh says his father's devotion to romantic love is in earnest. He doesn't cheat, and he's not a hypocrite about it. And, as hard as it is to get that man to think about anything besides Farzin, I've been grilling him all day, and there really weren't any spare women hanging around. Everyone in that palace is in each other's space, and he'd have known."

Isaac nodded, digesting the information. "Shula, if it doesn't feel like an intrusion, I'd like to see your notes after we finish up in here."

Shulamit nodded.

"As for my part of the research," said Rivka, "his military philosophy's exactly what I'd expect from a petty dictator in a very small nation. He tries to make up for their size by beefing up their ego--"

"Which is bad news for our rescue efforts," Shulamit interjected.

105

"We swoop in there with swords waving to rescue that engineer -- he'll see it as an act of war," Rivka continued. "No way would he believe for a moment Farzin was ever the point. He'd think the whole workers' wages thing was just an excuse for Shulamit to show off how much more powerful we are over here than he is, and he'd retaliate, even to his own great loss."

"He loves his City," said Isaac softly, "even to the point that to have it be called Great, he would destroy what makes it so."

"He's insecure because he's small," Shulamit observed, looking around the room at her loved ones -- all bigger and taller than she. As usual, she was painfully aware of her own smallness -- in stature if not in political power or military might.

"All the more reason to make this not to prove who has the bigger army," said Isaac. "Let's see those notes."

"Even so, if we fight, we'll be ready," said Rivka, flexing her muscles. "It doesn't make sense to feed into his delusional fantasies. Why should we hold off on justice we're all too well-equipped to provide, just because he thinks his patriotism is worth twenty armies? It's not, and we're--"

"You can keep training," Shulamit reassured her, "but I'm going to keep searching." She got up, and her two friends followed her, headed for the Hall of Records.

Outside, in Aviva's garden, Kaveh wound his way between the fluffy and fragrant bushes of basil, lost in thought. Sunlight streamed down on him, and he figured he needed it, after so many days inside recuperating, even though it was making him sweat. After all, was this not still the Month of the Sun, even though he was exiled from those who celebrated it?

106

The garden was beautiful, and he wished he and his beloved engineer were walking its lush paths together. It was all too easy to relive his kisses, sending jolts of spicy sensation down his entire body. His vivid imagination gifted him with the touch memory of having Farzin's tongue in his mouth, and he was so distracted he had to stop walking for a moment.

But then his treacherous mind betrayed him, and into his head flashed a darker image of that tongue... hanging out frighteningly from between dead lips on a frozen face, the noose scrunched up underneath his chin. *No!*

Kaveh tripped over a cucumber vine and went sprawling. He put down a hand to stop his fall, but it landed on a cucumber and fine spines buried themselves in his palm. He groaned loudly and picked himself up, examining his hand. This was ridiculous. Even though that was his father's word.

Determination coursed through his veins. He would remain a victim of his own emotions no longer. Whirling through the garden like a violent gust of wind, he barged into Aviva's kitchen, startling the cook as she stood weighing out dried chickpeas. "I'm sick and tired of feeling so useless and lost in misery. I want to *do* something with my time. Teach me to cook!"

Chapter 13: Cucumber Salad

"The secret to dicing an onion," said Aviva, "is to make sure you don't chop down the whole tree at once." She demonstrated by rocking her knife into the large white orb in quick movements. "See how I'm leaving the root intact? That'll keep it easier to handle because it won't come apart. You can get rid of it at the very end, and by that time the rest of the pieces will do whatever you say."

Once more, Kaveh picked up the knife she had lent him and moved toward the onion she had just showed him how to peel.

"Remember what I said about hiding your fingers. They're shy -- don't want them to get their hearts broken."

Clumsily, he shifted the hand that held the onion, making sure to keep his fingers away from the blade. With great deliberation he mimicked her rocking motions. As Aviva expected, the pieces of onion were of uneven thickness when he started, but he noticed his own mistake and began to correct.

"Good! Onions are wonderful. They add depth to flavor. Soaking them in lemon juice takes away some of the--"

Kaveh cried out in pain. "My *eyes!* What's happening?"

"Oh!" Aviva giggled slightly as she realized that the prince, for all his sorrowful life, was privileged enough never to have cut into a raw onion before.

"It's poison!"

"No-- no, it's okay. Onions are angry. Don't worry. She'll calm down quickly."

"Doesn't it bother you?"

"I cut so quickly that she won't be able to yell too much before I'm done."

"I've seen you chop food -- you're so fast it almost looks like magic," Kaveh observed. "I'd like to get that fast. I want to be good at something again."

"You'll get there, with practice."

Kaveh was still blinking in pain, and he put the knife down so he could wipe the tears from his eyes with the back of his hands without accidentally stabbing himself in the face. "Ugh. I feel ridiculous. So weak!"

"It's okay -- it's your first time! You're doing great."

"I'm so glad you're here giving me something to work at," he said. "What my eyes are doing now is what my heart is doing all the time anyway. I miss Farzin so much, and not truly knowing if he'll be rescued or not makes me feel like I'm drowning in my own nightmares. I'd much rather be in here, learning honest toil. Before I walked through that door, I felt completely useless, like a forlorn... I don't know, a captured maiden in a legend."

Aviva lifted a sunny face to his and asked serenely, "So feeling useless makes you a woman?"

"I didn't mean it like that. I--" He picked up the knife again.

"Now we're going to cut across," she said in a low voice, wanting to make it clear she wasn't finished with the other conversation. She began to demonstrate, and he followed her lead.

"Okay, so some real women aren't like that. But women in legends -- somehow in stories, it's always--"

Piles of neatly diced onions gathered in the wake of their knives.

"Yes, women in stories. Here's another onion." She plunked it unceremoniously next to his pile of translucent white squares.

"Tell me, Highness, the people like *us* in stories. What are *they* like?"

Kaveh grimaced, and he stared off into space for a moment. "Maybe you've made your point."

"Then stick *your* point into that onion skin and keep going!" She flashed him a sparkling grin and fished another onion off the pile for herself.

"Why do they hate us?" Kaveh's words fell from slack lips, and the rest of him was drooping morosely. "What's the point? I've done nothing wrong."

"They don't hate me. They just like me for the wrong reasons." There was a rare hint of sadness in her voice.

Kaveh nodded in understanding and kept chopping. "They don't see us as real people, do they?"

"Not really. I don't just like men, and I don't just like women. That doesn't mean I like twice as many people as everybody else. I'm just as picky. I like brains. I love the way Shulamit gets excited about something and then learns everything she can about it all week. I like to be needed, and appreciated. I like to dote on someone. I like intensity. Not everybody has that." She gathered up her diced onion with both hands and placed it in a nearby bowl. "The queen makes me happy. And then there's these." She gestured to her chest. "They're just fat. I could show you just as much fat floating around in a stew. Do you think that makes the stew crave passion? I mean, I guess it's *warm.*"

Kaveh chuckled, keeping his eyes on his knife. "I know what you mean. I mean... my father thinks of me as *distracted,* and Farzin as... as some kind of predatory monster. He rambled on and on about how I had been *damaged* by something that was so sacred to me that if I were to die this instant, all I'd be able to say to the Sun over and over again is thank you, thank you for Farzin..."

"No, no, stop it."

He froze. "Huh? What?"

"Don't dream about him while you're holding a knife. If you hurt yourself, the queen's gonna blame me."

Kaveh nodded. "Got it. So... what about your parents? I mean, they live here. Do they accept your choices or do they pretend you're only the palace cook?"

"I'm not the palace cook -- there's a real palace cook in a different kitchen. I'm the queen's personal chef. Neither wheat nor fowl ever darkens this door. We can't really trust everyone else to take that seriously." She handed him another onion with which to practice.

"Oh, okay."

"But Aba and Ima are our sun and moon and shine on us -- the way every parent should."

"That's so incredible." Kaveh beamed and paused in his knife work for a moment. He looked as though he needed a minute to savor the idea. "I wish... this place is such a paradise. I feel like I made it up in desperation. What about King Noach? Was he also as kind?"

Aviva considered her words. "He loved Shulamit more than anyone else in his world, and he wanted what was best for her."

"It doesn't sound like that was *you,* in his opinion."

Aviva shrugged. "I wash the dust from my feet, or else I can't walk."

"I need to learn how to do that. I've got a lot of dust."

"So do I. It hasn't always been easy for me. I even left the palace at one point. Took the heart right out of my body, set it on a shelf, and crept quietly away..."

"Because of King Noach?"

"Someone thought he'd gain the king's gold by paying for my mother's surgery in exchange for me becoming smoke and a memory. My feet left the palace grounds... and my mother's touched the dirt. You see her walking with a cane now, but she was in bed most of my life."

"And you came back when the king died?"

"The queen found me and brought me home."

"I wish Baba had just tried to pay off Farzin like that. He'd have taken the money and given it to the poor, and we'd have met anyway, in secret."

"I'm sure it happens all the time. The queen read about something like that in your city, during her endless gorge of books."

"Oh?"

"I know because it upset her -- it reminded her of what happened to us." She didn't tell Kaveh how Shulamit had needed Aviva's arms around her for a good five minutes, soothing her, reminding her that she'd promised she wasn't going anywhere. "Too bad, because to me that sounds like dessert reading. Something about... *Memoirs of the Marketplace?* Do you know it? It's a pretty old book. Most of the stories are from before I was born. I think the writer was Nouri or Naveed or something starting with 'nun' anyway."

"I may have looked at it. I don't know."

"It's very funny. I think the man who wrote it sells scarves or shawls. Anyway, he wrote down all these stories from all his years in the market, and one of them was about a craftsman who was bragging in a tavern how he'd sold some jewels for twice the price they were really worth, to an important man who was trying to keep his son away from the craftsman's daughter. Hidden in the price was a bribe. The craftsman had been sworn to secrecy, but, well, there was wine involved, and we all know about how Lady Wine loves to flirt until you'll tell her all your secrets."

"I know. I remember being overcautious that I'd betray myself as a lover of men if I ever drank. Even before Farzin, when the only men I looked at were my father's guards."

"The girl who sold shoes at market," Aviva commented, daydreaming a little.

"That's how you knew?"

"M-hmm. Speaking of things we like, do you like cucumber salad?"

He nodded enthusiastically.

"Then that'll be your first complete dish. Here, I'll show you how to peel and chop these."

After they'd been through the lesson on peeling, coring, and cutting up cucumbers, Aviva showed him the best way to juice a lemon. As she held it close to the fire for a moment, she explained, "If you warm her up a little, she'll give you more of herself."

"You can get more juice out that way? I never would have thought."

"Watch out for the seeds. We don't want them poking around in the salad."

Lemon juice went on top of the cucumbers and onions, which were soon joined by dill, mint, and other flavors. "This is amazing," said the prince. "There was -- nothing! -- before, and now it looks like real food! I made real food!"

Aviva pointed at his bowl. "Eat. Eat your usefulness."

Reverently, Kaveh lifted a small handful to his mouth.

"How is it?"

"It worked! It really worked! And I didn't wreck the kitchen!"

There was barely time to notice the large shape blocking the long afternoon sunlight from the doorway before Rivka was suddenly between them, seizing Kaveh's knife. Next thing they knew, she had flung it straight into the wall opposite them, where it loyally stuck.

Kaveh and Aviva, still as trees, stared at her. She grinned back at them, tossing her head brazenly. "What's this about?"

"I learned to make cucumber salad," Kaveh stammered.

Rivka reached into his bowl and tasted some. "Tastes pretty good! Hey, if you want to learn other things too, I'll be in the far courtyard by the coconut palms." She cocked her head toward her left hip, the hip where she wore her sword.

Then she was gone as quickly as she had come. *Rivka,* Aviva observed to herself, *is downright obnoxious after she and Isaac make the trees bloom.*

Chapter 14: Heavy Lifting

It was morning, and Queen Shulamit was wandering around in figure eights by herself in a stand of bamboo in the garden between the palace and its outer walls. Sunlight made the blond stalks and green leaves glow, and her fingers slipped over their smoothness as she paced.

In order to find the mystery woman in King Jahandar's past, she reasoned, she had to run down the list of everywhere one might meet a woman. The most obvious persons, those wives he had married and then lost either to death or disharmony, she ruled out due to the poem's clue of unconsummation.

The next thing she thought of was "willing women," simply because in her adolescent desperation when Aviva left so many years ago, she had herself thought of turning this way for comfort. But Kaveh had ruled that out; he characterized Jahandar's disdain for those who participated in the sex trade as sincere and heartfelt, come from a mind that placed the love between man and woman as something not only set apart from love between those of the same sex, but too sacred to sell. Shulamit knew a son may not know if his father visits whores, but the objective literature, if there indeed was such a thing when dealing with monarchy, verified his claims. Besides, Jahandar had respected the mystery woman too much.

If she'd been a notable woman of the court, her name would have come up in the many texts Shulamit and her household had read. But there was nothing. Clearly, she wasn't "important" enough to have been noticed by historians.

Where does one meet a woman?

Like his son, Jahandar had gone to an expensive school with the other sons of noblemen and rich commoners -- all boys. Before that, his tutors had all been male, which ruled out Benjamin's theory of a wise and beautiful young female tutor who quit her post when she realized her pupil's passion -- romantic though it might be.

But male classmates had kin. Sisters, cousins -- even mothers. And Jahandar's father, King Omeed, had plenty of friends, and they might have daughters, nieces, sisters, and wives.

Fiddling with one of her braids, which weren't tied back behind her head as usual, she resolved to start at the beginning and piece together an organized catalog of every one of Jahandar's classmates, with special focus on those he treated as close friends, and every one of Jahandar's father's close friends as well. Hopefully, somewhere in the sea of female names they'd turn up attached to those men, there would be a woman of strong moral fiber and large breasts, someone either in the nobility or born to a rich common family.

And someone with whom the king hadn't lain.

The task seemed endless. Leaning against a stalk of bamboo, she closed her eyes and prayed. *God, I just want to know that I can do this. I'll work as hard as I have to if it'll only come to something.*

"Majesty!"

"Hmm?" Her eyes snapped open.

One of her ladies-in-waiting had entered the bamboo grove, shooing away wild birds that had come begging for scraps. "The horses are ready to leave for the Games. Would you like me to fix your braids? They've come down."

"No, that's fine... I'll leave them down for today." Swallowing her irritation that she had to leave her Great Quest behind for the day but always aware that monarchs can't do everything they want, she left the grove.

Meanwhile, Aviva rushed through the palace and poked her head into Kaveh's room. "Are you ready yet?"

A manservant was helping him put on a formal yet airy suit of clothes. "Almost," he called back to her. "How do I look?" He held his hands out at his sides.

"Great! We're ready to leave, so they sent me to go harvest you." She didn't mention that Shulamit had required fetching as well.

"Do I ride up in the *howdah* with Shulamit, or is that only for once we're mar-- what?"

Both Aviva and the manservant were giving him awkward looks.

"The queen doesn't ride elephants anymore," said Aviva quietly. "She'll be on a horse like the rest of us."

Kaveh's brain switched on. "Oh. Oh, sorry. Wow, I'm sorry. Still? After all this time?"

Aviva's face twitched as if worms were crawling under her skin. "It cut deep."

"I was there when it happened, Your Highness," the manservant commented. "It was horrible. He was a good king."

"I'm really sorry. I didn't mean to bring up tragic memories. It's just that, in the city where I'm from, we're too built-up for elephants. I guess I was kind of hoping... never mind, never mind!"

"It's okay. Come on! Before the horses forget the way there."

117

When the procession was finally ready, the queen and her retinue made their way out of the palace gates and down the road toward the field just north of Quiet Lake. Shulamit was relieved to see that the shaded tent over the royal platform was already set up. The sun had been baking down on her the whole way there. She was also happy to see more than one man selling coconuts to drink.

"Here," she called, motioning to one of them as soon as she and her company were settled on the platform. He lit up at being chosen, and everyone was grateful for the sweet refreshment.

Settling herself into her seat, she alternated between sipping her drink and playing with one of the braids that rested over her shoulders. She didn't particularly care for sports -- it didn't interest her whether or not one of the shawl sellers could lift more coconuts or jump farther than one of the woodcarvers -- but the Marketplace Games were a beloved event in the culture of her capital, and she knew it made her people very happy to see her there.

Energy was in the air, and everyone around her was talking about something different.

The announcer was celebrating the agility of the man on the field, who apparently sold chickens and eggs.

Aviva was animatedly explaining to her parents that the lady vendors had successfully organized so that next year the Games would have women's events as well. Shulamit knew Aviva was happy to be here, to cheer on her favorite vendors -- those men from the marketplace who, in her expert opinion, sold the best raw ingredients for her culinary masterpieces.

Tivon, who was on duty at Shulamit's side, was telling Rivka's mother, Mitzi, some anecdote that was making her alternately laugh and quizzically ask him what a word meant.

"He's pleasing to look at, isn't he?" Kaveh said, admiring the man on the field. He turned to Shulamit. "I can't thank you enough for giving me a place where I can say that out loud, without fear you'll throw me off the platform."

She gave him a distant smile. Her mind was still on the Jahandar problem.

Only Rivka and Isaac were silent. They stood as grim sentinels at each forward corner of the platform, eyes on the crowd, as "on duty" as two human beings could get. There may as well not have been games going on before them; their "game" was watching the population. Isaac was even wearing armor for once.

Shulamit was more than safe behind the watchful care of her two towering northern guards.

"*Yessss!*" Aviva shot up from her seat, arms in the air. She nearly knocked her father's coconut askew in her zeal to cheer on the shepherd who produced her favorite cheese, as the announcer officially declared that the shepherd could lift more coconuts on his back than anyone else.

Everyone else was content simply to clap. Shulamit clapped without caring. Had Jahandar gone home for the High Holidays or Passover with one of his classmates? Were princes even allowed to do that? Her father certainly never would have allowed it, but he was exceptionally protective. Plus, she was a girl.

Wait, they don't have those holidays over there... She felt sun-silly that she'd forgotten that for a moment, and took another sip of coconut water.

Then she noticed Aviva's parents were looking at her, or more accurately, sending fleeting glances in her direction, and talking quietly to each other. What was that about? She wearily hoped they weren't pointing out how little their queen and de facto daughter-in-law was focused on the games.

Finally, Leah spoke up. "Majesty, darling?"

"Hmm? What?"

"I didn't know if it was important enough to say anything, but Ben talked me into it." *Oh, so that's what the whispering was about.* "I started reading some books about Jahandar's father, in case there were more clues."

I guess there were books I still hadn't gotten to yet, thought Shulamit. "King Omeed? What did you find?"

"There was a story," said Leah, "about a necklace of jewels that King Omeed had bought for his wife, the queen. The book said that he'd paid far more for the necklace than it was worth, and a rumor sprang up that it might have magical powers, to justify the extra cost. Do you think it--"

Trembling and leaning forward, Shulamit stared at her. "Jewels? He paid more for jewels? Oh, my God. How long ago? How old was Jahandar when this happened?"

"I--I think--maybe... thirty years ago? Jahandar must have only been in his teens."

"That's it, that's it, that's it!"

"What?"

"The man who was paid off to keep his daughter away from the wealthy man's son! That wasn't just a wealthy man, that was the *king!* It was King Omeed! And he paid off the jeweler to keep his daughter away from Jahandar, because he was the Crown Prince at the time! Leah, Leah, you did it! *Yesss!"* She sprang out of her seat with both fists raised.

On the field, a poor honey seller squinted into the sun with a smile on his face, happy that the queen had cheered the length of his jump. He didn't know the queen was such a fan of his honey, and he swelled with pride.

"Are you sure?" Leah blinked in happy bewilderment.

"Covered in jewels! The poem said, covered in jewels! All we have to do is find the jeweler and we've found her!"

"I visited a jeweler while Isaac was with Farzin," Tivon offered helpfully.

Shulamit's brow furrowed. "A jeweler? For what?"

Mitzi fidgeted conspicuously and played with her hair, clumsily trying to draw attention to a silver hairpin Shulamit couldn't remember having ever seen before.

"I wanted to welcome our captain's mother to our household," Tivon explained gallantly.

Mitzi batted her eyelashes.

"Was it a good transaction? I mean, if you went back and... pumped him for information, do you think it would go well?"

"I was happy with how much I paid, and I'm pretty sure he was too."

"I'm not saying he's our jeweler father, but hopefully all the jewelers in the city know each other and he'll be able to tell us something. Kaveh, what about you? Do you know anything about the necklace?"

Kaveh shook his head. "I liked my grandmother, but I don't remember any of her jewelry. Sorry!"

"That's okay. This is great! We're making progress!"

"So once you find her, you beg for her help... and she goes to my father and pulls his head out of his ass," Kaveh speculated.

"And then Farzin goes free and his men get paid," said Shulamit. "All their wages."

As if on cue, the crowd cheered. Shulamit didn't care that it was for something else.

A little while later, a woman with a baby in one arm and holding a toddler's hand in another worked her way through the crowd and called out, "Your Majesty!"

Tivon turned toward Shulamit with questioning eyes. She responded by standing and approaching the edge of the platform. "Yes?"

"Majesty, I wanted to thank you for cheering for my husband. He's so shy he couldn't bring himself to meet you himself, but it meant the world to him."

"Your husband?" Shulamit flushed and fiddled with her left braid. Who had she cheered for?

"Yes, my husband Simon. He sells honey in the marketplace and competed in the jump."

"Oh, the honeyman! Yes, okay." Inside Shulamit's head, an army of kittens were scrambling around, hoping she could fake her way through this. "I love honey with yogurt."

"So do we. Do you hear that? She likes her honey on yogurt just like you do!" The proud mother was talking to her toddler. Then she turned back to the queen. "Will you hold my baby to bring her luck?"

Shulamit drew in her breath sharply. This was the future, calling to her.

She reached out her hands and accepted the child. Her arms shook, and she felt as though she was holding the whole world. *Well, I guess this* is *someone's whole world -- its parents'.* It was warm and snuggly in her arms and winked up at her as it wriggled slightly.

Shulamit's heart was beating heavily.

Then the baby shifted around harder than she was expecting, and she had to hold on tighter so it wouldn't fall. It whined. Then it began to wail. Panicked, she whipped her head around to Mitzi and Leah, those who had mothered before her.

But she needn't have panicked. Aviva was at her side, taking the squalling child and soothing it against her chest. She bounced it up and down gently. "They like this," she commented under her breath to Shulamit. It stopped crying, but then it started pawing at Aviva's chest for its next meal.

Aviva handed the hungry baby back to its mother, who bowed slightly to the queen and thanked her again before going off to breastfeed.

Shulamit remained standing, watching them go. Aviva squeezed her hand. "We can do this together," she said quietly.

Two mothers. Shulamit tried the idea out in her mind. Ima and... and something else. Perhaps they could use Rivka's word for her mother -- Mammeh?

For the first time, the thought of a baby -- their baby -- began to make her smile.

Chapter 15: The Jeweler's Daughter

Isaac landed at a conservative distance beyond the City of the Red Clay just as before, and, once Tivon was on the ground, quickly turned human so King Jahandar would have no idea that a Serpent-Master had entered his kingdom. They walked down the red clay together, as real lizards darted in and out of crevices in the large rocks that lay to either side of the path.

"You made *really* good time -- unless he's closed up early, I'm sure the shop'll still be open."

"Thanks," said Isaac. "That was the idea." The part he didn't tell Tivon was how much his back and shoulders were burning with exertion, and how much he wished for Rivka to be there to pound on his shoulder blades with her fingertips. After all this was over, he wondered if Shulamit would let him and Rivka spend a day or two at a mineral spring.

"Do we have a plan this time, or are we just going in and asking?"

"I'll be a lizard and hide in your cloak," said Isaac. "That way, if you're unsuccessful, I still have a chance to go back in there and try another way. But I think you'll do fine."

"I know some of your philosophy," said Tivon. "Don't worry -- I won't volunteer too much information."

"No, no, actually, I *want* you should overshare. Tell him all about Mitzi and giving her the present and anything else you can think of, as long as it's unimportant." Isaac turned to face him and looked him in the eye as he added, "People say a lot when they feel like you've shared first."

"Hm. I guess that's true."

"Mitzi loved that present, but I'll tell you something else," said Isaac. "She loved that you gave it to her."

Tivon smiled. "I'm not a complicated man, and I don't need a woman to be complicated, either. She's easy on the eyes and thinks I'm interesting. What else is there?"

Isaac could have said a lot of things, and was certainly thinking them, but instead he returned to the mission. "Here's another thing you can do. People love to correct. Not always to be mean or show off, but -- well, I'm sure this has happened to you. It happens to me, anyway. If the sky is blue and someone stands up and says, 'No, it's green,' there's a feeling you get -- the knowledge gathers inside and bursts out, and if you try to keep it inside it becomes an irritant."

"How does that help me?"

"Say something you know *isn't* true. It might get you further than just to ask."

Tivon pondered this for a moment. "Maybe I could suggest that the stories in the book are all made up."

"Sounds good."

"You might as well transform again now. If we walk any closer, someone might see you disappear."

Isaac took Tivon's outstretched hand in his own and began the transformation. When he was safely a lizard, he crawled up Tivon's arm and settled on his shoulder, just inside his collar.

Once inside the city, they headed straight for the marketplace. Tivon walked past the fruit sellers and the ladies with cheese; he passed the man putting chairs together out of pieces of wood, and the man selling shawls. "That one would go with Mitzi's hair," Tivon murmured in a voice so low it was intended only for Isaac.

"Later," was Isaac's only reply.

125

"Buy a parrot?" A young woman, almost a girl, darted directly into his path. The bird on her wrist flapped angry red wings at both of them.

"No, I'm sorry." Tivon jerked his head to the side to avoid a faceful of feathers, and Isaac darted further inside Tivon's shirt. Ultimately, he was safe and could have just transformed back to human form if the parrot had gone after him, but that would have blown their cover.

Cats chased each other across the pavement, but Isaac was relieved that in none of them did he sense a human soul.

They passed a shop that, from the decorations and sign, usually sold the meat of geese, but during the Month of the Sun, when no meat was eaten, it had switched to selling feather pillows. "That's clever," Isaac whispered to Tivon admiringly. "Most likely they save the feathers all year round to make sure they'll have an income during the sacred month."

"Here it is," Tivon murmured, entering a pleasant stall just beyond the goosedown pillows.

The jeweler inside was hard at work with his tools, but when he saw Tivon come in, he jumped up and smiled. "The gentleman from the foreign Guard! And how did the lovely lady like her present?"

"Very much, thank you," said Tivon. "She wore it to the Marketplace Games. You don't have those here, do you?" Isaac smirked, as much as a lizard could smirk, anyway; this was a great plan for dragging the conversation toward *Memoirs of the Marketplace.*

"What, where all the vendors take a day off for sport and see who can run the farthest or whatnot? Not here." The jeweler shook his head and smiled cynically. "Too much going on -- nobody wants to close the whole thing down at the same time.

Maybe some of us meet and throw a ball against the wall when we have someone else who can watch the shop."

"Do you all get along pretty well?"

"Some of us. It's like with anywhere. You make some friends, you make some enemies, and everyone in between you just, you know... get on with. What brings you back here? I have some earrings that match the hairpin..."

Isaac, perched just inside Tivon's cloak, felt his pulse rise as the conversation drifted away from the culture of the market. "Buy the earrings and then tell him how you entertained Mitzi with stories out of the book," he whispered, hoping Tivon would be able to understand him at that volume, especially with his odd northern accent.

Luckily, he did, and Tivon made a big production of choosing between the two sets of silver earrings the jeweler showed him. "I was a little worried at first that she wouldn't feel at home down here, but now I think she's starting to enjoy herself," he chatted, his tone far more casual than his tense muscles betrayed to the creature riding in his collar. "And who knows? She may even like me for more than the presents. I read a funny book the other week, and while we were at the games I told her some of the stories. She didn't always understand the words I was saying, but she looked like she was having a good time."

"Of course she was -- you're a respectable gentleman of the Guard!" Then the jeweler told him the price.

Isaac was glad that Tivon pretended to haggle to avoid suspicion, even though they both cared more about finding out where the other jeweler was. "You might even know the book, as it's from around here," he added after he named a counter price. "*Memoirs of the Marketplace*. Picked it up last time I was here."

Good, thought Isaac. *That sounds natural.*

"Oh, yes, yes! An old one, but a classic. About the earrings, I really have to insist on..." and the jeweler went back to talking about prices.

Tivon counter-offered yet again. "It's definitely a fun read, but I think most of the stories in the book came out of the author's head. Imagine someone offering a jeweler twice the price of something to split up a pair of lovers! Sounds like something from a legend. What happened next, they throw themselves off the bridge at the full of the moon?" Here Isaac knew Tivon was speaking from the heart. The guard made no secret that he found the old, "beautiful" tragedies a bit laughable.

"No, no, the stories, they're all true." The jeweler smiled up at him frankly. "Even the one you mentioned. I was there the night Old Grey-Brows got drunk and told a whole roomful of other merchants, even though the man who bought the jewels had made him promise not to tell. Well, okay, maybe *he* was lying. I guess we'll never know. But Nouri was telling the truth when he wrote it down, all those years ago. And I didn't hear anything about any suicides," he added. "Probably they both just went off and forgot about each other. It's been decades. They'd both be growing older surrounded by their families by this point. As you say, life isn't a legend."

Life is weirder than legends, thought the lizard who had spent three years under a curse as a mare, being ridden by the woman he had been cursed for loving, without being able to tell her he had survived.

"Old Grey-brows?" inquired Tivon.

"That's what a lot of us called him," said the jeweler with a look of nostalgia. "He was my rival for thirty years. He's gone now, but his daughter Delara still runs his old shop on the other side of the marketplace. Fine woman. Good head for business."

"Did he have many daughters?"

128

"Just the one... had several sons with his second wife. Much younger than the daughter. Well, there was the daughter who died." Isaac held his breath, and he was close enough to Tivon's skin that he could feel the human doing the same. "Think she was about five or six. Very sad." Human and lizard exhaled with relief, Isaac a little self-conscious at feeling anything but grief at such a sad tale.

Somewhere in the middle of all this, Tivon and his jeweler managed to settle on a price for Mitzi's earrings, and then Tivon escaped from the shop. He walked out of the marketplace as quickly as he could and then hid in an alleyway so Isaac could transform.

"So. Delara. Other side of the marketplace."

"Good work, Tivon. That was perfect."

Tivon nodded slightly. "Thank you."

"Wait for me in the inn," said Isaac. "I have my own plan to talk to Delara."

"I'd love to know how you're going to get a woman to tell you whether or not she slept with the king," Tivon commented.

The wizard simply smirked at him calmly, enjoying his secrets as usual. "Let's just hope I can do it."

"See you back at the inn."

Isaac walked away from Tivon, back toward the marketplace. He walked past people selling musical instruments and clothing and food and things to put on the wall that held flowers. Sweet smells came from the shop selling pastries, and he stepped to the side to avoid the children chasing one another around with glee.

At the far edge of the marketplace stood a grand shop that looked established and venerable. A youth teetering on the edge of puberty hovered outside, arms folded across his chest, a knife strapped at his waist. He might as well have been captain of the Guard, so seriously did he take his position as shop security.

With a deferential nod to the youth, Isaac entered the shop. He noted the presence of a woman in extremely fine clothing out of the corner of his eye, but instead of moving straight toward her, he prowled the shop a bit, exploring. After a few minutes he had selected a few necklaces, each focusing on the color lilac. One looked like freshwater pearls; another, opaque beads with a dragon pendant. A third alternated between lilac and clear crystals.

He pretended to snap his head up with surprise when a soothing female voice beside him asked, "She likes that color?"

"Oh! Yes, yes, she does. Although, who knows what young girls like... Just when we think we can explain them, well..." Isaac flashed her a warm smile. "What do we know? They know everything, right?"

He could tell from her carriage that he was successfully charming her.

"At least, even if you guess wrong and you come home and she's thrown away all her lilac, she'll still treasure it because her Baba gave it to her." The jeweler unconsciously fingered the jasper beads she wore at her own throat.

"She loves her father, yes," said Isaac. As with the king, he hadn't uttered a single lie and didn't plan on doing so, but his answers led her down a false path. Such games amused him.

"Do you need help choosing? Maybe I can help." She took the necklaces from him and laid them out on the table in front of her. Standing back, she considered his selection. "Would you say her style is more... showy or more shy?"

Isaac waited a very calculated moment, then threw up his hands. "I don't know. One minute, she--" He turned around and looked around the rest of the shop with a wounded expression.

"Can I help? I raised three girls -- and two boys. And I'm discreet."

Isaac turned back around. "Do you think it's possible to pay a... rather ragged young man to go away and leave her alone?"

A complicated expression that wavered between sadness, wisdom, and amusement veiled the jeweler's face. "My honest answer? I'd say you'd have better luck if you just found a way to make him look a fool in her eyes, without saying so directly. That payoff ruse doesn't work. I don't want to scare you too much, but millions of years ago when I was a young girl, my father took a payoff... but I kept sneaking out to meet... a *boy.* It wasn't Baba's fault -- I'm pretty sure he never knew."

Isaac didn't have to feign dismay. If *sneaking out* meant what he thought it meant... "Sneak out? Do you think she sneaks out?"

"I couldn't say. I don't know your daughter at all. It's different from girl to girl -- but I can tell you that what we got up to at that age, you know -- hiding inside gardens -- that was exactly what the money was supposed to prevent. So, save your money -- or spend it with me! -- and find a way to embarrass the poor idiot instead. Make her see him as less than a man. You probably don't have far to go with boys that young, anyway."

"Thank you so much for the advice. I think I'll take this one with the beads and the, er, what is this?"

"It's a dragon. Supposed to be, anyway. That's purple jade."

"Oh, yes! Now I see. Very pretty."

"I hope she likes it. Can I help you find anything for your wife?" It was a sales pitch; it was also a probe.

"No, no, just the necklace for my little queen," said Isaac. "My wife, I gave her something big and silver when we first met, and that'll always be her favorite."

Rivka's sword had originally been Isaac's spare.

They discussed prices and the weather for a few minutes, and soon Isaac was out in the street again with his present for Shulamit packed safely away. He walked toward the inn with a heavy heart. Delara had lain with Crown Prince Jahandar, then -- how nice for them both, but it meant she obviously wasn't the woman from the poem. And someone who would take money with one hand while committing the very acts the money had been spent to prevent with the other didn't have the strong moral convictions of the mystery woman, either.

He figured that he should have known; her breasts had fed five children, but they weren't the size that would inspire poets to speak of melons.

Thunder cracked, and the beginnings of the afternoon rains began to soak his sherwani jacket. It helped him decide his next move. With a sudden jerk, he ducked behind a tree and dwindled down to his lizard form, the necklace safely in his pocket so it would reappear with the rest of his clothing. Going back to Shulamit without a solution would be embarrassing; even though they'd been successful in their mission, all they'd found was a dead end. Hoping Tivon would stay put and not try to come find him, he scurried across damp walls toward the palace.

The key to this whole mess was King Jahandar. Isaac resolved to spy on him until he learned something useful -- even something small, but something he could take back to Shulamit that would be more useful to her than a necklace of lilac jade beads.

Chapter 16: Shabbat in Flames

"Blessed are You, Milady, Queen of the World..."

It was Shabbat, and those closest to the queen were seated as usual around the big wooden table waiting patiently for her to kick off the day of rest with the usual blessings. Moments ago, Aviva had brought her a firestick she'd lit at a nearby torch, and now she held its blazing end toward the two candles placed in front of her.

Kaveh leaned in closer to Aviva and demonstrated his lack of skill at whispering. "I know you said that your god must be bigger than male or female, but I'm still not used to the way she--"

From across the table there came a sharp "Shhh!", and Kaveh flinched. Riv was glaring at him from beneath the dark-brown kippah that was somehow -- as if by magic -- taming the captain's usual mop of wild golden hair. Shulamit was relieved to see him shut his mouth, and she resumed her prayer while he watched in silence.

Shulamit shut her eyes as she sank into the familiar rhythm of the blessing, and then withdrew further into herself for the silent portion of the prayer. She hoped Isaac and Tivon's prolonged absence was a sign they had found the jeweler's daughter and were negotiating with her, or even better that they stood now by her side as she pled with Jahandar to come to his senses.

In her secret heart where she stood naked before God, she abandoned herself to selfish prayer -- the mystery woman from Jahandar's past was her only rescue from the unsavory choice between leaving her country in the care of strangers after her death, marrying a man who would inevitably demand her body, and making an enemy or possibly even starting a war. She couldn't live with herself if she ended up starting a war or leaving her throne to the whims of fate just to avoid having to sleep with a man on a regular basis -- what kind of a queen would she be?

But could she do that to herself?

God, help!

She started when she opened her eyes. Behind the friendly, flickering light of the candles, she saw Isaac standing before her on the other side of the table.

"Isaac! Tivon!" she added, seeing the other man standing in the shadows. She noticed a change in the body language of both Rivka and her mother, and she was momentarily amused. But as she studied Isaac's face for a clue to their adventures, she began to feel a weight in her stomach.

Isaac often sought to be mysterious, sharing only what he wanted to, and his face revealed nothing. But over the past few years, Shulamit had figured out that pride was also a powerful force within him, and she knew that if he had good news to tell her, his inscrutable expression would have been covered with a thin veneer of smug.

Instead, she saw nothing -- nothing at all. Not a good sign.

She found it hard to swallow. "Wh--what happened?" she stuttered softly.

"Bless the country, Queenling," he prompted her *sotto voce.* In other words, she had duties -- not now.

As the parents in ordinary homes bless their children at their own Shabbat dinners, Queen Shulamit blessed the nation under her rule. Tonight, especially, she felt the weight of that surrogate motherhood.

Aviva poured out some wine, and Shulamit was able to stutter out a blessing over that as well, her mind on other things. Isaac

135

sat beside her and tried his best to radiate a calming aura, but her jittery nerves were powerful even against his charisma.

Shulamit lifted Rivka's hand and nodded at her as she did each week, and then the captain proceeded to perform the blessing over the bread. This nod was a ritual passing of the torch that helped the queen not to feel so left out of that part of Shabbat, although she still longed to reach out and grab a piece of the fluffy golden braid with everybody else, stomach cramps or no stomach cramps.

When dinner itself was finally on the table, Shulamit finally turned to Isaac and asked, "Can you please tell me? I'm too tense to eat. I have to know."

Isaac paused a moment before speaking. "You were right about the jeweler's daughter, but she's not the woman from the poem."

"What?"

"She and Jahandar had an affair back when he was a teenaged prince, like you thought, and you were right that her father was the one who took the bribe from King Omeed. My smart little *malkeleh!* But they ignored the deal and saw each other anyway, in secret, and what's more -- they did lie together, years before the poem was written. Also, her chest is too small."

Shulamit opened and closed her mouth like a fish.

Isaac, who had just carried a full-grown man a full day's ride on his back, clearly didn't have any of her reluctance to eat and attacked his plate with nearly as much ferocity as if he'd still been in dragon form.

"So, I was right," she observed, "and it still did me no good."

"I'm sorry, Queenling." Isaac looked genuinely distressed. "I knew it would upset you terribly, so I stayed behind to spy on the king after I found out. I hoped he'd say, or do, something to give me a clue about his childhood love, so I turned lizard and spent

136

hours in his palace. The only thing I found..." Here he lowered his voice. "...was worse news."

"Worse? What do you mean, worse?" Shulamit began to play with her fingers nervously.

Isaac leaned his head toward hers and continued in a soft voice. "Late at night, the king sat in conference with his executioner."

"I don't like where this is going." Shula lowered her head and rubbed her forehead.

"He wants to get rid of Farzin as soon as possible, but according to their religion, executions are forbidden during the Month of the Sun."

"Right... We already knew that."

"The executioner was summoned in case he had any ideas around the religious prohibition," Isaac continued. "Originally, they planned to hang Farzin at dawn, as soon as the sun came up, so that the spectacle of his death would serve as an example to his followers and any others who want to act as he does. But technically, they're allowed to kill him at sundown the night before -- their holidays are like our holidays, starting at sunset."

"So he didn't want to hang him at night because then nobody would be able to see? I really, really don't like this man."

"Exactly. But the executioner pointed out that there are ways of killing people that are still very, very visible at night." Isaac's face darkened. "Even if they're far more cruel than the instant death of a neck broken by hanging."

"What are you--?"

Then she noticed Isaac's eyes were no longer on her but were staring to the front of her, at... the Shabbat candles.

137

"No. What? Really? That *bastard!*" Then she covered her mouth quickly, but Rivka wasn't even listening, and Mitzi was engrossed in whatever Tivon was saying, as usual.

Kaveh, however, was -- somehow. Their efforts to hide the conversation from him hadn't gone as planned. "What are you whispering about? Why is she staring at the candles? Why does he look like he just got a death sentence?"

Shulamit, panicking, remained silent. Isaac turned away from Kaveh. Their reticence to answer only made the prince more anxious. He sprang from his seat, attracting everyone's attention. "Tell me! Has Farzin -- is he still alive?"

"He's alive," said Isaac gravely. "Your father's just moved up the execution half a day."

"You mean after nightfall? How can he do that? It's at night! Nobody will see-- will see-- Oh, oh..." Kaveh trailed off as his eyes fell upon the candles. "No...no, he can't! Not fire! Oh, my poor love! What pain!" Pale-faced and breathing oddly, he lurched forward. Several pairs of eyes watched the unsteady man warily, unsure if he was about to faint or vomit.

"That way he'll be easier to see against the darkening sky," Isaac explained to those on the other side of the table who were just catching up.

"How horrible!" Mitzi exclaimed, groping around on the tabletop vaguely for Tivon's hand.

"Watch him!" someone shouted, just before Kaveh stumbled sideways and knocked roughly into the queen. Kaveh, wide-eyed, shaking, and clearly oblivious to his surroundings, began to scream. He stumbled out of the room, and Shulamit was close enough to the courtyard that she could hear him throwing up.

"Riv, please go help him." Shulamit struggled to regain control of her own emotions, but all she wanted to do was cry.

138

Chapter 17: The Amazing Shulamit's Juggling Act

"Ugggh," groaned Shulamit, collapsing into her usual chair within the safe confines of Aviva's kitchen-house. "What happened to Shabbat? So much for peace and contemplation. I feel worse than ever!"

"This Shabbat we peeled a litchi, and all that was inside was the seed," Aviva commented, rubbing her shoulders. "No fruit at all."

"Just a rough little nubbly husk thing," Shulamit agreed, picking apart one of the aforementioned litchi husks with agitated fingers.

Aviva quickly swept up the rest of the discarded husks before Shulamit's discomposure could cover the table in vegetative confetti.

"I'm sorry," Isaac murmured distantly.

"Oh, Isaac, we don't blame you! I'm grateful that you stayed and tried to find out who the woman was. It's not *you* that wants to set people like us on fire." The queen grinned manically, a smile with no joy.

"Someone loved him... once..." said Aviva in disbelief.

"If we could just find her again -- if he'd listen to her--"

The usual unselfconscious clatter announced the approach of Captain Riv. "Shulamit, you have to make a decision," said Rivka as she entered. "Kaveh's under guard right now because he threatened to castrate himself if Farzin dies."

Aviva gasped, but the queen was nonplussed. "You don't have to watch him so closely," Shulamit pointed out. "If he does it now he loses his bargaining chip."

"Bargaining chip?! *Gottenyu*, this man risked his life to come to me for help, and I gave him my word that--"

"I know, I know, and I want to help him too. I keep thinking, what if it was Aviva--"

Rivka sat down across from her and next to Isaac. "I know you worry about a lot of things. I know you have the whole kingdom on your shoulders, but you have to focus for a second."

"*Focus?* I haven't been thinking about anything else in weeks. Look. Here's my problem. If Kaveh doesn't let me marry him, I'm caught between letting people I don't know or trust inherit my kingdom whenever I die someday, or having to-- my body--" Words failed her and she sputtered and panicked, and Aviva put her arm around her in comfort.

"I don't like either one of those, either. Which is why I say we attack." Rivka took both her hands and fixed her in her gray-blue gaze. "Queenling. Let me sound the call. There's no time left. I know it's Shabbat, but everyone here knows what you're up against, and so does God. When this is all over you can give yourself a week's rest, and it'll all come out in the wash. If we leave now, we can be there with plenty of time for you and I and Isaac to talk to the king, free Farzin and pay his workers -- and, by the way if you don't like that idea, let me introduce you to my Royal Guard. We have the might! Why do you hold back?"

"It's going to start a thing," Shulamit insisted unhappily.

"A *thing?* Do you mean a war? I can handle a war. Jahandar can't put up that much of a war, anyway. Our men are strong, well trained, and clear-headed. They're ready to fight for you."

"I know -- I know we have the strength, but people could still get hurt. This could have lasting... Besides, the City of the Red Clay has never been our enemy. I hate the idea of making enemies out of nowhere."

"Please tell me this whole agonizing mess isn't just you trying to avoid *being disliked.*" Rivka's elbows hit the table with a thud, and she rested her face on her fists. "They're *gornischt* -- just one little nothing city."

"They still *have* an army! And no, I don't want to make enemies."

"Why do you even care what King Jahandar thinks of you? If you hate him, why do you need him to not hate you?"

"It's not just that."

"You don't need him to like you, just to fear us enough that he won't attack you."

"I thought you said he'd take it personally and attack even if he was outmanned."

"You think too much. Handsome prince shows up, begs for help. We give it. You get a free husband who won't touch you except to make babies. Why make it so complicated?"

"Rivka, if this starts a thing--"

"War. Say it. War. If it starts a war. Stop being scared. We can handle it."

"If this starts a *conflict,* then I basically just sold out my army because I can't bear the idea of laying with a man on a regular basis. How do you think that makes me feel?"

"I'm the captain of your Guard, and I signed up to do everything I can to protect you with my life. That includes protecting your body."

"I have the whole country to look out for, not just the army."

"Do you really think the City of Clay folks have enough of an army to provide a real threat to Perach? Because I don't. I think--"

"I know I'm probably going to have to send you and your men in there," Shulamit said wearily. "I just want more time to try it my way."

"You've had weeks! We found a... some jeweler who *shtupped* the king a million years ago. Not the glorious moral goddess you were hoping for. We tried it your way."

"She wasn't the one. It wasn't her. She's still out there."

"This *meshuggineh* poem was always a farfetched long shot!" Rivka barked. "I know you want a peaceful solution, but this isn't it. This one's a waste of time. If you really wanted a diplomatic way out you should have dropped this and spent your energy thinking of a different--"

"I *have* been trying to think of another one! My brain hurts from trying! There's something profoundly wrong with the fact that all I can think about morning and night is King freaking Jahandar. He's there when I fall asleep, and there right there all over again when I wake up. Maybe you're right -- maybe there *is* another peaceful way. I just wish I had more time to think."

"We don't have more time. And now we have even less time, because of this insane execution-by-fire business." Rivka stood up, throwing up her hands. "You go on and wait 'til the very last minute, but if something goes wrong with this rescue because we ran out of time, it's on your head."

"I can't just worry about my head -- I have to think about my country!" Shulamit called after the captain as she stormed out of the kitchen.

Isaac stood up and sighed.

"She thinks I'm only worried about making Jahandar mad at me, and that's not it. I mean, it's part of it, but it's not... It's my responsibility as queen not to go starting up conflicts with other nations. Even if she thinks they're not worth worrying about. I don't agree with that, anyway. They're not as powerful as we are but they're not *nothing...*"

"She's very confident," Isaac admitted. "And she loves you and she knows that she has talents that she can use to protect you."

"I wish I didn't need protecting."

Isaac circled the table so he could lay a heavy, comforting hand on her shoulder, and then exited into the clear night air.

Shulamit looked at Aviva. "You keep saying that Kaveh's attractive."

"In the conventionally accepted way, yes."

They remained in deep conference for a good while.

When Shulamit reached the prince's room, she found guards inside just as Rivka had mentioned. She ordered them to the outside of the room and then shut the door. Kaveh didn't acknowledge her, remaining tightly curled into a ball of emotion in the corner of his bed. She sat down beside him and put a hand on his shoulder.

"I promise I'll let Riv and the others leave in time to save Farzin if I can't find the mystery woman in time," she said gently. "I won't let him die."

Kaveh responded without moving, or even looking up at her. "I see him burning in my mind. His face torn with pain, the charred remains of his limbs--"

"Shh... Stop... stop." She ran her hand lightly over his back. "My brain does that too. It's so busy that sometimes it likes to make up nightmares to keep itself entertained. I hate it."

Kaveh rolled over to face her. "He's the best man ever born, Shulamit. All he wanted was for people to be treated fairly."

"Then you're lucky that you met him, and that he loves you."

"I'll die if he does."

Shulamit nodded. "I know. I've asked you this before, but -- is there anything else you can tell us about who the woman from the poem might be?"

Kaveh shook his head. "The only romances of his I know about are my mother and stepmother." He snorted weakly. "It feels strange to think of anyone loving my father. He's become such a monster."

"At least he'll be nicer to you now that he thinks you're paired with a woman."

"You look like the idea makes you want to throw up."

"It does, a little. My stomach feels like there's a big rock inside."

"Maybe it won't be that bad. You're close to me now, right? It would just be... a little bit closer."

Shulamit lifted an eyebrow skeptically, but she didn't stop him because she wanted desperately to see if she could handle this. She still wanted to rescue Farzin and see justice done, but it frustrated her and made her feel like a child that so much of her motivation these past few weeks had been the simple selfishness of avoiding what for many people was ordinary intimacy.

145

Kaveh pulled her down beside him onto the bed and ran a featherlight hand down her arm from her shoulder to her wrist. She took a long, slow breath, trying to pretend he was just massaging her to calm her nerves. For a moment, she was tempted to pretend she was somewhere else.

"Does that feel good?"

She didn't know how to answer. But. This was nothing. She could handle it.

She forced herself to put her arms around him, and he responded in kind. Not kissing -- she *couldn't* -- instead, they just held each other in an awkward, sweaty silence. Shulamit was drowning in the smell of man, and it was scary and unfamiliar. His body was harder, bonier, more toned than Aviva's, but he was trying to be gentle, and she appreciated that.

I don't like this! she screamed to God.

"Keep going," she said in a tiny voice. She was a queen, daughter of her father. Weaknesses were made to be conquered.

Then two things happened at once that broke her courage. Kaveh timidly slid his hand inward to wrap three fingers around her breast, and she felt the beginnings of his body starting to respond against her pelvis. It was as if someone suddenly blew out a torch. She panicked and pushed him away.

"I'm sorry... I'm sorry... Are you okay?" Kaveh babbled nervously. "Please don't call off the deal. I wanted to show you it wouldn't be so bad, so you'd try harder to save him. Oh, my--"

"Please go away." She sat up and crunched her body into a curled-up knot, her hands cupped over her nose and mouth. Her skin was crawling all over. "I'm sorry. I need to be alone." She had even forgotten for a moment that this was supposed to be Kaveh's room.

146

He disappeared, and she sank into her own mind, thoughts scattered, not even knowing what form her prayers should take.

The next thing she knew, she was surrounded by two pairs of very familiar, muscular arms. "Oh, *Malkeleh, Malkeleh,* what did you do?" cooed Rivka, plaintive and soothing, holding her almost too tightly -- but Shulamit needed it.

"Do you need me to transform?" Isaac asked, probably worried that in the body of a human male he might be upsetting Shulamit to be so close to her at this vulnerable moment. Not waiting for an answer, the room suddenly filled with his dragon form, and he wrapped both wife and adopted daughter in his wings.

Shulamit burst into tears. "I'm -- so-- *weak!*"

"Shhh..." Rivka patted her hair over and over again. "No, you're not. You aren't now, and you never were."

"I just couldn't bear it. It was like someone was trying to get my blood to flow the wrong way in my body. Like I was swimming against a strong current. Oh, and, Rivka--" She couldn't even describe the unsettling feeling of Kaveh growing hard against her.

"You did good," said the dragon in his deep, echoey rumble. "Don't be ashamed if you try things that wind up not working. Trying means you have courage. You don't have to succeed for that to mean something."

"Isaac, how am I ever going to go all the way through this with *anyone,* enough to get myself full with an heir?"

"Maybe you don't have to."

"What do you mean?"

"Maybe I can figure out a way to get Kaveh's seed inside you with magic," he explained. "After all, when Rivka and I... I have magic spells that kill my own seed -- there must be a way to reverse the spell and reanimate seed outside the body... and get it back inside of you somehow. Maybe even with Aviva's help, so it'll feel like she's the one impregnating you."

"That... would mean the *world* to me," Shulamit said to him, slowly and deliberately.

"Come back to our room," said Isaac brightly. "Nothing to do with this, but maybe it cheers you up. I just remembered I've got a present for you."

Shulamit woke up the next morning determined to give the search for Jahandar's mystery girlfriend one final attempt before acquiescing to Rivka's plea for marching orders. She was, therefore, thoroughly distracted by her own thoughts as she tried on her wedding dress for Aviva's father, who was a tailor.

"I keep forgetting how thin you are," said Ben, looking over his handiwork, "but I think I've finally gotten it right."

"Everything she eats just goes straight to her hair," quipped Aviva. Shulamit's long black hair was thick and unruly even for her people's already robust hair, which was why it usually lived so highly restrained.

Shulamit rotated completely so the present company could admire her wedding outfit. She had chosen a color between yellow and green that reminded her of new growth (and Aviva of unripe bananas). Ben also carried, in a neat folded pile, the white lace chuppah Leah had crafted. It was stitched here and there with thread of the same yellow-green as the wedding outfit in patterns reminiscent of young leaves and tendrils.

Mitzi, who couldn't resist being involved in anything to do with new clothes and thus had insinuated herself into the fitting session, gazed dreamily at the chuppah. When Ben and the servants had left and only Shulamit, Aviva, and Rivka remained with her in the room, she commented, "Ahh, Rivkeleh... you know, I made you a chuppah when you were a little girl. You never used it, but I brought it with me."

Rivka looked embarrassed, but Aviva jumped up. "Oh, Lady Miriam, I'd love to see it!"

Mitzi beamed and floated out of the room. Meanwhile, Shulamit continued to think about Jahandar. *Maybe she was one of the court musicians... but she'd have to be either rich or highly ranked. How would I find out if there was a rich musician...?*

When Mitzi returned she carried not only the chuppah, of undyed wool lace, but also a large dark-brown evening gown. Rivka's jaw dropped when she saw it. "Why do you have that?"

"It's your dress from Cousin Bina's wedding," Mitzi reminded her.

"I know. You brought it... why?"

"I don't know, don't you think Isaac would maybe like to see you in it? You looked lovely that night."

Rivka clapped her hand to her mouth with an exaggerated sigh.

"Let's see the chuppah," said Aviva. "Oh, lovely! And you made this all by yourself?"

"Yes, I made it when Rivka was a little girl. I didn't know she'd grow up so... different." She turned to face her daughter. "And then you went away and got married somewhere else without it, and it's never been used."

"Sorry?" Rivka said awkwardly. "Sorry I didn't wait until you could be there, but I waited for three years, and honestly given my mood at the time it was get married that day or risk not getting married before we--" She flailed her hands around in the air in a

149

gesture meant to indicate *I am not talking about sex with my mother.*

"Oh, honestly, Rivkeleh, he may be *literally* a dragon, but he's so calm and restrained that I just can't imagine him being any kind of a dragon in the--"

"Aaaaah!" Shulamit suddenly squeaked. Three pairs of eyes swiveled straight to her.

Mitzi blinked. "Wha--?"

"She is a bird! He is a dragon, and *she is a bird!* Literally!"

"Who's a--?" Mitzi's face was a perfect flower of confusion.

The other two had followed her line of thought. Rivka's jaw was hanging open -- it almost reminded Shulamit of the day when Isaac had been saved from the curse and Rivka's mare had suddenly turned into the man she had loved and thought lost three years ago, buck naked. Aviva, however, had burst into giggles and had started to twirl around the room. "I've been beaten at my own game!" she said to nobody.

Shulamit turned to Mitzi. "The mystery woman. She's a shapeshifter -- like Isaac. Only, instead of serpent powers, she has bird powers. 'She is a bird, and she has flown.' He loved a shapeshifter! This will be *easy!* There can't be that many people like her -- as long as she's still alive."

"Isaac said the Cat-Mistress he met mentioned another like her," Rivka supplied helpfully. "I bet you anything that's her."

"It's got to be." Shulamit started shucking off her wedding dress.

"We just have to get her to tell us where she is," said Rivka as she and Aviva helped bundle Shulamit more quickly into the lilac-colored clothes she'd been wearing before the fitting session. Meanwhile, Mitzi picked up the wedding dress where Shulamit had tossed it in a heap, and folded it into a more suitable shape.

"We will! Between the four of us. We've got to leave. Now. I'm coming, this time. We're all coming. Rivka, go get Isaac. Aviva, go put on pants that don't have turmeric all over them. Mitzi, I love you!" She sprang over and kissed the surprised woman on both cheeks.

"There aren't any," Aviva called after her, still grinning like a crescent moon.

Chapter 18: The World Is Held Together By Simple Syrup

The City was cloaked in darkness when the dragon and his passengers arrived. Shulamit's heart pounded with excitement as Isaac gently touched down on the path just outside the city. What if it was too late at night, and the cat woman had already closed up shop? That might easily waste time they didn't have, waiting around an empty tavern until dawn.

"*Oy*, my back," said Isaac as he transformed back to human flesh.

Biting her lip, Shulamit started to ask, "Do you need to res--?"

"No, no, I know we need to get to Mother Cat's before I can recharge."

Rivka put her hand to his back and rubbed it haphazardly as they walked.

This was Shulamit's first time in the City of the Red Clay, and she inhaled every vista, dimly lit as they were. Winding paths, some steeply inclined, led them through the alleyways between the red clay buildings. Lanterns and a nearly full moon illuminated block after block of quiet dwellings, guarded in front by fig trees or grapevines. Every time she saw a stray cat, sleeping on steps or cleaning itself in the middle of the street, she flashed a questioning glance at Isaac. But he dismissed these as ordinary animals.

Aviva fished something out of her pocket and handed it to the queen. "Eat."

"I'm sick of almonds," Shulamit fussed.

"If you're hungry when we get to the tavern, we'll need something from Eshvat besides what we really want," Isaac pointed out. "Then we start out at a disadvantage."

Rivka shrugged. "We have something *she* wants."

Isaac lifted one eyebrow high enough to bump clouds and gave her a look.

"Those figs... Shulamit, give me a coin." Aviva had stopped walking and was inspecting a tree in somebody's yard.

"What? Here."

Aviva picked a few of the figs and then hopped across the green to leave the coin on a windowsill. "Eat."

Shulamit dutifully consumed the fruit as they continued walking.

Soon they reached the great river that ran through the center of the city. After walking some distance down the riverbank, Isaac stopped and pointed ahead. "See that light coming from that alley? That's Mother Cat's. And now, if you'll excuse me, I need to rest." He melted down to the ground in the form of a huge python, butter-colored dappled with gold.

Rivka scooped him up and draped him around her muscular shoulders. He gave her an affectionate squeeze and rested his head on one armor-covered breast. Thus arrayed, she strode purposefully toward the light. Shula and Aviva trotted after her, still looking curiously around them at the beautiful and exotic foreign city.

The hour was late, but the door to Mother Cat's stood wide open. A small group of women were standing in the doorway chattering to each other in the tones of an extended goodnight. Their clothing varied from the rags of the most overworked cleaning woman to the subtle finery of rank. As each bade good-bye to her companions, she was sent down the street with warm smiles and waving hands.

Shulamit crept closer. She could see inside now. A woman in her forties or fifties with long, wild hair and a face more striking than beautiful was cleaning utensils and putting them away. Her face was unreadable, but the women closest to her wore expressions that were at once both affectionate and regretful. Eventually, they peeled away like the others and left, and the tavern owner called out after them. "No, really, thanks. Have a great night!"

When the last of the women had disappeared into the alleys, Rivka flashed a look at Shulamit and Aviva and then stepped inside the tavern.

"I'm closed," said Eshvat, her eyes still on her polishing. Then, as if sensing something, she looked up and straight into Isaac's eyes. "Oh. Hello."

"Snake form, as requested," said the snake.

Eshvat chuckled in a low, throaty voice and rubbed her temple with the hand that held her polishing cloth. "So you're back."

"You said I was welcome even when you were closed," said Isaac.

Eshvat spent a few moments staring him down, her work on pause. "So what are you up to?"

Isaac slithered down Rivka's body to the floor and transformed back into his human shape. "We were hoping you could help us." His tone was deep and seductive, and there was a mesmerizing look in his eyes as he stepped closer to the tavern owner.

Eshvat flashed him a saucy grin. "Hmmm," she purred. "With what?"

"You and I have something in common, obviously," said Isaac, every word a caress.

Eshvat nodded and said, "Mmm-hmmm," in an almost-meow.

"The last time we met, you said there was another one like us -- someone who'd studied the arts with you -- someone you hadn't seen in a long time." Isaac was hitting her full blast with charm

154

now. "I was wondering if I could get you to help us find her. I've got the evening free if you need time to think."

Eshvat folded her arms across her chest, threw her head up, and laughed heartily. "Oh, please. All that?" Now she was shaking her head. "I'm not betraying her privacy."

"We really need to speak with her," said Isaac, liquid and low.

"Look, first of all, I may not have talked to her in years and years, but I'm always loyal to my lady friends. All those women you passed on the way in -- everyone from countesses to seamstresses and fruit sellers -- they're my family and I love them all. I'd never sell them out to please a gentleman. And *second* -- *you* come back here expecting me to get pulled into your little vortex of handsomeness after telling me quite frankly and definitely that you were otherwise occupied. Yours isn't the only male body in this town, and I've had plenty of entertaining evenings since our little encounter."

"Let's forget that for a second," said Isaac, relaxing his seductiveness a little. "It's important. Would I embarrass myself like this if it wasn't?"

"Probably not," said Eshvat, "but then, who knows? I don't know whether or not you have any kind of honor. You never even told me your name."

"If I tell you my name, will you tell me where the Bird-Mistress is?"

Eshvat's pupils reformed into the vertical black slits of a cat's. "I never said she was a bird."

"No, you didn't."

"We can do this all night, and I'm not changing my mind. I can tell you're tired. Save your energy." She sat down at the table and returned to cleaning her supplies.

155

Shulamit approached the table and fished a handful of coins out of a pouch at her side. "I don't know if this is enough, but does this change your mind?"

Eshvat looked down at the coins, then up at Shulamit. "No. That's just selling her out in a different way." Then she squinted at Shulamit, standing before her with her two braids fastened behind her head as usual, and looked back down at the coins. She then returned her eyes to the queen with a hard stare. A pointing finger jabbed toward the coins. "That's... *you.*"

Shulamit opened her mouth to speak, but Isaac interrupted. "If it is, surely you know that means there's more to be offered."

"Not just coin, but jewels!" Shulamit interrupted. "Think about it. Anything you wanted to do with the restaurant, any improvements -- artwork, new plates, fixing anything that's broken -- all those worries, taken away. Let me help you... If only you would help me." She spoke earnestly, her little chest heaving as she waited for an answer.

Eshvat continued to shake her head. "This is my restaurant, and if I do anything like that I want to have pride in what I do. I'd rather have my little clay tavern with its charming problems here and there that I've improved with my own sweat and labor than some gilded palace someone else bought for me. Whatever I have, I want to be proud of." Since Shulamit didn't move to retrieve the coins, Eshvat covered them with her hand and slid them forward on the table. Then she went back to her polishing.

Shulamit stepped back towards Isaac, and Rivka was at the table in two bounds. "And what happens if we try to force it out of you?" she asked menacingly, towering over the seated woman. She began to draw her sword.

Eshvat sprang up, her hands on her hips. "I'd like to see you try to get me. Don't you know cats -- even ordinary ones -- are made of smoke? You can't hold a cat that doesn't want to be held. You make one move at me, and I'll scratch that mask right off your face before I disappear."

"Maybe, maybe not," said Rivka. "Only one way to find out." With one swift flourish, she drew her sword.

The room became a whirlwind of fur and steel as Rivka hacked and slashed at thin air. Eshvat, in her cat form, leapt from table to table, practically bouncing off the walls, hissing and squalling. Isaac, clearly too worn out to use magic, simply sat down and watched his wife try to swordfight with a cat.

Eshvat ran between Rivka's legs to try to trip her, but Rivka was too sturdy on her feet. She still, however, couldn't subdue the practically flying feline as she tore through the room.

Finally, Eshvat perched on one of the rafters. "Are we done yet?"

Rivka stared up at her, then burst into laughter. "Yes, fine. Cat wins, I lose." She rehomed her sword and sat down in a wide, open-legged stance. "I bet that looked really funny from the outside."

"Basically," Isaac agreed, flashing her the impish look that was much more genuine than all the sexy nonsense he'd been aiming at Eshvat earlier. The contours of Rivka's cloth mask rose to betray the shape of grinning cheeks beneath. She was still breathing heavily from her exertions.

"Look, everybody, I'm sure this has been a real party," said Eshvat, bounding down to the bench at the nearest table and transforming back into her human shape, "but I have to ask you to clear out. I really do have more pressing things to worry about keeping my friends' secrets from strangers. I'm serious. Please. Go away."

"What's the matter?" asked Shulamit, remembering the concerned faces of Eshvat's friends.

Eshvat opened her mouth, then shook her head. "Oh, business owner problems. Nothing for warriors and wizards and queens. Just a simple, everyday, *horrible* piece of luck."

"Sometimes we have everyday problems," said Shulamit. "I still want to know what it is."

"I had a pastry cook here," said Eshvat. "I'm great with savories, but I can't bake to save my life. I trusted him, and he--" She shook her head, and a feline growl came from somewhere in her skull. "Tomorrow we were supposed to deliver fifteen hundred pieces of baklava to the amphitheater, as concessions for the Month of the Sun concert -- and he knew about it, and yet he chose today of all days to run off with the milkmaid!"

"Before baking the baklava?" asked the queen.

"Exactly. He knew I was counting on him, and he let me down. The guy's an *ass*." Eshvat started to get really and truly agitated, scratching at her head and being rougher with the utensils she was polishing.

"And if you don't have it..."

"I'll lose my reputation. This was a big order. The word will go out that I can't be trusted. Think what that does to a business."

"I can imagine."

"I tried to bake it myself, but... I... and my friends, they were all trying to help me, but none of *them* know how to cook. That's why they're my regulars! All we did was make a mess and waste my honey and rosewater." Eshvat sighed. "See what I mean? Everyday problems. I have until tomorrow morning to figure this out. That's why I'd really appreciate it if you'd all scram and let me think."

Shulamit's mouth dropped open slightly, and in her astonishment, she said nothing. Neither did her companions.

Eshvat, likely wondering why her visitors were all silent, looked up again from her polishing. "What?"

Three of them -- Shulamit, her warrior, and her wizard, were all looking at Aviva, the only one who hadn't spoken yet. She was standing in the middle of them, an elated smile lighting up her face and her hand in the air.

"I got this!" said Aviva.

Aviva felt flashes of lightning in her body as she waved her hand, every nerve ready for work. She met Eshvat's eye with confidence as the tavern owner looked her over quizzically.

"She's my cook," Shulamit explained. Eshvat's eyes bugged out in shock. "That's why her pants have turmeric all over..."

"Stop fussing about that," said Rivka. "Nobody notices it but you."

"Her Majesty looks at me more than anyone else does," Aviva reminded her. "Anyway. Mother Cat, I'll be happy to bake your baklava for you. All of it. Overnight."

"You would?"

"Of course! Well -- if you help us!"

Eshvat scrunched her face in a sulk for a moment, then relaxed it. "Oh, fine. I don't see any other way out of this mess. I love my friends, but I can't see my restaurant go down the sewer. Bake them all by sunrise, and I'll tell you where she is."

"Deal."

"How can we trust you?" Rivka asked.

"I'll tell you part of it now, but it won't do you any good until later. She's far away from the city, on a very large farm that she manages."

Aviva was already preparing herself for the all-nighter, piling her hair on top of her head and holding it in place with a pair of sticks. She did a couple of stretches to loosen up her muscles. "Okay, where's your honey?"

"Over there."

"And what do you have for nuts? Are they already crushed, or do I have to put them to work?" She cocked her head at her three companions.

"No, he'd already crushed up all the pistachios before Little Miss Milk Jugs showed up this morning." Eshvat led her into the kitchen. "Oh, over there is the batch I made, the one that... well, you see."

"I do see," said Aviva. "You only used honey. You have to mix your honey with simple syrup, or they'll never set."

Eshvat nodded slowly. "I knew there was something."

"What about the butter?"

Eshvat continued showing her around the kitchen. Aviva could see the other three, their faces a mix of happiness and disbelief at their good luck, sitting around one of the tables out in the restaurant. The place had an open floor-plan, so they would be able to watch Aviva working -- at least, until they fell asleep.

"Aviva, you need any help in there?" Rivka called.

"Yes! Rivka, your job is to stay out of the kitchen." Nightmarish images flew through Aviva's head of Rivka's beefy warrior hands breaking sheet after sheet of phyllo dough.

Rivka chuckled. "I'm guessing Shulamit can't help because of all that wheat dough flying around."

"You'd be right. Isaac, I know you have to sleep, but I'd love it if you could help get me started by singing to me."

"I can manage some," said Isaac, standing up and joining her in the kitchen. Listening to his pleasant bass voice was like a jolt of sugar to fuel her work. Sometimes, if she knew the tune, she sang along in harmony.

That was how they spent the evening, Shulamit and Rivka sleeping in the restaurant on one of the cushioned benches, Isaac singing to Aviva until he, too, had to sleep (in lizard form on Rivka's chest), Eshvat curled up in cat form on her own hearth, and Aviva buzzing around the kitchen preparing tray after tray of the sticky triangular treat.

As usual, she made something wheat-free for Shulamit, after taking care to thoroughly scrub her hands and reach for an undisturbed pouch of nuts. A funny little bar made of almonds, honey, and simple syrup sat on a piece of cloth near where the queen was sleeping, so she'd have something different to eat for breakfast when she woke up.

Aviva worked late into the night and into the gray of the morning. She brimmed over with purpose, knowing that with this night of hard work she was doing her best to protect her precious beloved from the beds of men. She thanked God for the opportunity, and she felt powerful.

Finally, Aviva counted all the trays and confirmed she'd reached her goal. Then she fell asleep without even cleaning the extra honey and melted butter from herself and slept so soundly she didn't rouse until they were already airborne and had been flying for hours. Her eyes snapped open, and she stared straight into an unbearably bright sky. "What happened? Did it work?"

"We're on our way," said Shulamit proudly.

"Who was she?" Aviva murmured. She blinked several times, hiding her eyes from the sun as they adjusted to the midday light.

"Her name is Aafsaneh, the Blue Swan," said Rivka, "and we're flying to her vineyard."

Chapter 19: Her Hair Out of Her Eyes, So She Can See Her Way Clear

Outside, in the fields and gardens, the men of the two valleys hacked and slashed at each other. Deep within the safe haven of the castle, eight-year-old Rivka scampered about the room, stabbing dramatically at the air with a candle.

"Stop that," urged Mitzi, holding out her hands to catch the whirling tornado of wild golden hair and flailing limbs as it careened past her.

"I have to practice!"

"Practice for what? You're just making a mess." There went Mitzi's shoes, careening across the floor. She had slipped them off to be more comfortable, and nothing stayed put in little Rivka's way for long.

"For when I have to go outside and fight with the others." Rivka twirled in a circle, the candle high above her head.

Mitzi blinked, growing dizzy from watching the gyrations. "Don't be silly, Rivkeleh. Do you see anybody out there as small as you are? They'd trample right over top of you."

"I know! I mean *later!*" Rivka insisted with the exasperation of confident youth. "I'm growing really fast. You *said.* I'm bigger than Frayda, and she's a whole year older than me."

Across the room, the haughty baroness sat with her three daughters, trying to ignore her sister-in-law and her wild-animal niece. Cousin Frayda's eyes were fixed on her book, but a grimace had come onto her face. Mitzi suspected it was because she'd heard Rivka mention her name, even though Frayda was trying to look as though she was ignoring both freakish cousin and disgraced aunt.

"When you grow up -- not soon enough for me, you funny child," -- Mitzi massaged her own brow -- "you'll be a lady, and you certainly won't be swordfighting. Even with candles."

"Yes, I will. I'm going to be a lady swordfighter."

"That's like saying you're going to grow up and sprout wings," said Mitzi. "There isn't any such thing."

Rivka shrugged nonchalantly. "Maybe I can be the first one."

"Don't you want to grow up beautiful and gentle and have men fighting over your hand?" Mitzi smiled fondly at her lost dreams. Tall gardeners might be cute, but they certainly had a way of ruining one's chances with anyone else later on...

"Not if I can fight them first!" Rivka's smile was a little manic and bloodthirsty, but on an eight-year-old it simply looked hyper. "Wheeee!" She jumped off the furniture, waving the candle around.

"*Miriam!* Control that garden-patch brat of yours, or I swear--" began the baroness.

Mitzi leapt up and wrestled the candle away. "Please! You're going to get me in trouble."

Little Rivka didn't much care about being in trouble -- it seemed to her like she and her mother were always in trouble anyway, by default. "Augggh," she sulked, rolling her eyes.

She wandered around the room, looking for something else to do. Frayda was reading -- not that Frayda was much fun to talk to. The Baroness was rocking her sleeping toddler. Both of their

164

attentions fixed elsewhere, nobody was attending to little Bina, the middle daughter. She was wrapped in a blanket staring with wide, terrified eyes at the windows near the top of the room, even though they were too high up to see anything but sky. That was where the sound of the battle was coming from, though, and it provided faint but insistent background music of unease.

Men screamed outside, and something broke, and there was a noise of weapons.

Bina was crying. She was crying too quietly for either her mother or her older sister to have noticed, but Rivka was bored, and Rivka saw. She bounded over to the youngster and put her arm around her shoulders protectively.

Instinctively, Bina leaned into the comforting embrace. Rivka felt her tears, cold and sticky, against her neck, and she felt strong and useful.

"Bina! Come here."

With reluctant but automatic obedience, Bina slipped from Rivka's arms and joined her mother.

"Leave her alone," Frayda commanded Rivka, glaring over the top of her book. "We're not supposed to play with *you.*"

"I know, but she was crying." Rivka stared up at the window, mostly so she could avoid having to look at her aunt and her cousins.

"Here, Rivkeleh, sit by me. Comfort me. I'm scared by the fighting too." Mammeh was beckoning to her, so she walked back across the room and sat down by her side.

"I wasn't playing. I was trying to help."

"I know... I know." Mitzi put an arm around her. "You're growing so fast..." Rivka replied by resting her head against her mother. "I wish they wouldn't punish you for my mistakes. You

165

did the right thing, and I'm proud of you. See? You do know how to act like a lady."

"I can be a lady swordfighter and still comfort people when they're crying," said Rivka, but she was mumbling and facing away from her mother. She was tired of arguing. Instead, she settled in and stared up at the window, imagining the adventures that were to be had outside, in a world where instead of a candle in her hand she held a great, big, flashing sword.

The dragon Isaac flew through the dark, angry sky. On his back, the fully-grown Rivka lifted one hand to brush a lock of thick, rain-soaked hair out of her face and then resumed the tight embrace in which she shielded Queen Shulamit from the storm.

"It's coming down even harder," Shulamit pointed out in her characteristic neurotic whimper. "Are you sure we shouldn't land?"

"If we land we can't get across the river," Rivka reminded her, "and Eshvat said the nearest bridge was four hours' walk."

"How far until we get to the river?"

"Isaac? Can you see anything?" Between nightfall and the rainclouds, Rivka's own eyes weren't doing her any good.

"The river's not too far ahead," rumbled the dragon beneath them, "and I even think I see some lights beyond that."

"We're almost there!" cheered Shulamit weakly, still glued to Rivka's breastplate. Then lightning struck close by, and she screamed, burying her face and shrinking into the smallest volume possible. Thunder cracked all around them, like the sound of things breaking.

Aviva squeezed Shula affectionately, but Rivka knew she was nervous as well. "I don't want to be a sufganiyah."

"What?" asked Rivka.

"Fried," explained Isaac.

Shulamit started to cry. Rivka rubbed her back, wondering if Shulamit could feel that her heart, too, was beating faster.

The three women held each other in a cluster of rain-dampened skin as Isaac gave the ride over the river a final push. He landed on the opposite bank, and they scrambled off his back, the younger ones huddling under his wings to get out of the rain. "I'm sorry," said Shulamit. "I know you probably want to transform so we can all walk, but I couldn't resist! It's just coming down so hard!"

"It's fine -- I just need to sit for a minute."

Rivka looked at him with concern as she stood unflinching in the torrential downpour. "If you're tired, I can carry you again."

"That might be a good idea. Even if this Aafsaneh agrees to Shula's plan, that doesn't mean Jahandar will definitely listen to her. *Ohhhhh,* yes, definitely keep doing that." Rivka had started pounding on his back on the spot right where his wings met his body. "Anyway, as I said -- you and I should go back to the capital and have the army ready at the City wall, just in case. And that means lots more flying in a hurry."

"But if the army shows up, won't Jahandar take it as a threat?" asked Shulamit. "Even if things are going well?"

"Not if we bring Prince Kaveh back with us," Isaac explained. "That way, if all goes to plan and Aafsaneh manages to convince him to be more compassionate, we can say we're there to deliver your bridegroom and provide royal escort for your wedding. If not, well... you would unleash Rivka anyway. Or so you said."

Aviva grinned. "Isaac, are you the reason people talk about snakes when they want to make something sound sneaky? Because I like your recipes."

"I'm just glad he's on our side," said Shulamit.

"Are you two ready to come out from under *Tateh's* wing? Because I'm tired, and it's Rivka's turn to carry me, but once I transform the wings go away."

Shulamit looked at Aviva, then said, "I guess we can brave it." They held hands and yelped as they ran out into the rain.

Rivka hefted her now-serpentine husband onto her shoulders, and the three women trudged through the muddy ground away from the riverbank and toward the vineyard.

By the time they reached their destination, dawn was only a little while away, but the rain hadn't slowed down. The first few peasant houses stood still and quiet, but soon Rivka began to notice noises behind her, near the houses they'd already passed. Twice she whipped her head around, only to see nothing but muddy footprints that hadn't been there moments ago, quickly being obliterated by more rain.

Soon she realized what was going on. The people in the first houses along their path had sent scouts down to the farther houses, and men holding farming implements in threatening poses were beginning to block their way.

"I'd better go on ahead and explain we mean them no harm," Shulamit began, about to take off.

Rivka caught her by the braids. "I'm supposed to protect you, and I veto that plan. I've got the sword -- we'll stick together."

"I thought I was queen?"

"That's why you have bodyguards."

"Those look scary," Aviva pointed out, eyeing the rakes and poles.

"Yeah, they do," Shulamit admitted. "I just thought maybe they'd put them away if--"

"Birds are territorial," Isaac reminded her. "Remember earlier, how you noticed I have a way of being... a bit slick? And Mistress Eshvat is an unashamed hedonist, like a cat? I think our Lady Aafsaneh has some bird qualities as well, and while I doubt these men are also Bird-Masters, if she's as wonderful as Jahandar wrote, I bet they're very loyal. They might repel you even if you came to them in friendship."

"So what do we do?" Shulamit eyed the men beginning to approach them from both sides.

"We try anyway. It's what we came here for." Rivka's hand rested on her sword.

By the time they reached the initial line blocking their access to the grand house at the top of the hill, they were surrounded by suspicious farmhands. "Peace," said Shulamit. "I'm Queen Shulamit bat Noach. I rule over Perach, to the east."

"We answer to nobody but the Swan-Lady," said one of the farmhands, both fists resolutely fixed on the pole he held.

"I'm not here to take away your freedom," said Shulamit. "It's very important that I speak with your Swan-Lady right away. At least one life is at stake, and the livelihood and well-being of dozens of workers like yourselves."

"We don't know anything about that," said another man. "Our orders are to keep everybody out."

"It's easy to make up a story to get inside," pointed out the first man. "Especially if you've come with an armed warrior."

"This is my bodyguard," said Shulamit.

"Fair enough -- and we are hers."

"Is there any way I can get inside to talk to her?"

"No. Please leave. Our wine merchants travel to your lands to sell in the marketplace. You can contact her through them."

"She doesn't see visitors," said a third man who hadn't spoken yet.

"But I can't wait that long," Shulamit said desperately.

"Yes, you can."

Shulamit glanced uneasily at Isaac, who was still draped over Rivka's shoulders in his gold-and-ivory python form. She wasn't nearly as good at being crafty as he was. But she knew she was small enough that this *just* might work.

With a sudden dart, she attempted to make a dash through the legs of the men standing guard. Immediately she knew it was a stupid, stupid move. There were rough hands everywhere, and something hard hit her on the shoulder, and then suddenly four powerful dragon legs were clutching her to a familiar scaly body. Isaac's wings closed around her. "I don't know if I protect you from them or from Rivka," he muttered. "That was too dangerous. I don't need scares like that when I'm this tired. I can hardly fly, or I'd got you in there myself."

"I'm so sorry!" Shulamit breathed heavily, leaning against his underbelly. "I guess we should have sent you in there as a lizard or something."

"Too late now."

"What's going on out there?"

"My wife tries to fight off a dozen angry farmers with one sword," said Isaac dryly. He opened his wings slightly for a moment to let Aviva slide inside. "In the rain."

"I'm sorry..." Shulamit continued to murmur over and over.

Aviva held her against her bosom, and Shulamit knew the gesture was intended to help her calm down. "Not being able to see is making this worse."

"I have to protect you two. Otherwise I'd be over there helping her."

"Can't we peep through your wings?"

"If you can..." He shifted slightly.

In the silver of predawn, Rivka battled off the farmers' assault as rain continued to pelt the vineyard. Gusts of wind pushed the rain sideways, and her hair swirled behind her in sodden gold whips. "She really looks like she's working hard, not just fighting those men, but also advancing into the wind," Shulamit observed.

"Yes, she works hard," Isaac agreed, "but to face the wind actually helps her because -- look -- her hair is blown behind her, out of her eyes, so she can see her way clear. Imagine having all that mess fly around your face while you try to swordfight."

"They're coming this way!" Shula grabbed on to Aviva and pressed them both closer to Isaac's torso as three or four of the farmers broke away from the skirmish and ran toward them, poles held high. Isaac continued to keep his wings closed tightly around them like a sleeping bat, only right-side up, but he twisted his neck this way and that so he could snap his great jaws at them, roaring. It was a great, deep sound that Shulamit felt as much as heard, shaking her in her bones, but in a comforting way.

171

Unfortunately, with his wings closed in front of him, Isaac couldn't shoot the buzzing, whirling whips of light out of his fingertips that the queen had seen him use in battle and in sparring-play with Rivka.

Shulamit could tell from watching her that it was taking all of Rivka's concentration to not only fight off the farmers' poles and rakes, but also do so in a way that left none of them permanently maimed. She was concentrating on destroying the weapons, but even that worried Shulamit. She tried to keep tally of how many poles wound up scraped beyond repair so she could pay Aafsaneh once they finally managed to find her -- if they found her. *Oh, God.*

And Rivka was still taking a beating. She was just ignoring it, and fought onward. But between her efforts and Isaac's mouthful of sharp teeth, Queen Shulamit and her sweetheart remained on Aafsaneh's grounds, and were not driven away. The sun arose, and as its pink-and-yellow glow flooded the sky, Shulamit saw a woman walking with stately carriage down the path from the great house on the hill.

Chapter 20: Milady the Swan

She looked about Isaac's age, mid-forties, with a fascinatingly unique face -- long and with large, exaggerated eyes. Dark hair gone silver here and there flowed in gentle waves past her long neck to her shoulders, and she wore about her voluptuous figure a filmy cloak of shimmering blue that reminded Shulamit of the sea.

"What's this trouble?" she asked, looking around her with an expression of concern.

As soon as the farmers saw her, those not in Rivka's immediate vicinity bowed at the neck and approached her. "Milady, these intruders appeared in the night," explained one of them.

"But we've held them off," said another.

"I tried my best not to hurt your men!" Rivka shouted at her, still struggling against a man trying to push her down with a rake. "Milady Swan, we mean you no harm."

"What is it that you want, young northerner?"

Rivka merely looked over at Isaac, deferring to Queen Shulamit.

The Lady Aafsaneh cocked her head as she studied Isaac. "Peace, Serpent-Master. Why have you come? And what is it that you hide within your wings?"

Shulamit's head popped out from where he was hiding her. "Lady Aafsaneh," said Shulamit, "I'm the queen of Perach. May we please come inside and talk to you?" She grinned nervously. "Oh, and I have plenty of gold coins I can pay you for anything my bodyguard broke while fighting to keep us here. I'm really sorry about that."

"You have honor, little queen," said Aafsaneh serenely. "Men, please lay down your tools and return to your homes. Or into the fields, those of you who have work to do. I'm grateful for your protection and love you all, each and every one of you. You've done well here tonight."

"Are you sure you can trust them?" asked the first man who had spoken to them.

"I can see kindness in the dragon's heart," was her calm reply. "Come." She beckoned to her visitors, no longer intruders, and they followed her back to her villa up on the hill. Isaac was once again riding on Rivka's shoulders in his snake form, fast asleep and probably dreaming of mineral baths.

The view was beyond beautiful; through brilliant green rows of grapes, growing neatly in diagonal lines, they walked toward a large white house with a red roof glowing against the morning sky. Aviva craned her neck as she followed the others, inspecting the fruit with eager curiosity. There were also fig trees, and here and there an olive, old sentinels, standing watch proudly over the younger specimens of horticulture beneath them. They reminded her of Isaac's role in the palace, since he also stood guard and doted upon younger beings not related to him by blood, but only by spirit.

Once just inside, Aafsaneh bade them sit in a cool room away from the sun, but open at the sides and lined with a delicate pattern of geometric tiles. A harp rested in the corner, in front of a little stool cushioned with blue velvet. Aafsaneh's hand brushed at the strings as she passed it, more of a distracted caress than a deliberate act. The result was an unfocused and random beauty, like the music of nature instead of human artifice. "Have you eaten?"

"Not really," Shulamit admitted.

Aafsaneh clapped her hands and gave orders to the servant who appeared for the visitors to be brought cheese and olives. "Will he need food?" she asked, pointing at the snoozing serpent.

"He needs rest more than anything else," said Rivka, stroking his smooth scales faintly, "but he'll probably appreciate a *nosh* once he wakes up."

"He likes rugelach... and live mice, of course," Aviva piped up.

"As he likes to say," Rivka interjected with an evil grin, "same size, same filling. Ever since he said that, the raspberry ones make me suspicious."

Shulamit looked a little bit nauseated, but Aafsaneh chuckled. "He sounds like a lot of fun. Your father?"

Shula opened her mouth to speak and ran out of steam.

"No, he's our dragon, and we're the treasure he guards. He's the father God gave us after hers died," Aviva explained, gesturing toward the queen. "King Noach -- didn't you hear about the accident with the elephant?"

"So she really is Queen Shulamit?"

"In the flesh!" Shula grinned uneasily. She fished out a handful of coins. "See? How many awkward portraits of myself do I owe you for the rakes and poles?"

"Oh, that must be so weird," said Aafsaneh, fascinated by the money. "Does it make you feel like you're giving away part of yourself when you spend it?"

"I already feel like my kingdom owns me," said Shulamit. "I have to put them first in so many ways."

"I know what you mean. This farm -- it's been my life, even since before my husband died. He brought me here years ago, and I've worked so hard to keep it strong."

175

"I'm sorry you lost him. May his memory be a blessing."

"And the same with your father."

"Thank you."

"So, my friends -- why are you here? Why did you fight for hours just to get a chance to talk to me?"

Shulamit took a deep breath. She had hoped Isaac would be awake for this part, but without a dragon, they were marooned here, and he couldn't fly without rest. "Milady Aafsaneh..." She considered her words carefully. "There's a man doing some terrible things, and he's about to do even worse things, and you might be the only one who could stop him."

All the joy dripped from Aafsaneh's face. "What man?" she asked in a voice of deceptive calm, her expression betraying that she already had some idea of whom the queen was speaking.

Shulamit licked her lips and fiddled with the edges of her scarf. "King Jahandar of the City of the Red Clay."

Aafsaneh's eyes were fixed on the corner of the room, her lips slightly parted. She was looking inward.

"You're the only kind of moral authority who could get through to him--if anyone could."

"I-- can't--" A servant approached with a plate of olives and cheese, and she jerked her head up, startled at the noise. "Oh. Thank you. Thank you. Please, eat." The servant disappeared the way she had come. "I didn't think anyone even knew." These last words were nearly a whisper.

"Months ago, Jahandar hired a group of workers to perform improvements upon the city," Shulamit began, taking a slice of cheese from the tray. "They built a new bridge so that the people living in a recently built neighborhood could get their things home from the marketplace more easily. They also repaired

176

decades of damage to the roads. When everything was finished --
oh, this was all something to do with the Month of the Sun --
anyway, he didn't pay them their promised wages."

"Let me guess. Something about how they should have been
proud just to work for him."

"Well, basically. But he rephrased it as patriotism."

"Sounds like him. None of what you say surprises me."

"It gets worse," Aviva piped up. Aafsaneh cocked her head,
blinking.

"The underpaid workers sat down on the bridge and refused to
leave," Shulamit continued. She told Aafsaneh all about the
miniature rebellion, and how some of the townspeople had
smuggled food to the demonstrators. "But the really horrible thing
is that the king had their leader arrested, and he's going to execute
him at sundown at the end of the Month of the Sun. Execute! Can
you imagine? And he's so bloodthirsty that he won't even wait
until the next morning, because he's so convinced that this man
was trying to steal his throne. All because they wanted fair
wages!"

"Sunlight and ashes, he's gotten worse." Aafsaneh looked sick.
"Is this because I left? Could I have stopped him from becoming
this?" She clutched at something hanging from her neck, and
Shulamit realized it was a heart-shaped locket. Was Jahandar's
picture inside?

"If you come back with us, you might be able to save his life and
get all those men their fair pay," said the queen.

"No! No, I can't." Aafsaneh looked so skittish that Shulamit
almost worried she'd transform into a bird right then and there --
something small and swift, not the swan form -- and disappear out
into the vineyards. "I still feel for him. I can't go near him. I can't
go near such a monster if it means risking my heart."

177

"Please, Milady," said Aviva. "We only have until sunset on the day after tomorrow. Imagine only having one more day to live, just because you had a good heart. They're going to set him on fire, alive."

"Do you love this man?" Aafsaneh asked, turning to face her.

"No, I've never met him," said Aviva solemnly, looking her in the eye, "yet he is my brother -- in some ways."

"I should get you girls some new clothes," said Aafsaneh, changing the subject. "The rain did you no favors."

"Milady, *please,*" Shulamit insisted. "I'll give you money. I'll make your wine the official wine of every Shabbat in my palace for the rest of my reign. Anything."

Aafsaneh had stood up and was rooting around in her wardrobe, not looking at them. "Here, this looks like it would fit you -- you share my large chest," she said to Aviva, holding up a long gown that was as bright a yellow as a lemon rind. "It goes with this." In her other hand, she held a bright yellow scarf covered with pink roses.

Aviva took the garments from her uncomfortably. "Thank you. They're very pretty. About those poor men--"

"I can't. My little loves, please understand. Your hearts are in the right place. But I've been so safe here, even without my husband. What I felt for Jahandar-- it was-- like the sun. I can't control it. Even as evil as he is."

"You must have controlled it enough to leave," Shulamit pointed out, trying not to be distracted by Aviva unceremoniously changing her clothing beside her.

"I left once," said Aafsaneh. "Could any woman have the kind of strength to leave twice?"

"You look like you're strong enough for a lifetime," Shulamit commented.

"I might be. But I can't risk it. My final word is no." Aafsaneh sat down again. "You're welcome to stay and eat as much as you like, but I'm not coming with you. I'm sorry about your friends, and I'll pray for that poor man, but I can't face Jahandar again."

Rivka, who had been stuffing her face and not saying anything, banged her fist down on the table so hard that olives flew into Shulamit's lap. "Milady," she barked, shaking her head with frustration. "Even someone as cruel and stupid as Jahandar could see how wise and how gracious you are. You're like the queen of this farm, and all your men look up to you and would obviously die a thousand deaths just to make sure you sleep through the night without being disturbed. All we need is for that wise, amazing person everyone thinks you are to come out and play -- not this scared, frozen woman I see in front of me."

Shulamit, horrified, froze and clutched Aviva. "Riv, be quiet!"

Rivka ignored her. "You're scared of your feelings. So, *nu*? Feelings are scary. Death is scarier. Tomorrow night, because you won't go meet up with your old boyfriend, we have to go in there with our army and start an international conflict where there was none before. Men will die -- my men will die. The men I'm sworn to lead. I'd prefer *not* to have to lead them to their deaths!" Aafsaneh opened her mouth to speak, but Rivka barreled onward, a verbal Red Sea closing in on anything Aafsaneh might have wanted to say. "Yes, I know Jahandar's forces are weaker than ours, but they'll fight valiantly, and if I lose even one man because of your cowardice, I swear, I will break every bottle of wine I ever see with your name on it."

"Oh, my God, Riv, *what--*" Shulamit whimpered.

"And I have to do it, because if we don't -- if we fail, if we can't go in there, if I can't make it back in time to my army and lead

179

them to the City before tomorrow night, they'll set a huge fire, and Farzin will be--"

Aafsaneh stood up suddenly, knocking over the table in front of her. Olives and cheese flew everywhere. "*Farzin?*" She was shaking, her eyes flung open wide, her limbs tense.

"The engineer who led the bridge project," said Shulamit. "What? Why?"

With fingers trembling so profoundly that she could barely maneuver them, Aafsaneh struggled to open the locket around her neck. "Does he look like this?"

Rivka, puzzled, scratched her head and said, "I don't know. *Vakht Oyf.* Wake up, Isaac."

With a growly voice, the snake murmured, "*Vos?*"

"Wake up and look at something. Here." Rivka approached Aafsaneh so Isaac could scan the locket with his beady eyes. "Is that Farzin?"

"It looks like him. Sort of. Only, that's not him."

"What's going on?" asked Shulamit.

"This was my husband," Aafsaneh explained, swallowing uncomfortably as she held both hands up to her temples and swayed slightly, "and our son looks just like him."

Chapter 21: Mama Bird to the Rescue

"It'll take me all of today and tonight to fly there," called Aafsaneh breathlessly from behind her dressing screen. Garments flew about like living creatures as she discarded her morning robe and prepared herself for the public eye. "And maybe part of the morning. I only hope I can get there in time! He didn't tell me where he was working. All he said was that I'd be proud -- that it was his biggest project yet, and he'd tell me all about it when it was finished. Oh, my poor baby!" She'd already spoken to her servants and was nearly ready to leave.

"It only took us a day and part of a night to get here," Isaac commented, still resting as a snake around Rivka's shoulders, "and that was with three people on my back and exhausted from flying the day before."

"But dragons are faster than birds."

"Aren't we almost all the way back home?" Rivka asked her constrictor consort. "What's the plan?"

"We go home and get the Royal Guard, just in case," said Isaac. "If we leave soon and get everybody out quickly, we should be able to bring our men there by nightfall tomorrow, which is..."

"Yeah." Rivka looked grim. "And Prince Kaveh can ride with me. I'll look after him."

"Kaveh? Jahandar's son?" Aafsaneh emerged from behind the screen in much more splendid clothes. "I remember him. Farzin was fond of him. I wondered--"

"You wondered right, but it's a long story," said Rivka.

"I'll explain on the way," said Queen Shulamit. "Can I borrow a pair of gloves?"

"On the way where?" Rivka asked quickly.

"I'm riding with her. Can I? Can we? Will it slow you down?"

"You both look small... probably not," said Aafsaneh, considering. She opened a small box and retrieved a set of embroidered gloves for Shulamit. "Will these work?"

"But we're your guards!" Rivka exploded.

"I have to go with her to make sure we're successful," said Shulamit slowly and deliberately. "I'll be okay. Aviva can look after me." She pulled on the gloves. They were much bigger than her hands, and a little too hot to be comfortable, but now she knew she'd be able to hold on to Aafsaneh in her bird form without aggravating her body's odd reaction to fowl.

"She's a cook."

"She's good with a knife. And she was younger than you were when you first went into battle, when she killed the sorcerer who tried to rape her."

Rivka opened her mouth and then shut it again. "Fine. Whatever. We don't have time to argue. Isaac, can you fly yet?"

He craned his neck up to face her, and shook his head from side to side slowly. "Give me another five minutes, and then maybe."

"I have just the thing." Aafsaneh rummaged through a small wooden box in the corner of the room, then emerged with a small vial of something that looked like wine.

"How will it help to get drunk?" asked Rivka suspiciously, but Isaac was already slithering to the floor so he could transform.

"It's charmed. Here." Aafsaneh rushed over to them.

Isaac rose up as a man and murmured a quick, distracted thank-you as he seized the vial from her hand and drank it in one swallow. "All right, Mighty One, we're off." He and his warrior wife scrambled out into the vineyard so his transformation into dragon form wouldn't disrupt the furniture.

"Don't forget my wedding dress! And the chuppah!" Shulamit called after them as they flew off into the bright morning sky.

When she turned back to Aafsaneh, she discovered that in place of the stately middle-aged woman there now stood an enormous swan, her feathers the scintillating blue of a morpho butterfly. Her large eyes were now ringed by black over a formidable beak the color of ripe mango flesh. "Now, girls! Quickly!"

They obeyed without a word, Aviva helping Shulamit get her balance and placing her firmly in front of her on the bird's back. She kept one hand on each side of Shulamit's tiny waist as the swan emerged from the building and flapped her giant wings, sending up a wind that sent loose strands of Aviva's hair to dancing.

"Thank you," said Shulamit quietly, and they were airborne.

The neat rows of viticulture beneath gave way to wilderness as the great swan flew into the sky toward the home she hadn't seen in over twenty years. "I'm glad we're flying west," commented Shulamit. "It's so bright today we'd have to ride the whole way with our eyes shut if we were going in the other direction."

"Hmm," Aafsaneh murmured in assent. She sounded distracted, and her distress was unmistakable. Beneath their legs, the young women on her back felt muscles as tense as a tabletop.

"We have to keep her mind off what's going on in the Clay City," Shulamit craned her head around to whisper in her sweetheart's ear. "I trust her, but I can also see us crashing into a tree!"

"We want to have a baby soon," Aviva blurted out. "In your magical studies, have you found a way to make a second mother give milk?"

Shulamit's face burned with embarrassment at the question, but it did exactly what it was intended to do. She leaned back into Aviva's bosom, satisfied to make the minor sacrifice to her dignity.

"Oh, yes, there's definitely a way to do that," said Aafsaneh. "I helped a woman on my farm nurse her baby nephew once, when her sister was too sick."

"That makes me feel the sunlight," said Aviva. "I know love makes a mother, but... I want to give something of my body too, like she will."

"I don't think you need to, though," Aafsaneh continued. "If the queen is the one having the baby, her body will probably make everything the baby needs. And if you nurse too frequently and Shulamit doesn't, she could go dry."

After a long pause, Aviva responded. "I'm used to feeding my loved ones."

"By continuing to feed your queen, you'll be feeding your child too. And after about six months, you can start to feed your child directly, with other foods."

Shulamit felt an effervescent joy at the way Aafsaneh referred to her future offspring as Aviva's child as well. She hadn't expected any ugliness, because of what Kaveh had repeated about Farzin's mother, but she still poignantly appreciated the validation.

"It'll come looking for milk," Aviva pointed out, poking herself in the side of one breast, "from these coconuts I drag around."

"So it won't be nursing for nourishment, but nursing for bonding. There are so many ways you'll be there besides this one," said the Swan-Lady. "Still, it's a generous idea. I like your heart."

184

"Me too," said Shulamit. She was less nervous than usual while discussing this sort of detail with a stranger, but she still felt a firm thumping in her chest.

"How did you find her?"

"She found me," said the queen. "I get sick if I eat wheat or fowl -- that's what these gloves are for. She's a cook, and she's the only one who figured out what was happening."

"We spent a lot of time together," Aviva added. "Our vines began to grow up around each other."

"What about the sickness when the child begins to grow inside me?" asked Shulamit, her memory tripped by the discussion of her teenage illness. "Is there magic for that?"

"Yes, I've helped ease that too."

"Thank goodness! Will we need to come visit you, or is it something Isaac can manage?"

"It sounds like woman's magic to me," said Aafsaneh, "but, you know, I'm not really sure! I don't know where his skills lie. I would have liked getting to know him better. It's been so long since I've been around another wizard."

"You'll probably get to see plenty of him. I mean, I hope you will," answered the queen. "If all goes right, you're going to be my -- I mean, let me think about this -- my legal husband's mother-in-law. So Isaac will be family! Family of choice, anyway."

"You're a lucky queen to have your throne guarded by a dragon," said Aafsaneh. "I'm interested in what kinds of other abilities he has. I'm sure there are things we can learn from each other. Isaac has the dragon and the python, right? Is he ever a crocodile?"

"He can, but he doesn't like it," Aviva explained. "He says it makes him feel sleepy. I guess crocodiles do spent a lot of time sleeping with their eyes peeping up in the water. And he doesn't have a turtle form."

Shulamit noticed Aviva didn't volunteer the existence of the lizard form, but somehow, she instinctively trusted Aafsaneh. She didn't add to the information herself, however, and she also stayed away from anything that might out Rivka's womanhood. Instead, she asked if Aafsaneh had any other forms herself besides the swan.

"When I want to be small I look like a little blue starling," said Aafsaneh. "My husband used to joke that he'd caught me one year when he put out nets to keep the real starlings and finches out of the grapevines. He was always saying things like that. That's where Farzin gets that never-ending sense of humor of his. Oh..." she added, "but, that's right, you haven't met him yet."

"It almost feels like we have," said Shulamit, "because Kaveh talks about him so much."

"Since they can't be together, Kaveh feeds voraciously on the crumbs of memory," Aviva agreed enthusiastically.

"I know those meals." There was a pang of pain in Aafsaneh's voice. "It's been years since my husband died, but I talk about him with the farmers all the time. I tell stories to their children, the ones who never knew him. It wasn't just that he made me laugh, although when we first met, I desperately needed it." Then she told them of how she, a young noblewoman with illicitly-learned magical skills, had fled into the countryside to escape her royal lover and met the wealthy farmer she had married. "He was a good man," she concluded, "and filled with so much optimism. Farzin has that part too. I hope it's helping him now."

"From what Kaveh says, it sounds like your son has your devotion to goodness and justice," said Shulamit, eager to draw her once again from her quite understandable rage and worry.

"I'm glad to hear that," said the Bird-Woman. "I did everything I could to raise him right. I'm so proud of my boy."

"I can't tell you how much it means to me to hear you talk about him that way even though you know he's in love with a man," said Shulamit, instantly feeling self-conscious about her honesty.

"Why should that matter?" said Aafsaneh, and Shulamit would have cried if Aviva hadn't instinctively cradled her tiny body more tightly. It wasn't that King Noach loved his daughter less than he would have if she had loved men. But she knew her aberration disappointed him, and no amount of Bens or even Isaacs could patch up the memories of hearing the words 'unconditional love' used in a twisted way, meant to brand her natural inclinations as something to be loved *in spite of.*

As the day waned on, they talked more about Kaveh, since Aafsaneh had never met him, and heard more stories about Farzin's father. Aafsaneh wanted to know lots of things about life in the palace, but stayed away from painful subjects like elephants. Her voice was gentle, but underneath all her stories and her polite and friendly questions lay a deep sea of anguish. Shulamit could hear the tension in her voice, and she hoped the conversation was calming enough that she could concentrate on flying and get there safely.

The queen and her consort took turns napping in the night, each making sure the other wouldn't fall off. Her dreams didn't bear repeating, the dreams one has while closing in on an effort whose failure could result in three different nauseating nightmares come to life. Would she have to lie with a man, after all, or would a war start because of her refusal to select one? Or would she let down her responsibility to her country and to her father's memory, and abandon her kingdom to the squabbling of third cousins once she was dead? She was glad to wake from those dreams and hold Aviva instead, squinting into the pink dawn. Today was the day. She eyed the sunlight uneasily, silently willing its glowing rays to go on forever. With the departure of that sun might end all her hopes.

Broad morning daylight streamed over the sleepy girls as their flying chaperone reached the City of the Red Clay. Aafsaneh's path took them directly up the river, and Shulamit soon realized she was quickly drawing closer to the new bridge. The workers Kaveh had told her about were still there -- dozens of tired, gaunt men with glassy eyes set in determined faces. Some of them were picking through a basket of fruit and passing its contents out to the others, but much of the fruit wound up back in the basket or even thrown into the river because of rot or mold.

Even numerous as they were, they seemed such a tiny, forgotten band compared with the rest of the teeming city.

A few of them spotted the enormous blue bird flying overhead, and although they couldn't have seen the women on her back, Aafsaneh by herself was enough to inspire a sensation. Within seconds, they'd told the others, and all the men were staring and pointing, momentarily distracted from their grim vigil.

Shulamit, with the wind around her face, swelled up with euphoria. These men were in their most desperate need, and she -- little Shulamit! -- had the power to save them. All she needed to do was speak the words, and her entire Royal Guard, with the notorious Captain Riv Maror riding "his" fearsome dragon, would rain like a thunderstorm down on King Jahandar, crushing him into submission. How dare he force these men into this position after the months of hard work they'd given him? It was a beautiful bridge.

She could practically hear trumpets playing.

Aviva caught the look on her face and said, "Hm?"

"I could save them." Shulamit bit her lip and played with the edge of her scarf.

"You *are* saving them."

Shulamit leaned into her and breathed deeply. That feeling had been like a drug. "I hope so."

Inside King Jahandar's palace, Crown Princess Azar sat in court, unable to take her eyes off her new husband. He had been ravenously attentive to her lately -- singing to her, asking her lots of questions about her ideas and dreams and opinions, and touching her in ways that truly made her feel valued and cherished. She was grateful for the attention, and often she interrupted her thoughts with thankful prayer.

It was prayer, in fact, that had brought them together this way. Some days ago, the Crown Prince had been in the garden at dawn, praying to the Sun for guidance in his new marriage. He could sense he hadn't yet captured the heart of the lovely and fiery Azar, even though her mind had indeed chosen him as a suitable companion. "The Sun answered me, dear Princess," he had told her in bed on that first good night as he caressed her well-loved body. "He spoke in a deep voice that I almost felt flow through my body like the heat of his rays. He taught me how to love you properly. I listened and tried my best to remember every word, and I swear to you, Azar, I'll do my best to be all that you deserve."

Azar adored him now. She was embarrassed that her attitude had ever prompted such prayer. "None heard your prayer save for the Sun, right?"

"None but a lizard," laughed the Crown Prince. "I was alone in the garden."

"Lizards also pray to the sun, in their own way," Azar observed, "basking in the heat on the rocks."

"I could bask in your heat," purred the Crown Prince, mounting her again.

These were the kinds of memories Azar's mind replayed as she sat in court with her husband and her father-in-law, surrounded by courtiers. She was therefore paying very little attention to the legal case King Jahandar was discussing with two lawyers who had come to arrange an arbitration. The Crown Prince was listening studiously, since he was in training for the throne. She contented herself with studying his expression of concentration.

Suddenly, the doors at the far end of the hall banged open and drew everyone's attention. Azar heard a crash and realized Jahandar had sprung up from his throne and was standing, frozen in place, the broken pieces of his teacup scattered around the floor. She followed his stupefied gaze and beheld, standing in the open doorway, a beautiful woman standing before them wearing a floor-length cloak of peacock feathers over a blue gown. Her hands were outstretched, and no guards could come anywhere near her. Dark, curling hair cascaded over her shoulders, held out of her face by a few pieces pinned back behind her head with blue feathers.

Behind her stood two darker-skinned handmaidens, or so Azar took them for -- one beautiful and bosomy, the other smaller and with hair bundled up into braids. The smaller woman was fidgeting with the ends of the lilac scarf around her neck.

The court had fallen silent. Jahandar took a step closer. Then the woman spoke, her voice calm and powerful and present, like a mountain.

"Free my son."

Chapter 22: The Last Day

Whispers rose up through the court like trees swaying in the wind before a big rainstorm. "That's Queen Shulamit of Perach!" called a man Shulamit recognized as a merchant who had visited her court recently.

The man standing at the door, who was fidgeting nervously as if he expected to be executed for letting Aafsaneh and her companions through the entrance without introduction, eagerly pounced on the tip. "Really?" he hissed. When the merchant replied with a quick nod, the doorman bellowed, "Presenting Queen Shulamit bat Noach of Perach, to the east."

Shulamit stepped forward as the crowd bowed to her, oblivious to the double-take coming from Crown Princess Azar. The little queen's mouth formed a grim semi-smile as she beheld Jahandar in the flesh, riding a wave of surrealism as she came face-to-face with the man she'd studied on parchment and obsessed about for the past three and a half weeks. Tall and olive-skinned, he towered over her, his dark hair elegantly sculpted in waves and his clothing brilliantly red and gold. Like his son, his features were aesthetically pleasing, but whereas Kaveh was a creature of beauty, Jahandar's face was hardened by cruelty. "Your Majesty," she greeted him, honey in her voice but hate in her eyes.

"I welcome my future daughter-in-law to my kingdom," said Jahandar in a calm tone that contrasted dramatically with his wide eyes and practically vibrating body. Shulamit could tell from her own experience on the throne that he now clung to automatic protocol to save him from whatever it was he might be feeling. "This is my son, the Crown Prince, and his new wife. My second son is traveling the world. Have you brought Prince Kaveh?"

"No, he's on his way separately," said Shulamit. "But instead, I've brought your friend." Inwardly she was floating on a sea of storm-tossed waves, bobbing up and down, and if she could only keep her head above water, she could get through today.

"I see that," said Jahandar, gazing at Aafsaneh until she had to look away under the power of his glance. He turned to the Crown Prince. "My son will take the court into the garden. I will hear no more cases or visitors today."

A hubbub rose up. "But, sire!" each of the lawyers exclaimed with twin agitation.

Jahandar held up his hand. "Don't worry -- you'll get your chance to assault my poor ears with your nonsense tomorrow."

The Crown Prince stood, nodded to Shulamit, then led the court away.

The three women now stood alone in the room with the king and his guards. "Where have you been all this time?" Jahandar asked in a softer, more vulnerable voice than Shulamit had thought possible.

"On my husband's farm," said Aafsaneh quietly.

"Then you're married? And have a son, you said?"

"My husband is dead. My son will be too, soon, if I can't reach that heart I once loved so well."

"What are you talking about? By all the holy Sunlight is my soul stirred by your presence," he added as an aside. "You should have been queen."

"My son... that you've bidden to be put to death tonight at sunset."

"What are you talk-- wait-- Farzin? You're talking about *Farzin?* He's your *son?*" He whirled around to face his throne, his eyes downcast and angry. "He tried to take over my kingdom."

"He tried to preserve your honor," Aafsaneh pointed out, "which you lost when you broke your promise to the workers."

"My honor..." Jahandar turned again and looked up at her, his face a mass of confusion. "We have to talk -- alone."

"As long as it takes," Aafsaneh consented.

Jahandar ordered the guards away, telling them to take the visiting queen and her "lady" into an adjoining antechamber. The heavy door shut, and they could hear and see very little through its carved open designs.

"Well," said Aviva, "we planted the seeds, and we watered them. Now we wait."

Shulamit gave her a weak smile and sat down beside her on an ornate cushion.

They sat for a long while, unable to speak as they strained to hear what was going on. The tones coming through the door were pleading, furious, frustrated -- from Jahandar and Aafsaneh alike. Shulamit was too tense to enjoy looking around the room at the various specimens of art that lived there, but it was the only occupation available. Aviva hopped up off the seat eventually and began wandering around the room examining them more closely, especially the ones that had to do with food and drink.

After an intolerably long time, a beautiful woman entered the room. It was Azar. "I'm sorry we didn't get to speak before," said Azar. "I don't know what's come over the king."

"That's okay," said Shulamit, more icily than she intended. All she could think about was Azar's double betrayal of Prince Kaveh. Words like *broken* buzzed around in her head like big ugly houseflies. She looked away.

Azar sat down across the little room and looked over at Shulamit as if she wanted to speak but wasn't sure if it was a good idea. Shulamit wanted to be *anywhere else*. Finally, the inevitable came. "Your Majesty... do you know... about Prince Kaveh?" Azar's expression was one of protective concern, not malice or amusement, but this didn't ease the awful cramp in Shula's stomach.

"Kaveh's been honest with me about everything," said Shulamit with serene bitterness. *In other words,* she thought, *I know what you did to him. You disgust me.*

"I've been thinking," said Azar, "that there's probably a cure."

"For being narrow-minded?"

The princess blinked, considering. "It's true -- people can be very judgmental," she said, completely missing Shulamit's meaning. "I mean, it's not like other forms of sickness. It doesn't get in the way of, you know, *life.*"

Shulamit's stomach felt like a kettle of boiling soup, and her heartbeat pounded in her heated face. She didn't say anything, instead concentrating on straining her ears to hear anything she could from beyond the closed door.

Azar continued, "Take Captain Riv, for example. I don't know why anyone cares what he does when he's off-duty. He's already proven how well he can fight and defend you, and that's what he's there for. If I were in your shoes I certainly wouldn't care *what* he was lying with -- other men, parrots, an oil lamp... When I met him, I immediately saw why you have so much confidence in him and why you're willing to overlook--" Tiny droplets of her feelings about the captain were leaving a misty residue around her tone of voice, and her eyes grew dreamy.

"When did you see my captain?" Shulamit interrupted sharply. Azar obviously didn't know that Rivka was female -- if she'd seen her someplace and felt an attraction, what did that mean? Was there any way to use this to teach Azar a lesson without outing Rivka?

"When he and the other man, the older one, came to ask the king's blessing for your marriage," said Azar. "I was there. I was in court. What a powerful figure he makes!"

Shulamit remained expressionless, but she longed to smack her face with the heel of her hand. *I should have known,* she said to herself. *Isaac being Isaac. Oh, well, I guess the cat -- lizard -- will be out of the bag soon enough.*

"Everyone knows him as a hero," Azar continued. "But the prince, I mean, that's different. Aren't you scared he'll look at men?"

Aviva, who had been trying to ignore the conversation by concentrating on a jeweled mosaic of an orchard, tensed up. She was behind Azar, so the princess saw nothing, but Shulamit could see raw fear in her sweetheart's eyes.

"You're married to the Crown Prince," Shulamit pointed out, "but do *you* never notice men anymore? Ever?"

Azar's eyes flickered, and Shulamit hoped she was self-aware enough to think of her crush on Isaac. "But-- but I'd never cheat on my husband."

"Exactly. I don't see why it shouldn't be the same for someone like Prince Kaveh or anyone else who likes both men and women." Shulamit, seeing Aviva's anxiety relax into a beaming smile, straightened her shoulders and held her head high and proud. Despite her growing anxiety about the raised, increasingly annoyed voices beyond the door, for a moment she felt eight feet tall.

Hours later on the open grassland, Queen Shulamit's Royal Guard rode their galloping horses toward the City of the Red Clay. Rivka led them, riding on her husband's back and clutching an overwhelmed Prince Kaveh to her chest protectively. She was in full battle armor, but Kaveh carried in his pack the wedding dress and chuppah, and they all rode with the hope in their hearts that they'd only be there as a honor guard, not to start a war.

Isaac was well-rested; when he and Rivka arrived at the palace, he'd immediately gone to bed as she gathered the Royal Guard and gave command. They left at once, riding on ahead because the journey by horseback took longer than that by dragon flight. Rivka, Kaveh, and Isaac caught up with them the next morning, Kaveh fast asleep because he'd been up most of the night terrified about Farzin's scheduled execution.

The prince sleeping against Rivka's chest awoke in a sudden startle, gasping. "Nightmare?" Rivka asked protectively. She had some idea of what devastating pictures his treacherous imagination had produced, especially since she'd spent three years thinking Isaac had died from similar violence.

"I thought we hadn't made it."

"There's still light."

"But it's almost sundown." Kaveh looked back at Captain Riv with pleading eyes, and she felt the sweat of his anxiety seeping against her. The sky before them was lit all over with orange fire, and below them the horses pursued it westward.

Rivka inhaled deeply. "From what Isaac overheard, the king will wait until it's dark enough for the bonfire to stand out against the night sky." Within, she didn't know if she could trust a man like Jahandar to stick to that plan, and she wished she could cast out a harpoon and use it to tow herself behind the sun itself.

"Look! There's the city!" Kaveh sat up straight on the dragon's back, a taut and quivering plucked string. Red clay walls loomed

196

before them, shadows in the dusk. Some glowed in the remnants of light.

"Onward!" Riv screamed to her men down below.

"Onward!" Isaac echoed, in a louder voice.

"Long live the queen!" the men called back in a unison roar.

"Can you see anything?" Kaveh squinted into the dusking sky. "It's getting darker, and my eyes hurt." With Riv's firm grip still holding his waist, he leaned forward against Isaac's neck to peer over his head, each hand grasped tightly around one of Isaac's gold horns.

"Isaac, speed up. We have to see inside the city. If there's a bonfire, we can drop down and retrieve the package." Rivka had slipped completely into combat mode. "Tell the men we'll go on ahead. They should keep going and wait for our signal."

"Company, continue until you reach the walls," bellowed Isaac. "Watch the sky for a golden snake and stop at the wall. Without the snake, proceed straight to the river. Repeat, proceed straight to the river."

"Yes, sir!" Tivon called back from the head of the company.

"Do it," Rivka hissed at her husband, and he zoomed forward. Her powerful thighs gripped him tightly as she held the prince safe with her upper body. He was so frantic that he was making it difficult for her to keep him from falling off the dragon, but she was determined and also very strong. Her thick, wavy hair streamed behind her, waving in the wind, and her cloth mask was plastered against her face.

They soared over the walls into the city. "Where would they be?"

"The bridge."

"Of course." It was very crowded outside, and there were torches all over, since the celebration of the closing of the Month of the Sun was about to start. People everywhere were craning their heads up and pointing at the dragon, but Rivka ignored them. Her eyes were fixed forward with single-minded purpose -- looking for fire.

When they darted around a corner onto the main drag of the river, Rivka's eyes snapped straight to the far-off bridge and beheld, to her horror, a brilliant yellow blaze twice as tall as a man. Kaveh went limp and tried to slip off the dragon, but Rivka caught him. "Stop it," she hissed. "We don't know yet."

"Get closer!"

"We *are!*"

As they approached, she saw the dark shape of a humanoid silhouetted against the fire. Kaveh had seen it, too. "Who's that?" Kaveh gasped. He struggled in Rivka's grasp, reaching out.

She strained her eyes. Was it Farzin? They were still too far away to tell if the figure was fat or thin, tall or short, merely standing there in front of the fire, or tied up and screaming, caught in its flames.

In his frenzy to see, Kaveh nearly fell off again as he leaned to the side, trying to see around Isaac's head. Rivka seized him as if he were an escaping criminal and held on.

Then the shape became more distinct. It was a woman, and she was waving her arms in the air at them. Finally, Rivka saw the shape of a braid sticking out from the woman's head on both sides. "Shulamit!" Rivka called out.

Queen Shulamit waved to them again and then danced around with her hands in the air. "He's free! Farzin is free! Come and join the feast!"

Chapter 23: In the Dark

In the streets of the City of the Red Clay, crowds of happy people thronged to celebrate the Month's End and the New Year. The bright yellow light of torches and lamps made it easy to see, and street vendors on every corner were ready to sell the Citizens their first meat of the year -- fowl, goats, and even more exotic things like frog. A group of little girls sang peasant songs on one street corner, and over across from them, a man sold streamers attached to sticks to anyone feeling frivolous enough to wave them around.

A marvelous noise was coming from the east, foreshadowed by a burst of light in the sky that looked like a snake of gold against night's blackness. Those nearest the city gates were first to see them -- a large group of men on horseback, wearing beautiful ceremonial armor and bearing the crest of Shulamit's house. They were singing as they rode, a steady, thrilling hymn in two-part harmony. Before them, the crowds parted, and ran beside them, and stared.

In front of them on foot strode three figures.

"Look! It's Prince Kaveh!"

"He's back!"

"Where did he go?"

"Where have you been all month? He ran away when the princess married someone else."

"He must have run to the east."

"Did you hear? He's going to marry the queen of Perach."

"He looks well."

"He certainly looks better than he did at his brother's wedding."

"Who are *those?* They're not from around here."

"Their hair's made of bronze!"

"Look at those muscles!"

"I've never seen such a big sword."

"Why is he wearing a mask?"

"Oi! That's Riv Dragonfucker!"

The one wearing the mask twitched slightly, but stood up even prouder and straighter as they continued the procession. The other one, an impish smirk seeping onto his face, sent a hint of scaly flesh over his body in a diagonal ripple of subtle delicacy, and then returned immediately to his human form. The crowd went wild.

"Did you see?"

"He's a wizard!"

"I thought I saw wings for a second!"

"Do it again!"

"Dragon! We want to see the dragon!"

A girl wearing a patched and ragged dress ran up alongside them. She confronted Riv. "I want to grow up and be a soldier like you, but my brothers say I can't, because I'm a girl."

"Of course you can. You have a body, don't you?"

The girl nodded.

"Eat the best foods you can and exercise so your body will be strong," said Captain Riv. "Figure out what techniques suit you

201

best, and when you're in combat, train your mind so you won't get distracted."

"I can't wait to tell them you believe in me!"

"You can be a soldier not just because I said so, but because you already know so in your heart."

The girl held on to Riv's left hand and kept walking.

A boy joined them a few minutes later. He stared up at Riv and Isaac, blinking, clearly not sure what to say. Finally, he just asked shyly, "Can I walk with you?"

Riv's smile was so big and welcoming that you could tell it was there from the crinkles around the captain's eyes even though there was no way to see the mouth behind the mask. "Of course." Riv's right hand closed around the boy's fingers protectively. "And when we leave to go back home, you should look to your own Prince Kaveh. He's a big hero too. He's the most determined man I've ever met, and he's very brave. You should be proud of him."

The boy looked up at Riv, then at Kaveh. The prince was preoccupied and overwhelmed because he still hadn't seen Farzin yet, but he nodded amiably at the youth.

Shulamit said that Farzin was alive, and everybody was celebrating, but he knew he wouldn't be able to relax until they were in each other's arms again. Where was Farzin? Up on the dais with his father? Still in the prison but alive? With Shulamit somewhere?

Now they were approaching the bridge, and beyond the bonfire, he saw his father sitting in a makeshift throne on the same platform from which he had underpaid the workers. His stomach flipped around like a fish on dry land, but with Riv on one side of him and Isaac on the other, he reminded himself that this time would be different. He not only had the queen's own bodyguards flanking him, but her entire Royal Guard was behind him on horseback. As for the queen herself, she was standing beside his father, very close to Aviva, who was dressed finer and looked prettier than he'd ever seen her before. Together they waved at him and his companions.

When they drew near enough, the king stood and moved his hands together in a single mighty clap. Trumpeters on either side of him gave a mighty blast, and the babble of voices nearest the royal platform died into a hush.

"Welcome back, my son." Jahandar's voice pierced the night.

"Baba," Kaveh responded in greeting. He tried to look his father in the eye but couldn't resist peering around everywhere for Farzin.

"I congratulate you on this... amazing match you've made. To captivate such a powerful and insightful queen and make her yours shows much sense." He reached for Shulamit's hand, and when she gave it, he held it high to the crowd. "Citizens, I give you Queen Shulamit of Perach, soon also to be a Princess of our City."

As they cheered, he lowered her hand and then placed it inside Kaveh's. Their eyes met. "Where's Farzin?" Kaveh whispered.

"Somewhere safe," Shulamit hissed back. "Shh." She giggled nervously.

"Queen Shulamit has given this kingdom a great dowry with worth beyond measure," Jahandar continued to the crowd. "The rumors are true. Soon, not only will you have a new princess -- you will have a new queen." He smiled broadly. "She's kind and just and wise, and honey for your king's poor heart."

"What do you mean -- new queen?" Kaveh blinked uncertainly.

"Yes, Kaveh. You'll have a new stepmother. She's the Lady Aafsaneh, whom Queen Shulamit found for me and salved my greatest pain without me having to breathe a word."

"Lady Aafsaneh is..." Kaveh couldn't believe it. He'd barely even had time to get used to the idea that Farzin's mother had been the woman they'd been searching for, all these weeks, and now this new surprise? They were going to get married? Did that mean Farzin would be his--

"Yes, Kaveh. I know she's Farzin's mother. Of course he wasn't after my kingdom. He was just trying to make sure I upheld my promises and didn't tarnish the honor of my crown, like any loyal Citizen." Kaveh swallowed, speechless. Jahandar leaned closer, so he could speak to Kaveh without the crowd hearing. "I understand how you and Farzin felt -- you must have just gotten confused. Now that you'll be brothers, you'll be able to express your mutual admiration more virtuously. You'll no longer have to resort to... you know." He waved his hand around dismissively.

The king couldn't see that the little queen beside him had lifted her eyebrow and the corner of her mouth sharply in a skeptical smirk.

"Thank you," Kaveh stammered insincerely.

Jahandar shifted his head so he was now facing the two bulky northerners who had knelt, each on one knee, beside Kaveh. "Captain Riv, we've already-- wait. Who are you?"

The captain looked up with proud blue-gray eyes. "Captain Riv Maror, your Majesty."

"Captain Riv?"

Riv nodded solemnly. "I'm the leader of Shulamit's Royal Guard."

"Then who's that?" Jahandar pointed at the man kneeling on the other side of the prince. Isaac met his gaze blandly, his face now uncloaked.

"He's my dragon," Riv said simply.

"I... see," said Jahandar, with a frown and a scrunched-up brow. His eyes kept moving back and forth between Riv and Isaac, and Kaveh could see in his father's face a touch of confusion that *both* members in a two-male pairing could so well represent manliness.

Unconsciously, Kaveh stood up straighter and puffed out his shoulders, wanting to defy his father's expectations.

At last, Jahandar's face cleared and he asked instead, "Why did he pretend to be you?"

"May I beg your forgiveness, Majesty?" Isaac's voice was deep and gentle and unthreatening. "The honor of appearing in your court to announce the prince's intention to marry should have fallen to the captain, who outranks me. I didn't have the heart to tell you it was only me. I didn't want you should feel insulted."

"Your humility is admirable," said the king. "I wonder why Queen Shulamit chose not to send her captain."

"I've been thinking about Prince Kaveh and can't remember," piped up the queen, smiling innocently.

The king smiled fondly. "I understand completely -- I feel somewhat the same about my future queen. And now, we feast!" Jahandar clapped his hands again, and the people cheered.

Kaveh allowed himself to be buffeted, like a leaf floating down rapids, towards a makeshift outdoor table and into a seat. His future bride sat across from him, in earnest conference with her sweetheart about which of the holiday offerings she could and couldn't eat. "Shulamit?"

"Hm?"

"Where's Farzin?"

"His mother's taking him back to the vineyard," said the queen. "She'll come back in a week or so to marry the king, but she wanted to get him away from Jahandar as soon as she could."

Kaveh wilted. "So he's not even in the city?" He felt as if his heart were missing from his body.

"Just be glad he's safe," Shulamit answered wearily, and sank her teeth into a piece of lamb. Aviva slid into the seat beside her, finally able to relax now that she'd vetted the queen's food sufficiently. There was barely any physical distance between them, and it drew out more of Kaveh's pain to see their shoulders touching, their faces far too close for ordinary friendship.

"Are you sure he's safe? Did you see him?" Someone tossed a roasted chicken leg to Kaveh, and he picked it up with a disoriented expression as if he'd never seen one before.

Shulamit nodded, her mouth too full to speak.

Kaveh picked at his food, unable to relax. He felt suddenly isolated, poignantly aware that he and Shulamit were very new friends, and he had no way of knowing if she even spoke the truth. It would certainly be nothing new for his father to speak falsely. But surely the queen didn't want to conceive his child badly enough to lie brazenly to his face? Surely Farzin wasn't already dead, heaped up in a pile somewhere--

He wrenched his mind away from such thoughts, glad the chicken leg at which he was picking was so obviously fowl and not flesh, not even close to human.

Other, less gruesome worries rose up in place of the more fantastical ones. Brothers? Stepbrothers, to be precise. Could stepbrothers still be lovers? Kaveh didn't see why there should be any impediment -- they weren't related by blood, and there was no possibility of children. But what if Farzin didn't feel the same way? What if the Farzin that Aafsaneh had taken with her out of the City was all too ready to greet him with the lukewarm embrace of a sibling rather than the passionate embrace for which he longed?

Whatever Farzin wanted, he'd have to go along with it. He loved him that much. He only hoped he could bear it.

The royal party departed the festival while the rest of the Citizens still reveled, for the next day the prince's wedding lay before them and it was important to get some sleep. Kaveh returned to his own room in his father's palace for the first time in a month, Isaac hovering just behind him at a respectful distance as his assigned bodyguard. Even Isaac, with whom he had so long felt kinship as a fellow lover of men, no longer felt like a friend in this night of loneliness and mistrust. He knew the man was capable of keeping many secrets. Was the dragon-man following Shulamit's orders now, calmly deceiving him along with the rest of them?

A trio of buxom dancing girls were waiting for him when they reached his chamber. The Crown Prince, trying to be helpful and brotherly, had already paid their fee as a bachelor party gift. Kaveh responded by waving them off. "Go perform for the queen."

"The queen?" asked one of the dancers.

"Queen Shulamit. The visitor. My intended."

The void produced by their puzzled silence was filled with gentle tinkling noises coming from their spangled costumes.

"It's my wish," Kaveh commanded, now louder and more assertive. He pointed at the door. "Go."

Nodding in respect, they scurried away quickly, their baubles jangling and jingling.

Kaveh looked sharply at Isaac. "I want Farzin." It was an order, a demand, a member of the royal family reverting back to habit.

Isaac, unimpressed, shrugged. "I want Riv."

"Yours is only a few rooms down the hall. Mine is... somewhere." Kaveh moved around the room, crossly putting out all the lamps and candles. "Alive? Dead? All I know is what you all tell me."

The wizard didn't argue. Instead, he moved toward the door. "I'll be outside."

"You do that."

Soon, he was alone in a room illuminated only by a thick silver moonbeam. He flopped down on the bed and stared at the ceiling. The room felt enormous after his long stay at Shulamit's petite, open-air palace, and he was hyperaware of how alone he was inside of it. The queen seemed so happy, and her captain and wizard were certainly acting triumphant enough. But was any of this real, or was he surrounded by a conspiracy? He wanted to be near Farzin so badly it hurt, physically, and he punched at the bed with frustration.

He didn't know how much time had passed when he realized Isaac was talking to him. "What? I can't hear you."

For some reason the man was refusing to raise his voice, so with a grumble, Kaveh hopped down off the bed and put his ear to the door. "One more time?"

"Do you need my help to get out the window or can you manage?"

"What?"

"Can you get out the window without my help? Yes or no?"

"I.... yes? I think so. It's not that high, and the ground's soft."

"Then go to the window."

Kaveh rushed across the room without another thought. Farzin! Finally, he would rush into the arms of the man he loved! He threw open the curtains, expecting to see the engineer standing there in the moonlight.

But instead of a man, he saw -- a cat.

Chapter 24: Lamb for the Lion

Kaveh was so irritated he nearly picked up a nearby pot of herbs to throw at the poor animal sitting innocently in the flowerbed beneath his window. But before he could move his hand, he remembered everything his new friends had told him about Mother Cat. "Are you--?"

The cat stood up and began to walk away.

Kaveh still couldn't tell if it was responding to his question or merely startled by his voice. He stood there halfway hanging out the window, peering at the creature.

It halted its departure and turned around to stare at him.

"I must be mad," he muttered to himself as he climbed out the window and dropped down into the well-tilled dirt.

Silently he followed the cat through narrow, moonlit alleyways. He could hear faint sounds of joy in the distance, where some of the evening's revelry still continued on the bigger streets closer to the river. Every once in a while he sensed other people and hid in the shadows until he could be certain to pass unseen, and each time he paused, the cat waited patiently.

He was certain now that she was Mother Cat -- some name like Eshvat? -- because, despite the circuitous path they took through the most tiny and winding of roads, he could tell they were approaching the restaurant. Sure enough, they popped out through a small passageway, barely big enough for a grown man, and emerged into the street across from Mother Cat's.

The doorway was open, and the cat ran inside. Kaveh followed her.

Dim light from a few lamps lit the room, full of tables in front and the open kitchen in the back, but empty of patrons. Kaveh peered around anxiously. Was he here? "Farzin!" he tried to say, but his throat was dry and his voice nervous, so it came out as a faint bleat.

Then he noticed the red curtains that covered the doorway to the tea room, where low tables were ringed by cushions instead of chairs. He and Farzin had sat here with some of Farzin's workers in days past, draining pots of tea and relaxing after a day of work on the construction project. It was a familiar room, but in this night of uncertainty, everything was ghostly and contained the prospect of nightmares.

His trembling hand drew aside the curtain.

Stepping inside, he saw Farzin lying motionless before him on the far side of the room. His eyes were closed but his mouth hung open; his body lay twisted in an unnatural position as if he'd been flung against the deep-red cushions and forgotten. Farzin who he had loved, but not as he had known him -- a month of starvation and occasional abuse had left its mark in that gaunt face and on those bruised limbs.

Kaveh's eyes flew shut after only a millisecond. He couldn't stand it. Farzin might only be sleeping, but the prince couldn't find within himself the courage to step forward and see for himself. What if he touched Farzin's face and found it cold? If he stayed here in the doorway he left himself standing in the threshold of hope. One step forward might be the first into tragedy.

But whichever way their destinies flowed, let them flow in the same course, forever united.

"Farzin," he gasped, his eyes still screwed shut, "if you're alive-- if you're alive, take me into your arms. If you're--" He couldn't say *dead*, not out loud. "--*not*, take me into your grave."

And then arms encircled him and held him very tightly, and Kaveh nearly hyperventilated with relief. "My grave? Really?" asked a familiar jovial voice. "Because I was thinking *bed.*"

"You looked funny when you were asleep!" Kaveh protested, bowing his head to rest it against Farzin's chest. He smelled of peasant soap and rosewater. The prince opened his eyes, and yes, Farzin was real, real and holding him, clasping him tightly. He could barely breathe, and yet he had never felt so comfortable in his entire life.

"I look funny when I'm *awake,*" Farzin reminded him.

"You're alive... You're alive..." It was a grateful prayer of thanks.

"All of me! And all of the workers have been paid too -- the full amount, this time." There might be dark circles under those eyes, but they twinkled; there might be whip stains across his back, but it stood up proudly straight.

"What about you? Did you get paid?"

Farzin gazed down on him with caressing eyes. "I told you before, all I want is you. If we'll really be together from now on -- if you'll share happiness with me as we've already shared so much pain -- if you'll let me kiss you awake in the morning and bore you to sleep at night babbling about projects... then, Kaveh, then my work will have been paid for, more than fairly. Generously. I love you."

Kaveh vibrated with sheer joy. "Always. Always! Then it doesn't worry you that we're going to be brothers while we're living that way?"

The engineer responded by kissing him. It was their first time their lips had touched in a month, and Kaveh threw himself into the kiss with energetic ardor. His body heated up as he swept his hands over Farzin's back.

Then Farzin broke the kiss. "Eww! You kissed your *brother!*" He was even laughing at his own joke.

Kaveh chuckled. "You goof. Anyway, it's not by blood."

"It could have been, if my mother had been queen from the beginning."

"I like it better this way."

"Me too."

"But why didn't you tell us how to find your mother? We didn't know about Jahandar, but still!"

"I tried to, a couple of times, but you were getting shot at, and Isaac ran off." He was breathing heavily. "She didn't know where I was because I knew she wouldn't like me working for Jahandar. I thought she'd try to talk me out of it. I just wanted to tell her how great the whole thing had been when it was all over. I had no idea why she... why she..."

Kaveh felt the grip around him loosen, and he noticed his partner's arms were trembling. "Farzin? Are you all right?"

Gasping, Farzin pulled away from him. "Yes, it's-- I'm just worn out from being hungry. I've been a month without good sleep or good food."

"Sit down!" Kaveh dragged him back to the cushions where he'd initially found him. "Have you eaten since they let you out?"

"It turns out my mother's friends with Mother Cat from way back -- her name is Eshvat, by the way -- and she fed me before going to get you. They also cleaned me up a bit. I had a beard, and longer hair -- although, not as messy as yours!" He flashed Kaveh a goofy expression.

So that explained the rosewater. "But you're still hungry."

213

"I'm a growing boy."

"Not lately." Kaveh looked him over, forcing himself to see Farzin's shockingly reduced weight for the first time. "But I'll get you back to normal. Wait 'til you see what I learned from the queen's sweetheart -- and personal chef."

A female voice at the doorway startled them both. "Feel free to use anything you want, but if you make a mess, either clean it up or pay for it." They looked up toward the curtains and beheld Eshvat, Mother Cat, in her human form, all bosoms and kerchiefs as usual. "My magic'll keep you safe within these walls until I get back. I'm going out looking for my own mess."

And with a flourish of skirts, she had disappeared again.

"We've got the place to ourselves," Farzin commented gleefully.

"I'm going to cook for you," Kaveh informed him, pulling his shirt over his head. Farzin grinned at the sight of Kaveh's lithe, muscled chest, and the prince beamed at the attention. He left the shirt on a table and drew back the curtains so Farzin would be able to watch him cooking in the other room.

Farzin leaned back against the cushions and admired the view. Kaveh bustled around the kitchen, aggregating rice and vegetables and some leftover meat he'd found together on the countertop. Now the rice was being heated in water, and with aggressive yet impeccably controlled motions, Kaveh diced carrots and leeks. He began to sweat in the heat of the kettle's steam. "If you could see yourself right now, you'd be too distracted to cook," commented Farzin, obviously enjoying himself.

Kaveh instinctively looked down, and grinned when he realized his lean, toned chest was shining in the lamplight. "Maybe it's your appetizer."

"Maybe I want seconds already." Farzin rested his head against a nearby pillow and kept watching as Kaveh kept working. He looked for a moment as though he might fall asleep again.

Then, out of the corner of his eye, Kaveh saw Farzin stand again. He walked over to the kitchen and slipped behind his partner. Kaveh was concentrating on pulling apart pieces of leftover meat so it would fit into the pot and had assumed Farzin was getting up to get a drink of water or some other mundane errand; he therefore felt a lightning current of surprised arousal as instead Farzin's hands appeared on both sides of his bare waist, Farzin's body very close behind him, pressing into him. He gasped and dropped the lamb shank back into the dish, splattering the juice slightly.

"I can't help it," Farzin murmured into the ear he was now nibbling. "You look like a statue come to life."

"You have to eat or you'll pass out on me if we start-- if we--" Oh, how could Kaveh even remember how to speak with Farzin grinding into him like that! And with those demanding hands now owning his nipples. Aviva told him not to handle knives while distracted. Well, he was done with knife work. The vegetables and rice were simmering in the pot. "I'm almost done. I just have--"

"You just have to add the *meat*, right?" Farzin grinned wickedly.

Kaveh blushed at the innuendo. Quickly sliding the rest of the lamb into the pot, he succumbed to Farzin's firm grip and let himself be spun around so his back was to the counter. Farzin claimed his mouth with a heavy, almost magnetic kiss and then brought his mouth lower to lick his nipples. Kaveh leaned back against the counter, seeing stars.

But Farzin soon paused in his embrace and leaned over, panting and wobbly. Kaveh held him for a moment so he didn't collapse. He helped him back to the cushions in the other room and returned to seasoning the meal, his body tingling. When everything was ready, Kaveh scooped it into a bowl and carried it into the other room, where he found Farzin fast asleep.

This time, he didn't close his eyes or say anything about death. He simply sat down beside him and put his hand on the exhausted man's cheek.

Farzin's eyes fluttered open, and he smiled. "Some beautiful bare-chested god is bending over me holding a bowl of... Wow, that smells amazing! -- and that he made himself, by the labors of his own hands. Maybe I did die."

"I'm going to fatten you up again," said Kaveh matter-of-factly, "and then I'm going to make love to you."

"I can multitask," said Farzin sleepily, reaching for Kaveh with one hand and the lamb curry with the other.

Chapter 25: Date Night

"Mmmm...." Shulamit submerged herself deeper in the tub of heated water and closed her eyes. "Is all that nonsense finally behind us?"

"Long day," Aviva agreed, leaning over the tub. She trailed a few fingers through the water and brushed against Shulamit's shoulder.

"Long *month.* I need to uncoil, and I don't know how."

"Are you hungry? I can have someone send up some mangoes or something. Hey, Rivka!"

"What are they arguing about?" Shulamit realized that far away, on the other side of the room, Rivka was arguing with Tivon through the closed door.

"I'll go see." Aviva hopped away, leaving Shulamit to soak.

Her departure was unnecessary – Rivka soon grew loud enough so that Shulamit could hear. "--a dozen angry farmers. I think I can handle a couple of dancers." Rivka rolled her eyes.

"Three," Tivon corrected. "I'm not even sure they're really dancers -- they don't have a musician with them."

"We sing and clap!" shouted an affronted voice.

"What's going on?" Aviva asked.

"There are some dancing girls out in the hallway," Rivka explained. "They said Kaveh ordered them to dance for Shula."

Aviva started to chuckle. "Manna falling from the sky... wheatless manna!" she added, bounding back across the room.

"What is it?" asked the queen.

"Dancing girls."

"*What?* Actual ones or are you teasing?"

"Kaveh sent them. But Tivon is pulling his usual thing where every lady for hire could have a knife between her breasts, and he doesn't want to let them in."

"Like I care what he wants!" Shulamit was already out of the tub and toweling off. She pulled on a dressing gown haphazardly as she darted across the room, nearly missing a table and two chairs. "Tivon, let them in!"

"As you wish, Your Majesty," said a weary voice.

"If you're that worried, come in and watch," Rivka pointed out as she opened the door. She gestured to the other guard. "We've still got him in the hallway."

"Fine." Tivon entered the room, followed by three beautiful ladies in clothing that jingled and sparkled as they moved. The expression on his face clearly read *Royalty... some want to bathe in wine, others love their own sex... while the rest of us have to work for a living.* But under all that, Shulamit knew he did care about her welfare and would have protected her with his life if one of the dancers really did draw a weapon.

Shulamit, enraptured, didn't know where to look first. One was in pink, the second in bright orange, and the third the deep, rich purple of a red onion. Their hair flowed long and shining over their shoulders, decorated with delicate strands of silver fastened to their headbands. Plenty of skin was showing in so many beautiful ways -- soft cleavage, sculpted stomachs.

Aviva took her hand and led her to some cushions where they could sit. Riv and Tivon remained standing, vigilant and detached.

"One, two, three!" With this cry from the one in pink, the ladies began to sing, dancing and clapping along with the music. The

218

song had very frivolous lyrics, a combination of nonsense syllables selected for their musical effect and innuendos referencing every vegetable that even remotely resembled the male sexual organ.

"This is amazing," Shulamit murmured into Aviva's ear, a little overwhelmed. "Those words are making me feel like I'm not supposed to be here, though."

"They could sing about melons instead," Aviva suggested.

"They're singing about what they like. I don't exactly have melons." She gestured toward her chest.

"Good point. Then they should sing about dates." When she saw that Shulamit was making a face, Aviva added, "Don't! Dates may be tiny, but think how sweet they are." She sidled closer. "'You are slender like a palm tree; your breasts are clusters of sweet fruit.' See, it's even in the Song of Songs. And you're also like a date tree because you're going to be hand-pollinated." Shulamit lifted one eyebrow to the moon, and Aviva grinned wickedly. "You did know that, right?"

"Yes, my 'book learning' is good for something."

When the song was over, the dancer in pink drew closer to them. "Your Majesty!" she said, bowing low. "We're here to celebrate the glory of the female body. Let us show you how to feel more proud of yours."

"But I already--" Then Shulamit realized the dancer was beckoning to her. "What do you mean?"

"If your Majesty accepts, we'll teach you to dance so that you can move sensually for your new husband," explained the dancer in orange.

With a wide-eyed look at Aviva, Shulamit stood and let herself be led into the clear area of the room amidst the dancers. She figured out pretty quickly from the things they said to her that the dancers had seen her body language -- her discomfort at the male-oriented lyrics, her gestures at her small breasts -- and decided amongst themselves that the reason Kaveh had sent them to her room was so they could teach her their craft.

Well, so what?

Two of the dancers started to sing again, clapping and moving around, as the one in pink instructed Shulamit how to sway and jerk her hips around. She was shy at first, feeling her awkwardness enveloping her like a cloak, but she soon realized the grin on Aviva's face was for her, and that she must not look so bad at it as she'd imagined.

By the time the dancers left, she was feeling terrific and completely juiced up. Tivon returned to his post outside the room, and she was left alone with Aviva and Rivka again. She wished it was only her and Aviva, for obvious reasons, but Rivka was taking advantage of the discarded bath water and the privacy and was now scrubbing away the dust and sweat of the past few days.

Shulamit paced the room, burning to touch Aviva, to sink into softness and lock together like the petals of a rosebud. Seeking distraction, she picked up the package in which Kaveh had brought her wedding dress and chuppah. As she unwrapped it, she realized there was something dark like chocolate mixed up inside the pile of white lace and chartreuse clothing.

"Hey, Rivka! Kaveh accidentally brought your dress." She rushed over to the bathtub, where Rivka had just climbed out and was drying herself off with a sheet of cloth. "From back when."

"Oh, please, Rivka, please put it on!" Aviva clapped her hands, her eyes wide. "I'd love to see your other plumage."

Rivka grunted. "Who says I'll still fit into it?" She flexed her muscles.

Shulamit shrugged. "Can we see?" She was beginning to have an idea of how to get Aviva alone even though Rivka was technically off-duty and had nothing to do.

"No harm there." The captain took the pile of brown finery and fiddled with it, looking for closures to open.

Shulamit and Aviva went back to the other side of the room to finish unpacking Shulamit's wedding clothes while Rivka finished putting on the dress. They had just finished spreading the lace chuppah out on a table to admire it when they heard a rustle.

Rivka was shifting around in front of a mirror glass, looking at herself. She was bundled into the brown cloth like a bunch of fruit in a market seller's tote, wet hair cascading over the bare skin of her upper chest.

"Wow," Shulamit couldn't help saying. "You look really good." Aviva was also looking at her admiringly.

Rivka was moving around awkwardly. "I can still move my sword arm," she observed. "But, *oy.* I can't believe I sparred with Isaac in this dress."

Perfect. "You should go show him!" Shulamit grinned.

"Oh, yes, Rivka, please let him see!"

From both sides they pressed in on her. "You look so pretty!"

"There's a cloak over there -- just throw it over your clothing and surprise him."

"It's dark in the hallways anyway."

"I love this pattern. I want a brown dress now."

"I'll tell Aba when we get back."

"It won't look as good on me as it does on Rivka -- with her golden coloring."

221

"*Oy gevalt,* you silly creatures!" Rivka threw up her hands. "Fine -- you want I should go, and I'll go." But she was smiling.

Shulamit and Aviva helped bundle Rivka into the cloak, and then she tied her mask around her face as usual. "How do I look?"

"Like usual," said Shulamit.

"Like a geode," said Aviva.

Rivka lifted an eyebrow at that one. "Back in a bit."

She opened the door. "Tivon? I'm supposed to go see Isaac and Kaveh about something."

Tivon and the other guard moved to the side to let her pass into the darkened hallway and then shut the door behind her.

Rivka moved smoothly through the hallways, illuminated in some places only by moonlight pouring in through windows cut high into the red clay walls. She fit easily into the shadows and wasn't noticed by many; here and there a servant passed her in the halls but she was cloaked and uninteresting, and if they were moving about this late at night it meant they had work to do and didn't care who else was there.

Here was Kaveh's room -- but where was Isaac? He should have been outside the door, standing guard. She tensed up, every muscle ready for whatever was to come. Even without her sword, she was still a formidable force.

She rapped on the door. "Isaac?"

"Mighty One?"

Relieved to hear his voice, she relaxed slightly. "Can I see you in the hallway for a minute? I'm alone."

"You should come in. Kaveh's not here."

"What? Where is he?"

"Come in and I'll explain."

Rivka opened the door and stepped inside. It was a large room, flooded with silver light filtering through the white curtains that veiled every window. Isaac was at the far side of it, sitting at a small table eating something. She kicked the door shut behind her and approached him. "Where's Kaveh?"

"At Mother Cat's, with Farzin. Here I sit -- here I watch."

"Farzin? I thought he left town with his mother?"

"She's leaving before sunrise," Isaac explained. "She had something important and private to do first, so she left Farzin with Eshvat so that he and Kaveh could see each other again before she takes him home. I didn't know either, but a little while ago I was standing outside the door, and suddenly I felt a cat brush up against my leg."

"Oh, you did?" Rivka smirked. "What are you eating?"

"She brought me a midnight snack." Isaac picked up another piece of food and gnawed at it, but didn't put the whole thing in his mouth.

Rivka drew closer and peered at the piece of leather that had held his meal, and now served as a makeshift plate. "Are those -- are those *mice?*" Even without the fur they were still unmistakable, and with their little intact paws curled up and their eyes shut they might have just been asleep.

"Apparently Aafsaneh repeated something Aviva told her about how I like to eat live mice when I'm a snake, and she... Don't ask

223

me how that woman's mind works." He returned the empty skeleton to the table. "You want to try one?"

"*No*," Rivka said quickly. She still hadn't taken off her cloak, and it suddenly occurred to her that they were alone. In a very large bedroom. She longed to take him in her arms -- even if he was eating mice.

"Were you looking for Kaveh or for me?" Isaac asked politely.

"For you," she said. "Shulamit wanted me to show you something." She opened the cloak and let it fall to the floor.

His eyes flashed, and there was an audible noise from his nostrils. "You were wearing that dress the night I first knew you loved me."

"My mother saved it and brought it down with her. Not that she knew."

"I remember seeing you, wanting you, thinking I had everything under control... that I could go the rest of my life without ever touching you but feeling you flavor my entire world... How arrogant I was."

You're still arrogant, but I wouldn't have it any other way, Rivka thought. Then she noticed he was looking down at the table and playing with something small and dark and solid. "What's that?"

"Nothing much." An impish smile spread across his face. "Only a privacy charm Eshvat gave me to keep Jahandar from finding out Kaveh had left the building." His gaze swept over Rivka's body, then fixed squarely on her eyes. "As long as I have this, I control who can enter the room."

His eyes might as well have been his fingers, his tongue, more. She felt him everywhere on her from just that stare, her body tingling with anticipation as she drew closer. "Kiss me, mouse breath."

224

Across the city, Farzin lay sated against the dark-red cushions, a very naked Kaveh sprawled to one side of him and a very empty bowl to the other. Kaveh was munching on dried dates, which Farzin regarded with a wrinkle of his nose. "How can you eat more than one of those things? They're so sweet!"

"You're sweet," Kaveh mumbled, staring up at the ceiling with a silly grin on his face. He had never experienced as much pleasure before as on this night. The muscles in the back of his legs were sore from unfamiliar exertion. Maybe it was a good idea to stretch before this kind of thing as if you were exercising...?

Farzin had picked up a date and was examining it in his hand. "So many people have to put in their hard work to make this little thing."

"How so?"

"Not just whoever sold it to Eshvat," Farzin explained, "but the worker who had to climb the tree to harvest it -- think how dangerous that is! -- and also the worker who had to go up there to hand-pollinate it."

"Why do they do it that way? Why can't they just do it naturally?"

"That way they only have to have one or two male trees for a whole orchard of females."

Kaveh chuckled. "Sounds like some guys I know."

"Count me out. Anyway, the female trees are the ones that bear the fruit, so it makes more sense economically to have more of them. Like with hens and roosters."

225

"I understand."

"So think about all those people... climbing up date trees, pollinating them, cultivating them, harvesting them, selling them... all for this tiny fruit." Farzin rotated it in his hand, then popped it into Kaveh's waiting mouth. "Everything we do, everything we accomplish -- lots of times, it's with other people's help, behind the scenes. People we don't ever meet. I think about them a lot. Who raised the lamb we ate tonight? Who made those candles keeping it bright enough to see in here? We all need each other, and, ideally, we all keep each other going."

Kaveh thought about the stranger far away, climbing the date palm, slowly struggling against gravity and up toward the sun to reach the fruit that would earn his livelihood. Or her livelihood. Suddenly, each date was so much more valuable to him. They were the product of human labor. So much was the product of human labor. He had never really thought about it that way before, and he vowed to take it to heart.

Love reigned across the City of the Red Clay that night. In Mother Cat's Tavern, Kaveh memorized Farzin's body, vowing to replace every tear and bruise from the prison with infinite kisses over the coming years. In the palace, Shulamit and Aviva quickly wore each other out and then lounged around naked talking about babies, while in Kaveh's room, Rivka writhed joyously, her bare skin reveling under the alchemy of Isaac's tongue. Even Eshvat was off somewhere in an alley, growling with pleasure over the shoulder of a young guard she'd found patrolling the river.

Only Aafsaneh was alone. Deep within the city in a tiny garden no bigger than two elephants side by side, she knelt in the moonlight before the simple stone monument that marked the grave of the old man who had taught her to perform magic. "Master," she whispered, tears falling down her cheeks, "I'm home."

Chapter 26: Created by Love, Surrounded by Love

Under the clear, blue morning sky, the wedding procession made its way toward the Temple of the Twenty Date Palms. There was considerably less pomp than there had been when the Crown Prince married Azar, for Kaveh was only a third son and the wedding date had been set so suddenly. Also, the Citizens for the most part were ready to get back to work (or sleeping it off) after their night of revelry. But there were still a few people following the procession, and as it wound through the marketplace, the shopkeepers and fruit sellers came to the front of their stalls to watch them go by.

They saw Prince Kaveh, a strapping figure of masculine beauty in his indigo garments with gold brocade, following his father on horseback. The change in his face between that last wedding and this one was remarked upon by more than one merchant. Where there had been distress, there was now peace; his panic had turned to potency.

Then came the foreign queen, Shulamit, her beautiful "handmaiden" walking beside her horse clad all in fuchsia, and her two northern bodyguards leading the way on foot. She was decked from head to toe in brilliant yellow-green, decorated here and there with the bright green jewels that had been her mother's. The cord holding her braids back behind her head was twisted all over with yellow flowers. Behind her came her entire Royal Guard, also on horseback.

Isaac noticed, when they passed the jeweler's shop where he had bought her the dragon necklace, that Delara was not outside watching with the others.

When they arrived at the Temple, Shulamit peeped inside and was relieved to see that the chuppah had been set up correctly. "It's so beautiful," she commented to Rivka. "Every time I look at it I'm uncontrollably happy."

"Leah does fantastic work," the captain agreed. She wiped sweat away from her face underneath the mask. "*Nu?* Are you ready?"

Shulamit nodded. "Completely."

"You gave us such a beautiful wedding," Rivka commented. "It hurts that I can't repay you in kind, and you're stuck up there with a man."

"No, really, it's fine." Shulamit smiled. "Even if I weren't different, and liked boys, you think they'd let me marry the cook? That's not what the life of the monarchy is like. There's a price we have to pay for all the money and glory and power. But it's okay -- he won't touch me in any way that makes me uncomfortable, and I still have Aviva. This is just business. Politics."

"Level-headed little one." Rivka squeezed Shulamit's shoulder affectionately.

"By the way, does Isaac have the magic worked out for... you know? Because." Shulamit licked her lips awkwardly. "There's... mucus. I think I might be ready for babies. I mean, from what Aafsaneh said..."

"He's all set. What, you want to try tonight?"

"If we can. Otherwise it means waiting another month. And Kaveh's already nearby."

Isaac drifted closer. "They're ready for us."

Shulamit placed her arm inside his, and together they stepped into the path made resplendent for them by women throwing flowers.

As she walked that scented aisle, she remembered her father's voice. Lying on his deathbed, his body broken by the fall from the *howdah*, and his head muddy from herbs that were supposed to ease the pain, he had murmured over and over again with great sadness that he wouldn't be able to walk her to the chuppah some day. The regret obsessed his mind in those final days, that he would be deprived of seeing his beloved little princess married.

But he is *here,* Shulamit realized as she felt the presence of God surround her and wrap her shoulders like a shawl. Aba was there in everything he had taught her to be, strong and fair with her country and living up to her responsibilities to lead them in peace and prosperity. He was also there in the strength and determination with which she protected herself, and in the way she refused to give up even when things looked bleak. He was even there in her face, in those heavy eyebrows she recognized as his each time she saw herself in a mirror or on a coin.

Isaac must have sensed her tears, perhaps from her grip tightening on his arm. "Your father is proud of you."

Shulamit didn't know if the present tense was Isaac's mistake in his second language or referring to him himself, and she didn't care. They were both right. "*Ikh hob dir lieb, Tateh,*" she said in a choked-off voice.

Under the chuppah, she and Kaveh joined hands and made vows to each other in the language of the north, so that they wouldn't have to lie. "I promise never to touch you in any way that makes you uncomfortable," Kaveh swore. He spoke with the great deliberation of one who has been coached in a language they barely understand.

"I promise to protect you and your stepbrother and anyone else like us with all the power and might of my rank," said Shulamit.

230

She didn't say Farzin's name in case someone would recognize the syllables and wonder what they were doing there.

"I promise not to embarrass your throne."

"I promise to be the best mother for our child that I can possibly be."

When they were declared married, Kaveh leaned forward and delicately kissed her cheek, the rest of his body an unthreatening distance away. Then they turned toward the spectators and raised their joined hands high. In the din of the resulting cheers, nobody heard her tell him, "We did it! We're a team now."

"Who wouldn't want to be on a team with you?" Kaveh replied. "After what you've done for me, I owe you enough babies to make a small orchestra."

"We're starting with one," she retorted with a smirk. "Good grief, that's gonna be hard enough."

After last night's heavy feasting on meat, everyone was relieved to see a light spread of cold vegetables and fish waiting for them outside. There was a brief amount of dancing and eating, Shulamit even dancing with Rivka in a moment of sisterly ecstasy over the success of their mission, and then the visitors prepared to leave.

King Jahandar's wedding present was a sumptuous carriage drawn by two horses, in which they'd be making the journey back to Shulamit's palace. Rivka volunteered to drive, to keep Jahandar from sending his own man. Isaac transformed into his dragon form, drawing noises of marvel and awe from the crowd, and flew on ahead with Aviva on his back, while Shulamit and Kaveh followed in the carriage with the Royal Guard as their escort. They parted the curtains on each side of the carriage to wave at the Citizens as they departed, smiles shining broadly on each of their faces.

Kaveh promptly fell asleep once they were beyond the city walls, having spent a good part of the night with Farzin, but when he woke up he was happy and full of chatter. Today had been an intersection of past and future, and they spent hours talking about both. "I'm really looking forward to learning how a winery works."

"So you and Farzin will be running the farm once his mother marries your father?"

"Isn't it perfect? And it's close enough to your capital that we'll get to be a part of the child's life."

"To be honest, I'm curious about the winery myself."

"Why are we stopping?"

They could hear Rivka yelling at something. Shulamit pushed aside the curtain and peered into the dusk. "It's Isaac! And Aafsaneh's with him."

Kaveh sprang up and stuck his head outside. In the sky, a dark-green dragon and a brilliant-blue swan flew about together, in tandem, each carrying a human on their backs. "Farzin!"

The flying creatures approached them, and landed gracefully beyond the group of horses. Kaveh tumbled out of the carriage and ran towards Farzin, who was dismounting from his mother's back. Then he stopped abruptly.

Shulamit followed along behind him, and he turned back to her with a jerk, a questioning look in his eyes. "It's okay. You're among friends."

Kaveh rushed the rest of the way towards the grinning engineer and grabbed him in a strong, grappling hug. They embraced tightly, and then unpeeled from each other to walk back towards the carriage. "My brother is so handsome," Farzin joked to everyone else.

"You're going to do that forever, aren't you," Kaveh realized out loud.

"Only if you stay handsome forever," Farzin retorted. "If you don't I'll have to start saying other things like 'so hardworking' or 'so eager to learn' or--"

"Can we meet properly?" Shulamit interrupted. "Your mother rushed you away so quickly I didn't see that much of you back in the City."

"Oh! That's right. Are you the queen? Majesty..." All frivolity dropped from Farzin's face. "I owe you my life. I--thank you. Thank you."

Shulamit grinned, taking Aviva's hand as she faced him. "Welcome to the family."

"I like it here already!"

Isaac and Aafsaneh were human now. "We caught up with them a little while ago and figured this might be a good place for everyone to camp for the night," Isaac explained.

Rivka nodded, surveying the land. "He means more than camping," she murmured to Shulamit. "I told him what you said before the wedding."

Shulamit cringed, but her discomfort floated away as she decided that Isaac knowing her medical details was better than the fate from which his magic was saving her.

Under the darkening sky, the Guard and the royal family prepared their camp, and then it was time for dinner. As Shulamit and Aviva were finishing their meals in the firelight, Isaac appeared between them, his head near their shoulders and his voice low and conspiratorial. "Are you ready to conceive?"

Shulamit grinned nervously. "I'm ready and I'm not ready and I'm scared and I'm really excited."

233

"We've been scheming," Aviva explained.

Isaac took Shulamit's hand in his right hand and Aviva's in his left. "Now, *mammelehs,* my magic will keep Kaveh's contribution alive until it reaches your body. The rest may happen tonight, or in a month, two months -- we hope. It might take more than one try, and even then there's no guarantee. But you have all of my blessings."

"Thank you." Shulamit smiled weakly.

"Give me your hairsticks," said Isaac to Aviva.

Down around her shoulders tumbled Aviva's thick, dark hair as she plucked out the accessories and handed them to the wizard. Shulamit watched, wide-eyed, full of intellectual curiosity as always.

Isaac drifted away toward where Kaveh and Farzin sat with Aafsaneh on the other side of the fire, talking about the vineyard. They watched him put a hand on Kaveh's shoulder and say a few words. Kaveh stood instantly, and Farzin joined him, more slowly because he was still healing from his month in Jahandar's prison. Together they followed Isaac away into the darkness beyond the campfire's glow. Aafsaneh squeezed Farzin's hand as he passed, a look of maternal devotion and nostalgia glimmering in her eyes.

"Why is Farzin going with him?"

"When he touches Kaveh, he'll be a part of it the same way I will when I give you the hairstick."

"I guess that's symmetrical," Shulamit agreed. "Wow, this little one's going to have two mothers and two fathers."

"Plus Isaac and Riv, and Aafsaneh. Created by love but also surrounded by love."

"And your parents. Thank you for giving me an extra set of parents since the baby will never know mine."

"He will. She will. We'll tell it stories. I remember Noach too. So do lots of people."

Shulamit sighed and squeezed Aviva's hands.

She tried to relax, but it was difficult, knowing how important tonight could be. Resting her head on Aviva's shoulder, she began to sing softly. Aviva harmonized with her in a rich, gentle alto, her arm around the queen, idly caressing the bare skin of her upper arm. It was more than simple physicality. Shulamit perceived the serenity of a divine benevolence in the way this touch made her feel. Jahandar and his daughter-in-law were tiny in the distance, their bigotry drowned out by a broad black sky full of watchful stars. This was the real truth, this existence out here, in which she knew that her love, *their* love, was as pure and blessed as any union of man and wife.

Out here in nature, away from the palace and between nations, was she really still queen? Was she not, here in the open, just a woman, one of millions, lucky enough to have been granted one amazing person with whom to share her life and her love? She'd never expected that a teenage dalliance with a cook could have led to this, back in those days when they were just friends who discovered they enjoyed each other's warmth. Over the years, the more she'd learned of Aviva, the more she realized the depth of her love. It was so right, so natural, so *intended* that Aviva should be sharing this next step with her.

Finally, the men returned to the campsite. Farzin and Kaveh were holding hands and trying to look innocent, but just before they reached the others, Kaveh darted forward and kissed Farzin for what was obviously not the first time that night. "They look so cute, all newlywed like that," Aviva commented.

"I guess they are," Shulamit realized. She was looking more at Isaac. He was holding one hairstick before him like a magic wand, his scarred right hand cupped underneath its tip. Deep breaths slowly coursed through her lungs as she tried to calm herself.

235

"Let's go. He's ready for us."

They met up with Isaac halfway back to the carriage. "Everything go as planned?" Shulamit asked awkwardly.

"Kaveh insisted on reciting some ornate verses I bet he stored up just in case," Isaac remarked. "Like son, like father. At least his rhymed."

"Did you have to watch them?"

Isaac lifted an eyebrow. "What, *that* part? No. I transformed and shielded their privacy with my wings. They were just holding hands and making promises, at first, but once the talk slowed down I kept my head up, watched for danger -- and stayed out of their business."

Aviva reached the carriage first. She held the curtains for her to let Shulamit slip back inside, then followed.

Isaac stuck the front half of his body in with them for a moment. "Aviva, you understand what to do?"

Aviva nodded, taking the hairstick from him carefully. On its tip glowed a pulsing light, coming from something white that looked a little bit like coconut oil. Aviva had seen it before. Shulamit hadn't, and looked away, feeling bile rise in her throat.

"It's okay -- you don't have to look at it," Aviva reassured her.

Shulamit lay down across the seat of the carriage, pulling out the cord that held her braids together. Yellow flowers spilled across the seat cushions, but she didn't care.

"I'll be out here -- I'll stand guard and keep this private." With a swish of curtains, Isaac left them alone in the carriage.

Shulamit removed a few layers of clothing, then pooled her dress up around her waist. "Can you see?" The carriage was lit only by the glow of the hairstick and some firelight that could slip through the curtains.

"Well enough," said Aviva. "Plus, I know my way around the garden." She ran her free hand up Shulamit's thigh and into the space between her legs.

"That feels good."

"It's supposed to. You tell me when the flower's ready for the bee, okay?"

"Just do it -- I don't think I can relax while I'm still waiting for it. How are you going to be able to get it all the way back there without the stuff coming off too close to the entrance?"

Aviva held her open slightly and then paused, the wand poised to enter. "Isaac's spell will keep it on until I command it to unstick."

Shulamit covered her face with both hands. "I'm so glad nobody can see me right now but you."

"Okay, I'll try. Wait, I'm going to put my finger in there first to make sure the way is clear and there isn't any mucus for it to get stuck on."

"Fine." She relaxed at the more familiar touch and even leaned into Aviva's hand a little. Then, when the finger was withdrawn, she bit her lip and waited.

Something long and thin and *hard* in an alien way entered her body. She worried for a moment that Aviva would stick it in too far and break holes in her womb somehow, but then she remembered the hairsticks weren't really *that* long.

"It's in," Aviva told her helpfully. Then she took Shulamit's hand in hers and closed her eyes. "Ready?"

"Yes."

"A sheynem dank." Thank you, she had said to the magic spell, in Isaac's language -- and the spell understood.

"How long do we wait?"

"I think I can take it out now."

"Try it. This feels weird."

With a swift motion, Aviva pulled the hairstick, now slick from Shulamit's body, back out. It no longer glowed. Isaac's magic was working. "The seed's in the earth."

"Now what?"

"Aafsaneh says I should make you purr," said Aviva. "She says it'll help make sure the pollen hits the stigma." She rolled up her hair and stuck the hairstick back into it.

"I can't believe you just--"

"I can't do this with hair in my face!"

Shulamit only giggled for another two seconds, because after that she was too distracted by Aviva's attentions.

Chapter 27: Mortar

"Why is this night different from all other nights?" said Prince-Consort Kaveh, with great portent.

Eleven months had passed, and he looked markedly happier, stronger, and more comfortable in his own skin. It wasn't just the line of dark hair around his mouth and chin, and it wasn't just his newfound muscles, grown from enthusiastic new work on the vineyard he now called his home and making his wiry frame look even more, as Farzin had once said, like a statue. The change was in the way he held his shoulders -- the sparkle in his eyes. It was in the comfortable smiles he shared with everyone else at the seder table. For the past several months he had finally felt glad to be Kaveh, instead of someone else.

When he first arrived at the vineyard, fear of being mistaken by the hardworking laborers for Farzin's pampered lapdog had driven him to work twice as hard as anyone would have thought possible. Between that and the food he cooked for the farmers, he quickly won the hearts of his new neighbors. But that wasn't his only reason to feel such joy. Beside him sat Farzin, comfortably pudgy again as Kaveh had promised he'd be, and in Kaveh's arms squirmed a little brown beauty wrapped in guava-colored cloth. Princess Naomi, his daughter, stared all around the room with big eyes full of wonder. He was actually asking the Four Questions on her behalf, since at fifty-five days old she was naturally the youngest one there. But it made sense for him to ask, because he hadn't grown up around seders and Passover.

"On all other nights, we eat all kinds of bread--" Here he met the eyes of the queen, and chuckled sheepishly. "We would eat all kinds of bread, if we could," he ad-libbed. From behind the look of harried happiness that enveloped her constantly in these early days of motherhood, she gave him a crooked grin. "And tonight, we eat only this stuff." He held up a matzo cracker, and Naomi's tiny hand waved in its direction.

"See that, little one?" Farzin murmured through a jolly smirk. "Someday, you, too, will be able to eat cardboard."

"That has seasoning," Aviva retorted saucily. "Be nice, or I won't let you have extra helpings of charoseth afterwards."

"He said this stuff was supposed to be mortar!" Farzin protested with a grin. "You can't deny a builder mortar. His bricks go everywhere!"

"It's good, isn't it," Shulamit agreed. She loved watching people new to their culture discover charoseth for the first time.

"The secret is letting the wine soak in overnight and get friendly. It's really time that works the magic." Aviva chattered. "Time is the key ingredient. Otherwise the other ingredients never really get to know each other."

"The secret ingredient is *love!*" said Shulamit with a silly grin.

"Let Kaveh finish," said Captain Riv. The table fell silent, and everyone's face turned back toward the prince consort.

"On all other nights, we eat lots of different kinds of vegetables, but tonight, we eat only bitter herbs."

Farzin's mouth twitched, but he didn't say anything until Rivka folded her arms and stared at him. "What?" He smiled at her innocently. "I'm leaving that one alone. It's too easy."

"All other nights, we--" Kaveh looked down at Naomi. "Shula, she's-- she's trying to-- no, baby, I don't have milk. I promise."

"I'd better take her. That was most of it! You two did great!" Shulamit stood to receive her infant, and then sat down, wrapping herself in her lilac scarf for modesty before letting Naomi latch on.

"We're here to remember that once we weren't free," Isaac began, his booming, low voice settling over the table like a soothing scent. "To be thankful for the fact that now we are, and not only free but surrounded by blessings. And to meditate on the fact that even today, plenty of people are still not free, or are still not fairly paid for the work of their bodies, and hope that God will show us a way to fight these injustices. Long ago, there was a king--"

They listened raptly as he told the story; Shulamit drinking in the familiar, comforting words and passing on that sense of peace to her nursing infant; Rivka stirred and inspired and feeling lucky that she was married to him; Kaveh fascinated as he learned for the first time about those who had been slaves, at least in legend, and about Moses who stood between them and their tormentor.

"That's like you!" he whispered to Farzin, his eyes full of love. "With the bridge and everything."

"More like you," Farzin pointed out, "since he was raised in the house of the king, but stood up to him anyway."

"--hailstones, of fire!" Isaac held up one hand with a pointing finger for emphasis.

A suspicious noise from the baby prompted the queen to surreptitiously check her clothing. "Oops, I think she needs changing." Shulamit stood up and kissed Naomi's forehead as she placed her carefully into Aviva's waiting arms.

"I can pause," said Isaac.

While they waited, Shulamit turned to her husband-in-name. "Your brother's baby was born just recently too, I heard?"

Kaveh nodded. "A healthy son. My brother's really happy."

There was an expression in his face that Shulamit couldn't understand. "What's--?"

"Azar doesn't want me to see him."

241

"What?" Her jaw hung open.

"She didn't come out and say it, but she wants Farzin and I to stay away from her children."

Shulamit shook her head slightly, her eyes narrowing. "It's...not... I don't..."

"I think she's scared he'll see us the way we are and think it's one of the ways to be normal."

"It *is.*"

"Why is it so important?" Isaac pointed out. "Neither of you wants King Jahandar too involved in Naomi's life, even though he's her grandfather."

"*Zayde* Isaac is a much better one," Shulamit pouted.

"If you don't like someone, why lose sleep if the feeling is mutual?" Riv shrugged. "The room is full of people who love you."

"I'm still working on that."

"You two are a funny pair of expert worriers," Isaac pointed out. "I wonder how much of it the little one got!"

"It doesn't matter," Riv pointed out. "We'll teach her to be strong and face whatever worries her."

Aviva returned, the now-cranky princess in her arms. "She fusses when we change her," she apologized as she sat down, bouncing slightly because she knew it would be soothing.

"Next, locusts settled over the fields..." Isaac had returned to the story.

Shulamit, with the others, listened and let herself be transported - - but not too far. Part of her was indeed in that far-off ancient kingdom, watching the power of God, working through Moses, teach the selfish king a lesson about human rights. But on another level, flowing through her, in the very familiarity of it she felt multiple branching veins of family connection. She was at seders throughout her life, listening as a teenager to her father tell the story in his own way, listening as a tiny child as her grandfather held up the matzo and explained what it was all about, thinking about her long-departed mother.

But she also relived recent seders in her reverie, as she welcomed Aviva's parents into her household, and the strange pair of warriors from the north whom she had come to love and cherish as well. All her family, living and dead, on both sides, plus her in-laws, plus her golden-haired guardians, plus the family into which she had married. Now there was her little one, Princess Naomi after Shulamit's father Noach, this magical little being who somehow made all the zooming in her head slow down every time she cradled her and felt skin as soft as flowers, and love like never before.

She had experienced it with them all, this tradition and this feeling. Each year happened one on top of the other simultaneously, mixing together like the fruit and wine and nuts in the little dish in front of her, and tasting just as nuanced and sweet.

END

243

My sincere thanks to:

My spouse, for tireless passion for justice and human rights. You are an inspiration and a moral center.

My family, for believing in me and for the connection to my heritage

My in-laws, especially Kat and Kiernan

The incomparably patient Katharine "Kate the Great" Thomas O'Gara, for honest but gentle sentence-by-sentence critique and guidance, and Dr. Tof Eklund, for answering all the questions I sent over like so many honeybees

James Ingle for a man's perspective, as well as his work on the Alachua County Wage Theft Task Force accompanied by Jeremiah Tattersall, Diana Moreno, Marie Dino, and everybody else whose activism brings justice to our community Their work has as of this date resulted in forty-five thousand dollars in lost wages recovered in just a few short years. Also now in 2016 I would like to add a special memorial note for Zot Lynn Szurgot, who we just lost.

Rebecca, Jane, Erika, and all my other beloved artists

Amir and Linda, for love, support, and Farsi names

Ducky, Erin, Nikki, Caitlin, Karen, Alissa, "Other Jane," Sarah, Rachyl, Rachel, Mindy, and Dr. Alana Vincent for all their help. Kitty Campanile for keeping me true to myself.

Jonas Kaufmann, Joyce DiDonato, Anna Caterina Antonacci, Boaz Daniel, and of course René Pape for an incredible amount of inspiration

Giuseppi Verdi, who was himself a revolutionary, and Friedrich Schiller, whose characters also strived toward the light

All the chefs I used to work with, and anyone who has made their kitchen my home away from home

Jessica at Prizm and her proofreading team, Jo and Anna, for their advice and polishing

As always, forever: Richard Wagner, for always being there in the background.

Glossary of non-English words in *Climbing the Date Palm*

Some of them seem like English to me, because they were a constant part of my upbringing and remain a constant in my life! But, I realize that many Gentile (non-Jewish) readers would like more information about some of those words, and likewise that not all Jewish readers share my background. It was my hope that I had incorporated them organically, so that they could be understood in context the way one would understand invented words in any other fantasy novel. But why not give people the opportunity to learn more?

The conceit of the Mangoverse is that Perach, the setting, is a Hebrew-speaking haven of tropical agriculture, and that up north, several countries away, there's a country whose primary language is Yiddish. "Perach" itself means "flower" in Hebrew, and is a reference to Perach's being based on South Florida, where I grew up. (Florida also means "flower", in a way.)

What follows is an informal glossary, starting with Chapter 1 of *Climbing the Date Palm* and continuing to the end of the book, maybe a little out of order. I don't claim to be an expert in Judaica, but I'd like to offer what I have.

Halvah – a sweet desserty thing that is so unbelievably sweet that thinking about it makes me sick. It's shaped like a brick and you break off little pieces and then die of sugar.

Maror – horseradish. Well, "bitter herbs", anyway.

Ir Ilan means Oak Town in Hebrew.

Riachinho Estrela – in a fit of affectionate punning, I named the Imbrian capital after a friend, whose name in English means "little river of stars." It seemed appropriate since her Portuguese heritage is one of the reasons Imbrio is Lusophone. I don't know if her parents had this in mind but in *The Olive Conspiracy*, Princess Carolina tells Princess Shulamit that the "little river of stars" means the Milky Way.

Schmendrick – another one of those undefinable Yiddish insults

Al tigu bo — "Don't touch him!" in Hebrew. Yes, I had help with this one.

Mammeh – Yiddish for "Mom". (Dad is "**Tateh**", and they're both the same words in Polish, which makes sense — Yiddish is in a lot of ways Polish-flavored German written in Hebrew letters.)

Fershtay?— Understand?

Tuchus — The Posterior :P

Eshvat—my Iranian friend named this character; he said her name is related to a Farsi word that means *flirty*.

Mazel tov—People use this as "congratulations!" but it literally means "good luck" – I've had it explained to me that it's like saying "wow, great luck!", not "good luck on this future event." Like you don't say *Mazel tov* when someone is about to have an exam, you say it after they finish and do well.

Aba – Dad in Hebrew (Mom is **Ima**.) Likewise, **Baba** is Dad in Farsi, although I seem to have copped out and didn't reference the Clay City people speaking a different language from the Perachis. Whoops, sorry! (If you're curious, Mom is **Maman**, but nobody needs this until *The Olive Conspiracy*.)

Malka – Queen (with Malkeleh meaning "little queen", commonly used for a little girl in one's life, even if she's not royalty–the way my dad used to call my little half-sister "Princess." Rivka's use of **Malkeleh** as a pet name for the queen is therefore a pun.)

By the way, the -eleh ending for a name to make a diminutive is a Yiddishism. Hence "**Vivaleh**" at one point, for Aviva.

So "Malka Shulamit bat Noach" is "Queen Shulamit, daughter of Noach", Noach being her deceased father. "**Bat**"—sounds like *bot* as in robot, not the Halloween flying puppy–is the "daughter of" name syllable. For "son of" it's "**ben**."

Sherwani—NOT a Hebrew or Yiddish word; this is an Indian men's long dress coat.

Kippah (Hebrew)/**yarmulke** (Yiddish) – those teensy hats that Jewish men wear in shul and at holidays and weddings.

Gottenyu—"Dear God" in Yiddish

Gornischt—Yiddish for "nothing"

Shtupped—To shtup is to screw. In other words, it's a crude way to talk about sex.

Meshuggineh—Yiddish insult

Chuppah—Jewish wedding canopy

Sufganiyah—Donuts without holes

Rugelach—Little pastries with filling. I've seen chocolate, raspberry, and more interesting flavors. They're about the size of a business card. Someone should take advantage of that and use them as a business card. Isaac would be a big fan of this idea.

Vakht Oyf—"Wake up" in Yiddish

Nosh—Snack (Yiddish that's crossed over into English)

Vos—"What" in Yiddish (see how similar to German it is? German is *Was*, pronounced vos.)

Oy gevalt—I'm not sure how to translate this other than "Oh, BLAH." Google is giving me some results about Yiddish getting

248

it from a Middle High German word for violence but that's already ice-skating well out of my wheelhouse. Yiddish, when it gets cranky, is not always translatable.

Ikh hob dir lieb, Tateh—"I love you, Dad" in Yiddish

Shabbat (or **Shabbos**, in Yiddish — Shabbat is Hebrew) is Friday night and Saturday morning. The Jewish Sabbath, involving compulsory rest, special food, candle-lighting, going to **shul** (Yiddish word for temple/synagogue which is the same as the German word for school), and supposedly, marital sex

Seder – the ritual meal associated with **Pesach** (Passover), a really awesome holiday about freedom and human rights and cleaning crumbs off of everything. **Matzo** are big square crackers that have no flavor unless you put things like chopped apples or horseradish dip on them, but fortunately, that's built into the ritual. Yay!

Shira Glassman is a bisexual Jewish violinist living in Florida with a trans guy labor activist and a badly behaved calico cat. Her books, inspired by her heritage, upbringing, present life, and favorite operas, have made the finals of both the Bi Book Awards and the Golden Crown Literary Society awards in more than one year.

Shira Glassman online:
Blog: http://shiraglassman.wordpress.com
Facebook: http://www.facebook.com/ShiraGlassman
Goodreads:
https://www.goodreads.com/author/show/7234426.Shira_Glassman
Twitter: http://www.twitter.com/shiraglassman

If you liked *Climbing the Date Palm*, leaving a review is probably a mitzvah.

Check out the rest of the Mangoverse!

The Second Mango
Climbing the Date Palm
A Harvest of Ripe Figs
The Olive Conspiracy
Tales from Perach/Tales from Outer Lands

Looking for excellent f/f fiction?
Check out:

Daughter of Mystery by Heather Rose Jones
Poppy Jenkins by Clare Ashton

For more pro-union fiction, try Kitty Campanile's UK mining strike romance *Mighty Like a Rose*

If you're not ready to leave the tropics yet, try Zen Cho's *Spirits Abroad*

For more Jewish fantasy, try Helene Wecker's *The Golem and the Jinni*

51660174R00144

Made in the USA
San Bernardino, CA
28 July 2017